WITHDRAWN

When Ghosts Call Us Home

KATYA DE BECERRA

PAGE STREET YA

To Jorge and my parents

Also to Rena, who always has the most excellent ideas

First published in 2023 by
Page Street Publishing Co.
27 Congress Street, Suite 1511
Salem, MA 01970
www.pagestreetpublishing.com

Distributed by Macmillan, sales in Canada by The Canadian Manda Group.

27   26   25   24   23   1   2   3   4   5

ISBN-13: 9781645679639
ISBN-10: 1645679632

Library of Congress Control Number: 2022952435

Cover and book design by Rosie Stewart for Page Street Publishing Co.
Cover illustration © Dolce Paganne

Printed and bound in the United States

"Mortal fear is as crucial a thing to our lives as love. It cuts to the core of our being and shows us what we are. Will you step back and cover your eyes? Or will you have the strength to walk to the precipice and look out?"

—Marisha Pessl, *Night Film*

PART ONE

The House

One

Ghosts are memories; we carry them in our blood. And no place taught me this lesson more clearly than Cashore House that summer five years ago, when my sister Layla made her amateur horror movie *Vermillion*, using Cashore as the set.

Vermillion turned into an underground cult sensation. I was twelve years old, and I became its star. There was no script—fans wrote one later via crowdsourcing. There were no notes to follow. *Vermillion* was a clever assembly of disturbing footage, bits and pieces stitched together by my sister in post-production. Even though I knew I was safe—while chandeliers swung and chairs smashed into walls as the movie's chilling final sequence unfolded—I was scared out of my mind. I still am.

My memories from that time may be hazy and disjointed, but one thing I know for sure—it was all pretend. Special effects. Layla explained it all to me. And I believed her, even if her eerily-moving homemade props looked a little too impressive in the moonlit hallways of Cashore House, the place that was our home that fateful summer.

The place that's haunted my nightmares for years.

Much has been written about my sister and her eerie creation in the years following *Vermillion*'s release. I used to keep a scrapbook of clippings and printouts, but when the euphoria of "fame" wore off, I threw away my collection. Still, some of the articles written about Layla and *Vermillion* stuck with me, especially when the writer asked questions that bothered me too. Take this one fanzine review I screenshotted—

The young protagonist's realistic fright imbues Layla Galich's macabre creation with verisimilitude, while the titular ghost's torments are sure to evoke empathy as well as bone-deep terror . . . the director's resultant fame should come as no surprise to found footage genre fans, sprouting countless amateur investigations into the film's enigmatic setting and its complicated history.

Were young Sophia Galich's blood-curdling encounters with the film's eponymous ghost real? Did Layla Galich capture authentic ghost sightings on camera? And does the dark lore surrounding the film truly extend beyond the original footage, with fans—or V-heads, as they call themselves—claiming to have supernatural experiences

after viewing the film, and with clues allegedly showing up in freezeframes and the grainy periphery? This
reviewer is certain that the main question every Galich
fan out there wants to ask our favorite director is: Will
there be a sequel?

—Esme Craig's review of *Vermillion* for *Basement
Ghosts,* an online fanzine of indie horror cinema.

Or that other piece that likened Layla's film to a "monstrous
child" of David Lynch, Carmen Maria Machado, and all the
found footage horror classics as if *Vermillion* was some Frankenstein's monster made of pieces, ideas, and vibes.

Layla rarely did interviews or discussed her vision, with a few
exceptions. When cornered by a persistent reporter at the Saturn
Awards, she said perhaps her most famous words: *Some believe
the house was haunted. Who am I to say otherwise? I was just a girl
with a camera.*

While reviewers and critics highlighted my "realistic fright"
and praised my "authentic" reactions, my childhood stardom
didn't hold a candle to Layla's cult status, which catapulted her
into fame before devouring her whole.

And she owed it all to a house on a cliff.

Cashore House.

In the summer of 2017, Mom and Dad's architectural business was contracted to restore this early twentieth-century

seaside estate located in the flourishing Californian town of Livadia. The way my parents worked often required long-term immersion. Layla and I would come with them, and we'd all take up residency on the property.

Not to disrupt our schooling, the work was always scheduled for the summer months, so instead of camping or going to the beach with friends, we'd spend our breaks trapped in some dusty building in some equally dusty town while our parents turned blueprints into reality.

Cashore House was one of their biggest jobs. And unlike my parents' other projects, we needed to change schools for this one, and then when the daily logistics of getting to school proved too complicated, we switched to online schooling. It was like the house wanted us all to itself. And so, as Mom and Dad worked to transform the building, the building was, in turn, transforming us.

We just didn't know it at the time.

Two

A patina of uncertainty covers my memories of the house. Some things I remember with painful clarity, while some are like remnants of long-ago dreams, the kind that wake you up in the middle of the night, teeth clenched and blood pumping. Strange events out of context, raw emotions, body-shuddering fright.

Our first three nights at Cashore House were so quiet we could have heard a mouse pattering across the mahogany floors if it weren't for the rumbling sea outside our windows. And when I sat up in my bed at night, distracted by Cashore's watchful still- ness, I would track the lighthouse's hypnotic beams gliding over obsidian waves. I loved it—in the beginning. The house charmed me with its quiet beauty—it charmed all of us.

Cashore House was built in the 1920s, then ravaged by the 1933 earthquake, after which it stood devoid of life for decades until its acquisition by a mysterious new owner who hired my parents to restore it. We remained in the house for nearly a year, in its undamaged east wing. We remained, and if my sister is to be believed, so did the others who came before us. But I am getting ahead of myself.

Shortly after settling in, Mom and Dad disappeared into their work, leaving Layla and me to our own devices. There was nothing new about this. Then, I thought Layla was the most interesting, beautiful, and intelligent person I'd ever known. I used to copy everything she did, from how she styled her hair and combined torn jeans with oversized blazers to imitating her considered speech. Every word was worth its weight in gold. I besieged her private spaces, the little spying brat that I was, looking for her secrets in the depths of her messy closet or between the pages of her diary. I marveled at her fast-growing occult collection, played with the crystals, and leafed through the pages of books with titles that sent ripples over my skin. And I loved it all, the thrill of it. No lock could keep me out, and no hiding place would remain hidden for long.

And yet Layla always remained one step ahead, unknowable, unreachable.

Long before Cashore, I became fixated on knowing my sister's whereabouts. My bloodhound sense served me better than any tracking app or GPS feature. I followed her—everywhere. Night after night, I went after Layla, climbing out of windows, retracing her steps. But I'd always lose her as if she could vanish into the shadows, become one with the dark. She knew what I was doing, of course.

One night when I went after her, she was waiting for me just off our suburban street, in the uneven shadow cast by the carefully-trimmed bushes. She was irritated—I could tell from the way she tapped her fingers against her side—but there was something else about her too. Something I couldn't decipher. A curious look in her dark eyes. Was she impressed by my tracking skills? Flattered by my single-minded devotion? I was, after all, her biggest fan—long before *Vermillion*, before all the V-heads joined the Layla admiration club.

"If I tell you where I'm going, will you please go back to the house and stay in your room?" she asked me that night.

We struck a deal. I'd remain behind, letting my sister live her mysterious life. In return, Layla would feed me stories of her night-time exploits. I lived for those stories. The boys and girls she kissed. Underground clubs she danced in. Bars she frequented—courtesy of a fake ID that allowed my sister, barely sixteen at the time, into places I could only imagine. Our parents didn't know. Layla was good at playing the role of a well-behaved, dutiful daughter around them. But I knew the real her. At least, I thought I did. And so I kept her secrets.

This equilibrium lasted until we moved to Cashore.

With this house, we'd soon break all the rules. My sister's

life and mine became so intimately intertwined that I no longer knew where Layla ended and I began.

It was only natural that when Layla got interested in the history of Cashore House, I did too.

Between wandering Livadia's sunbaked streets and feasting on iced coffee and white chocolate muffins, we spent our days riffling through the town's dust-infested archives and chatting up locals. As a kid, I didn't really question why, so soon after we moved in, Layla was already in the middle of an intense research project. Maybe our parents asked her to, and perhaps they wanted her to locate Cashore's original architectural plans. But, as it turned out, architectural plans were not what Layla was after. I didn't know that my sister was looking for something specific—she was looking for a ghost. A real ghost. And then she found one. At least, that's what fans of her movie believe.

We learned that the house was designed and built for Baron Pyotr von Hahn—a disgraced dark magician. A charlatan of Russian heritage, the Baron claimed to be Madame Blavatsky's long-lost brother. In addition to horror movies, Layla was seriously into the occult. Crystals, candles, incantations, all of it. So, when it came to Cashore's history, nothing held Layla's interest more than a dark magician.

Von Hahn modeled Cashore House after his family's estate— the Swallow's Nest—in Yalta. With Livadia's neck-breaking cliffs, this place was perfect to pay homage to Cashore's predecessor. Some claimed the name of the estate was a dedication to the Baron's doomed lover, the celebrated émigré ballerina Adrianna Kashoroff. Her brief but turbulent life ended during the earthquake of 1933 when the cliff foundation of the house developed a sudden crack. It threw a sunbathing Adrianna into the sea along with a large chunk of the outer patio.

Her body was never recovered.

There were other stories, too, that *Cashore* was the anglicized name of a demonic entity summoned by von Hahn in some Faustian pact. The demon, who coveted a human body and favored the color red, tricked the Baron and refused to be sent back. It inhabited the house instead.

Only after Layla started capturing our life there on film did I truly begin understanding the place we called home. Had I been more aware when I was younger, I might have realized that Layla knew exactly what she was looking for. But I was too infatuated with my sister to see anything suspicious in her actions, or understand she was involving me in something dangerous.

Early in our stay, I lived as if I was breathing through a wall of fog. I remember having this constant *bad* feeling, dizzying vertigo, tightness in my chest, a sick feeling in the pit of my stomach. When I told my parents about it, they dismissed it as nerves, or dust, or my getting my first period (which did come that summer, but only later).

It wasn't until our fourth night in Cashore House that strange things started to happen. That night I remember with a raw clarity that many of my later Cashore memories lack.

With Mom being in bed when the lights flickered and then went out, it fell on Dad to go searching for the switchboard. From the darkness of my room, I listened to his retreating steps. And then Layla came in, aiming a flashlight at my face.

"Time to get up and explore, Queen Sophia-the-Wise," she said, making a theatrical bow. "The night is ours. The house's secrets await." (She started calling me that, Sophia-the-Wise, when I was about six, as a joke. I wasn't particularly wise, at least I didn't think I was, but I had the appearance of a learned owl from some cartoon, with bushy eyebrows over huge, round eyes. That, and my name literally means wisdom.)

With Layla beckoning me to follow, our established roles changed—I no longer chased after her as she set off to have her fun and adventures. But I wasn't her equal in this particular adventure either. Now, I suspect Layla was already planning the film, complete with my role in it. If I had any suspicion of her motives then, I must've ignored it. I feared being alone in the dark, so I trekked after her, her lone flashlight guiding our progress.

That night we found a secret room filled with stage costumes and props. Wigs, curling Poirot-esque mustaches, lacquered masks with cracks for wrinkles. Vintage fans made of swan

feathers. Facial prosthetics. Hands, ears, noses. Under the flashlight's scrutiny, the room and its contents looked sinister. It didn't
require a giant leap of imagination to see the props as body parts,
or discarded skins worn during some unholy ritual.

White sheets covered each of the room's walls. Layla
screamed after pulling down the nearest one. A pale ghoul
seemed to jump at her from the wall. But then Layla stepped
back, and the ghoul imitated her movement. A mirror. We both
laughed off her fright.

The remaining sheets came off, a mirror behind each one.
Particles of dust floated in the air. We sneezed and sneezed.

We didn't notice it straight away, but there was a fifth mirror
in that room. Mounted into the ceiling. In that mirror, Cashore
House was turned inside out.

Layla picked up a pair of old-fashioned spectacles from the
props lineup. The octagon-shaped glasses had one lens missing,
and the other cracked. Layla put them on and aimed the steady
flashlight beam at her face. Then she danced in the dark, twirling and making silly faces.

Later, she'd recreate this moment in *Vermillion*, in the scene
known as "The Discovery of Baron von Hahn's Preparation
Room." Layla would be off-screen, holding her digital camcorder,
while I danced around in those glasses, the flashlight in my hand
making a pale specter of my face.

One would think that since Layla named her feature after

the color so beloved by von Hahn's alleged demon that there'd be rivers of blood flowing from the ceiling or something equally gory, but it wasn't anything like that. My sister's creation wasn't a slasher film, it was something else entirely.

Three

My sister's movie, and our family's time in Cashore House, may be in the past, but the events of five years ago continue to influence my life, shaping my actions.

Two years ago, my sister disappeared.

The last time I heard from her was the night she vanished.

I'm doing this for you. I love you, and I'm sorry.

That's what her last text message said. The words implied I'd know exactly what she was referring to, but I had no idea then, and I still don't know. In my book, the only thing Layla should have been apologizing for was using me in her movie. As for the rest of it, your guess is as good as mine.

In my initial attempts to reconstruct the events of Layla's disappearance, I came across a 911 transcript from that night. A resident in Layla's dorm placed the call, citing the stench of acrid smoke coming from my sister's single room. As I read that account, it was as if I was on the spot, inhaling the fumes. But it wasn't a raging fire that the first responders found upon arrival. No. Blood-painted walls greeted them, as well as the remnants of a black salt circle marring the carpet—and no Layla.

That led the police to believe, at first, that a fan obsessed with *Vermillion* took my sister. But then, new evidence came to light. Campus surveillance cameras captured Layla leaving her dorm not long before the 911 call. She walked to the nearby parking lot, got into a car, and vanished into the night. Though the car's license plate was an indecipherable smudge, cops theorized it could've been a rideshare, even if there was no record of the transaction on Layla's credit card or anywhere else.

My sister carried no bags or personal belongings, aside from what might have been in her pockets. Her digital path became patchy as the mysterious car traveled along Route 101 toward the ocean, until it . . . wasn't. It seemingly blinked out of existence—there one moment, gone the next—just like the titular entity in Layla's movie. But unlike Vermillion's ghostly lead that always reappears in the film, the car never returned, and neither did my sister.

Cameras glitch. Digital records become corrupted. That was what the police told my parents. Aside from Layla's initial trajectory, nothing tangible linked my sister's path to Livadia, to Cashore.

But I know that's exactly where Layla was going.

What I don't know is why. Was someone making her do this? Was she being threatened by a fan?

Nearly a year following Layla's vanishing, a shocking new piece of evidence emerged. But because it only existed for a short time, the authorities didn't take me seriously when I called them with this information. They didn't see what I saw: a photograph of Layla, looking the way she did when she left her dorm that night. Entering Cashore House.

The photograph vanished so quickly from the web, it was almost as if it briefly came into existence to be seen by me and me alone.

The site hosting the photo was CrimsonDreadNet, a closed online community that treats Layla's creative lore like a lived experience, not some pop culture construct. No one knows exactly how CrimsonDreadNet started or who's behind it. The first time I'd heard about the site was soon after *Vermillion* was picked up for a wider release after starting its life as a YouTube freebie. A review mentioned the fast-growing forum, where fans flocked to share their unsettling "encounters" after seeing Layla's film. Talk about haunted art . . . or, in this case, a haunted screen.

I first looked up CrimsonDreadNet out of curiosity. I was promptly turned away, denied access. The site isn't like other online fandom spaces. Joining isn't as easy as signing up for an account or paying a membership fee. Actually, there is a fee to pay, but its currency is stories—authentic narratives of experiencing that which can't be explained, all to do with my sister's film.

There are forum threads for all things *Vermillion* and Layla, no matter how far-fetched—from necromancy and summoning manuals to fashion and makeup. One massive thread alone is dedicated to comparing the shades of red lipstick to the color of the dress the film's eponymous entity wears. Another thread called **__CanDeadDance?** offers step-by-step reconstructions of the twisted ballet moves I perform in some of the film's most horrifying scenes. And then there is a whole below-the-surface section of the site dedicated to The Path, outlining a series of mysterious signs associated with the film. I was never able to gain access to The Path section of the site; it's like a citadel, or a temple's inner sanctuary, where only the priests, or the initiated, are allowed to enter.

And then there is **__LaylaGalichIsAlive**, which fans created to report the alleged sightings of my sister. The thread popped up shortly after Layla's disappearance, and I have been haunting it ever since I'd managed to obtain my login credentials via a shady online business that offered complete anonymity and didn't shy away from dealing with minors. For a while, the thread proved useless, but then something happened I couldn't explain—the photo of my sister entering Cashore House.

As far as I could tell, it wasn't a manipulated image or something stolen from Layla's social media, and it wasn't a photo of me edited to look like Layla. It was Layla, her face bathed in moonlight as she reached for Cashore's front door. Her expression, terribly sad, but also desperate, even frantic, stuck with me. I've seen my sister look like this only once before, when filming *Vermillion* got out of hand, and I nearly died.

Seeing the photo, this proof of Layla's last known location, was a brief, bleary-eyed moment of heart-pounding panic. It was as if Cashore itself reached out to me across space and time, its clawed hand wrapping around my wrist and pulling me in. It was as if the house was calling me home.

I sat frozen in my room, and stared at the image until my eyes started playing tricks on me. Did my sister's head turn in the grainy photo? Did her lips move, saying my name?

CrimsonDreadNet doesn't allow screenshots or downloads—I didn't know it then. As I hit my laptop's PRINT SCREEN button again and again, the website reloaded, then locked me out. By the time I found my way back, the photo was gone.

My parents didn't believe me. The police didn't take me seriously. They said I saw things I wanted to see. Or worse—that I was crying out for attention.

The police searched Cashore eventually, albeit reluctantly. They found nothing but cobwebs and decay. Since my parents' reconstructive work, the house remained empty, shunned by the living. I wonder what happened to Cashore's most recent owner, why they abandoned whatever plans they had for that house.

As for my sister, I know Layla didn't run away. She didn't hurt herself. Someone took her—perhaps the same someone who had snapped a photo of her entering that house. But no one who witnessed my sister's movements that night—from the mystery driver to the photographer watching from a distance—stepped forward with information.

The truth about what happened to Layla is still out there, and it's linked to Cashore, and, I believe, to *Vermillion*'s fandom. To find my sister, I must think like a fan.

That's why I'm coming back to where it all began and where Layla was last seen.

I'm returning to Livadia where, perched atop an eroding cliff, Cashore House sleeps fitfully. Instead of settling into a rustic lake cabin with my friends for a glorious month of summer sun, I'm spending hours in a bumpy van with a tight-lipped camera-woman and a nervous producer who never stops typing on her phone. But in just a few hours, it's all going to be worth it. I'm going to meet the man who made my return to Livadia possible. He's waiting for me in Cashore House, along with the secrets my sister left behind.

I've spent a year setting this up in secret from Mom and Dad. My parents' anger if—*when*—they learn of my real plans for this unsupervised summer is the price I'm willing to pay for the answers I'm looking for. I hope that my carefully constructed alibi holds, that my friends keep my secret. I'm too far gone not to see this through.

I must know what happened to Layla.

Four

I don't believe in ghosts, never did—at least not in ghosts as a tangible presence, felt or seen. Even living in an allegedly haunted house and starring in my sister's horror movie didn't change my mind. I've seen what Layla could do, what unsettling props she could devise to manipulate the world to induce a reaction from me. She was always nearby, her camcorder ready, to capture my fright.

But I do believe in the power memory holds over us; I believe in ghosts as remnants of powerful emotions we have experienced. Over the years, I've learned that—for the most part—our ghosts stay silent. But there are times when our busy world quiets just enough for the ghosts to emerge. I've been hearing the ghosts of that summer for years and I've tuned them out. But I'm not a twelve-year-old child anymore. I'm seventeen, the same age Layla was when she made her film. I'm finally ready to hear what Cashore's ghosts have been trying to say.

There's a split in my head, a demarcation line drawn between my year with Layla at Cashore and everything that came after. I know this is an obsession, but I don't want to fight it. I fear the moment this fuel inside me burns out. But perhaps what I fear more is the moment when I get what I'm looking for. The moment I find Layla. What'll drive me then? Who am I beyond this preoccupation with the ghosts of my past?

My fingers twitch with impatience; I want to grab my phone and navigate to CrimsonDreadNet. Losing hours at a time to scrolling, studying V-heads' creepy posts, has become a habit ever since that photo of Layla. I'm scared of missing something, another photo, another clue.

But I know better than logging in to the site now. I'm not alone and, worse, there's a camera on me, recording my every move. This is the price I'm willing to pay to gain temporary access to the house that devoured my sister. I have to partake in a documentary being made to commemorate *Vermillion*'s fifth anniversary of release. My parents don't know what I'm up to, and I hope to keep up this charade for as long as possible. The documentary's mastermind, Erasmus Sawyer, managed to secure Cashore House for a few weeks of filming. As this place attracts V-heads like moths to a flame, I can only hope the low-key production will remain secret, at least until the filming is over.

We're running late, which means money's being wasted. I overheard Petra, the producer, say so during our last stop about an hour after we left Fresno. The van's driver has barely let go of the gas pedal since then. Layla would be green in the face from motion sickness, but my sister isn't here. I am.

By the time we reach Livadia, the sun is setting.

Part of me is grateful we're rushing; the van's frantic tempo gives me little chance to dwell on the things I see. Another part of me is secretly scared stiff.

On the surface, the manicured seaside paradise doesn't seem to have changed in the past five years. Picture-perfect townhouses, overshadowed by their luxuriously landscaped gardens, still stand blissfully unaware of the terror that lurks in Cashore House. White cobblestone fairy tale streets still curl in on themselves.

My phone pings.

I ignore it, despite the chill that rushes through my body at the sound. The van's air-conditioning is arctic, but that's not it.

My phone stays in my pocket where it belongs. It's likely just another message from a friend anyway. Another selfie by the lake. I don't have a lot of friends, but the few I do have are loyal, their trust hard-earned. They are my alibi during the documentary.

What I try not to dwell on is that, every time I hear the familiar ping, I think about my sister. Even if I stopped hoping for a text from Layla a long time ago.

"One last bit of commentary before we get there?" Petra snaps me out of my thoughts. I glance outside, seeking inspiration.

The camera glides over me. Miriam, the camerawoman, is efficient and a little bit mysterious—she may be quiet, but her presence is magnetic. I wonder how she sees the world through her camera, how she sees me. Fleetingly, I see myself reflected in her aviators. I look away.

"That's the famous DeVore ice cream parlor—over there." Ignoring the camera in my face, I point at the blur of hot pink awning that's already too far behind us to be captured on film. "Best mint chocolate chip in the county," I add. Nobody needs to know that I barely remember eating any. There are gaps in my memory of that summer, but it's no one's concern but my own.

As we approach our destination, it grows unnaturally quiet inside the van. Miriam never stops filming, not even when I turn away and rest my head against the window, pretending like everything's fine and I'm not about to face all my childhood ghosts.

There's a security checkpoint at the foot of the cliff. That's definitely new. The van makes a quick stop, while a friendly guard verifies our identity. It seems Erasmus Sawyer doesn't want unauthorized visits from Layla's fans.

Cashore House stares down at Livadia like a sovereign overlooking its domain. The more of it I see, revealed anew with each turn of the serpentine road, the less I believe I once called this place home.

A few more minutes, another turn of the road, and we arrive.

Petra gets out first, followed by Miriam, who proceeds to film me as I scramble out of the van. The crash of the ocean absorbs the sound of my feet hitting the ground.

Wispy fog clouds Cashore House, congregating around the building's turrets. Layla's fans often refer to Cashore as a castle. Perhaps they're right. Compact and reinforced with steel and thickened glass, it does look like something out of a fairy tale. Time and distance haven't erased any of the building's charm. It still takes my breath away.

From where I'm standing, I can't see the house's ocean-facing observation deck. But I know what it looks like when viewed from the beach below the cliff.

Whenever Layla would head down to the beach to scout for cinematic angles or to film external footage, I'd shadow her, our bare feet soaked in sea water and encrusted with fine grains of sand. As Layla trained her camcorder at Cashore, we'd move along the beach until we reached the tide pools at the cliff's base. When I stood by the pools, Cashore House's shadow blocking out the sun, a strange chill would spread through me, beginning in the tips of my toes and climbing up until my eyelids grew heavy.

Layla was drawn to those pools, but they made me uncomfortable. The pools stank—of stale water and decay. Of drowned flesh. When I said so to Layla, she dismissed it. "The pools aren't stagnant," she'd say, meaning whatever had died in there would eventually be dragged out to sea.

But the smell remained.

While Cashore House's outer patio had been completely restored by my parents, as a kid it never occurred to me to wonder whether certain segments of the old structure, the one that had collapsed, could still be found at the bottom of those pools. Then, I entertained the morbid idea that Adrianna Kashoroff's bones were there, half buried in the sand and muck, her algaefied crevices providing shelter for scuttling crabs. But I know now that logically it makes no sense. Surely, they searched for Adrianna's remains in the pools, and those bones would be nothing but rot by now.

I stare at Cashore for so long my eyes begin tearing up.

"I can only imagine how much you miss Layla," Petra says. "I think she's with us in spirit." But she's misinterpreted my tears.

I know when people say *in spirit*, they don't mean it literally, but I sincerely hope Petra's wrong about the spirit thing. One tormented ghost is enough. I'm not sure that I, or Cashore House, can handle two.

Five

The camera follows me as I proceed up the brick driveway toward Cashore House's front door. I stop there, staring at the elaborate door handle shaped like a swan. This swan appears in *Vermillion*'s opening sequence: The handle turns slowly, as if of its own volition, and the door opens. If the viewer pauses the footage at just the right moment, they can catch a sliver of my shadow. I was the one operating the handle from inside the house.

The swan's polished bronze hasn't lost its gleam. I think of Layla's hand gripping it, turning it, the metal creaking. I stand where my sister stood the night she vanished.

"In your sister's cinematic oeuvre, the image of a swan symbolizes an invitation, a mystery to be solved," Petra's off-camera voice prompts. I know she wants me to say something meaningful.

But I'm at a loss.

Amid all the information Layla dug up about the house, she never found anything that unequivocally explained the abundance of swan designs. A local history buff she befriended told her that Cashore House is believed to contain ninety-three cygnus objects and images scattered throughout its rooms. But no matter how many expeditions we launched, we only ever found eighty-five. The Baron's swan obsession was likely a decorative choice, which only acquired a sinister connotation thanks to Layla.

I doubt that's what Petra wants to hear.

"Layla had this idea. . . ." I gather my scattered thoughts and turn toward the camera. "Baron von Hanh's mother came from the Lebedev dynasty, and 'lébed' means swan. Perhaps the bird is a reminder of the Baron's heritage."

"And what about you, Sophia?" Petra asks. "What do you think?"

I sigh, then compose my face into what I hope is a wistful expression. "I always thought the swan had something to do with Adrianna Kashoroff. She was a ballerina, educated by a celebrated Russian émigré ballettmeister. Her stage presence was often likened to that of a willowy swan."

I reach for the handle. Its textured surface imprints against the sensitive skin of my palm. A faint shudder goes through me. I half expect the phone in my pocket to emit another one of its pings, but it stays silent. I open the door.

Dragging my suitcase behind me, I enter the spacious lobby of the house where I'm immediately bombarded by extravagant luxury. It's not at all how I remember this place. When my parents were completing their restoration work on the house's partially-collapsed patio, most of Cashore was covered in plastic and roped off with safety tape. While filming *Vermillion*, Layla had to carefully move things around without our parents noticing, to clear out space for me to have my staged encounters with the ghost. But what I'm seeing now is an expansive space, filled with natural light and beautiful things. Embroidered silk wallpaper. Brocaded curtains shot through with golden thread. Art deco furniture—well-preserved originals or lavish imitations. The comparison may be off by a decade, but it reminds me of the *Titanic*'s opulent interior. All that's missing is a doomed string octet in the corner, playing "Nearer, My God, to Thee."

Once upon a time, the Baron and his beloved Adrianna would greet their guests right in this glittering lobby. Writers, academics, politicians, and an assortment of émigré intellectuals were rumored to socialize right here under von Hahn's glamorous roof. They held séances, played risqué sex games, and discussed politics. The Baron's scandalous soirées would last through the night. And in the morning, mostly sobered up, exhausted but fulfilled, the hosts and their guests would proceed down the rocky stairs cut into the cliff to the pristine sandy beach, just in time to catch the sunrise.

Now, Cashore House teems with a different type of crowd.

The documentary crew is already here, installing lighting and motion activated cameras, all of which appear to have their lenses instantly trained on me. Five years ago, I could never shed this feeling of being constantly watched while in this house, and I don't mean Layla's ever-present camcorder. It really felt like the house itself was watching me. At last, that feeling is justified now it's not just my imagination—I'm indeed being watched, but at least it's by technology, and not the ghosts that Layla created.

I'm really here. I'm back.

The thought is like a punch to the gut: What have I gotten myself into?

Why do I feel like I want to turn around, run away, and never look back?

I look up and meet the gaze of Erasmus Sawyer, the director. He descends the spiral staircase from the second floor and moves across the room toward me. I've only ever seen him on screen and in photographs; his mesmeric eyes stay trained on me long after I've averted my gaze. We've chatted on the phone, on Zoom, and exchanged emails, but seeing him in the flesh now, tall, broad-shouldered, adorned with a majestic black beard, he's much more imposing in person.

"Sophia, a pleasure," Erasmus says as we shake hands. His skin is dry and scaly against mine, weird to the touch. "Thank you for joining me here, and for trusting me to tell this story. I know it can't be easy for you."

"Thanks for making this happen," I reply, diplomatically refraining from speaking what's really on my mind. I'm here because Erasmus is my ticket back to Cashore House, my access to Layla's last known whereabouts.

When Erasmus first reached out to me over a year ago to pitch the idea of a documentary that would celebrate my sister's legacy, I wanted nothing to do with it. Even his impressive reputation wasn't enough to convince me. I've been burned by *Vermillion*'s toxic fandom too many times. Whenever I hear "I'm your sister's biggest fan," my first impulse is to stay far, far away.

But that damn photo of Layla entering Cashore changed everything. It beckoned me, its siren song thrumming in my veins.

I wanted—needed—to return here, desperately. It didn't take long to become completely obsessed with the idea of making my way back to Cashore House, to search its holes and its shadows, looking for any signs of Layla's presence.

Layla's fans say *Vermillion* is a puzzle, and the film is intimately connected to this house, to its history, with ghostly clues woven into the footage. If I were to solve this puzzle, could I bring my sister back?

I wrote to Erasmus and said yes. If cooperating with him was the only way for me to return to Cashore, so be it.

Come to think of it now, his idea for a movie celebrating *Vermillion*'s fifth anniversary was nothing short of serendipitous. It was like the universe heard my call and provided me with a solution exactly in my time of need. There's a suspicious part of me that wonders why Erasmus is interested in Layla and her film, but if I question the director and don't like the answer, my time at Cashore might be over before it even begins. Without Erasmus and his project, I'd have to resort to V-head tactics of breaking and entering, likely to be caught by security within minutes of making my way past the door. At least, I assume that's what would happen. The police said Cashore was alarm wired, and yet somehow my sister evaded getting caught that night. As if she simply walked through the door and then immediately vanished into the shadows of the house.

Now that I'm here, and Erasmus expects me to actually act in his movie, I feel my toes curling at the thought. The way I understand it, his project is part documentary, part reenactment. He's claiming nothing quite like it exists, and the whole thing depends on my participation. But I'm not the kid I was five years ago, with innocent eyes full of earnest dread. Plus, I've done nothing resembling acting since *Vermillion*. And I wonder what his take is on Layla's story—Erasmus must have an angle, right? Is my sister a teen genius? One-hit wonder? Strange, disturbed girl with a twisted view of the world?

Surprisingly little is known about Erasmus Sawyer aside from a few personal details he mentioned in interviews. I remember reading somewhere that he married his high school sweetheart, but is now a widower, and that's about it. He's not a scandalous celebrity; he's not on social media. He doesn't even talk about his movies to the reporters that much. Erasmus is practically embodying the whole "death of the author" thing. In that way, he's like my sister. Brilliant, aloof, mysterious.

This mystery extends to Erasmus's current project. It hasn't been officially announced, only hinted at.

I was so desperate to find a way back here, for Erasmus's people to negotiate access to Cashore House, that we never really talked details, just big picture stuff.

"I look forward to getting started," I say. "Officially, I mean. Miriam must've filmed every single moment of our drive here."

"Your old room has been prepared for you," Erasmus tells me, his features soft.

My old room.

The room where I used to fear every corner, every shadow.

I conceal my mounting anxiety behind a smile, then discreetly scan the lobby.

"My son will help you with your things . . . Arthur, come here, meet Sophia," Erasmus calls out.

"I don't need help . . ." I start to say as a much younger version of Erasmus Sawyer, sans beard, comes over. He—Arthur, apparently—takes my suitcase.

I didn't know Erasmus had any children, let alone that his teenage son was going to be on set. He never mentioned that. I study Arthur in short glances as I follow him up the stairs. He's about my age. Tall like his dad, but lanky rather than impos-ing. Torn black jeans; t-shirt endorsing some Scandinavian band I've never heard of; dark reddish-brown hair that frames his face in unruly, soft waves. His gaze is elusive, but I do catch a hint of tiredness nestled around his hazel eyes that are slightly red-rimmed. I wonder how many nights he's already spent here, helping his father prepare the set for filming. I wonder what he thinks about this house. Does he see the shadows move the way I did when I lived here as a kid?

We proceed up the wrought iron staircase, and I try not to think about a certain infamous sequence in *Vermillion* involving these stairs. One of the earliest scenes Layla filmed took place right here, and landed us in hot water with our parents, nearly ending the entire *Vermillion* endeavor before it began. But in the end, Layla persevered. She always did.

As we move up the stairs, Miriam trails behind, while another cameraperson films our ascent from the second floor at an angle that must conceal him from Miriam's lens. This multiple camera business is going to take some getting used to.

"So, what do your friends call you? Sophie? Soph?" Arthur turns his head to look at me as we near the top of the narrow staircase.

"It's Sophia, actually." Better to nip it in the bud, this nick-name business.

My phone chooses this exact moment to ping again.

"Sophia it is," he says, a playful expression on his face. My phone pings again, then *again*.

"Boyfriend? Girlfriend? Significant other?" Arthur teases, looking at me like we're friends. I catch a long glimpse of his eyes before looking away and frowning.

"I'm really tired," I say, for some reason burning with embarrassment at this exchange being recorded. "Can we just get to my room?"

"Sure thing, Sophia-the-Wise."

Layla's label of endearment coming out of his mouth grips me with foreboding. I want to warn him to never call me that *ever* again, but I don't want that to be caught on camera. I seethe silently.

Arthur carries my luggage toward the familiar door at the end of the corridor. I'm glad he can't see my expression. I have no choice but to put up with Erasmus. But Arthur is . . . I don't quite know what to think of him, how to behave around him. He's an unknown. I don't like unknowns.

"'Sleep you will, gentle spirit, night itself cradling you on its feathered wing,'" he recites, eyes latched on to me.

"You're a fan, then?" I ask. As if his quoting verbatim from *Vermillion*'s dreamy voice-over doesn't speak for itself. "Midnight screenings? Tracking the Seven Signs?" I keep my voice flat, already annoyed at myself for taking the bait. Was Arthur coached to do what he could to get me talking? Or is the situation worse than I thought and he actually *is* a fan, a V-head?

His face turns serious, thoughtful even. "I guess you can call me a fan," he admits. "Can you really blame me? Your sister managed to create something unprecedented—something that still resonates with so many people."

"And now she's gone." I don't bother to hide the bitterness in my voice.

He's not wrong about Layla's art resonating, but what if there's a tragic catch here, what if her creation has resonated with a certain person, or certain people, a bit too much. *And now she's gone.* Homicide detectives assigned to Layla's case eventually hit a dead-end. My sister was gone. Missing. Vanished. Vague, passive words that don't hint at a culprit or issue blame. But someone took that ghostly photo of my sister. Someone was there to capture the moment of her entering Cashore, never to be seen again.

I never stopped believing that Layla may still be alive. But what if she is being kept against her will? After all, V-heads have always been obsessed with her, with our family.

"I'm sorry," Arthur says, and he sounds like he means it.

But sincerity can be faked, and I've been fooled before. You'd be surprised at the lengths Layla's fans have gone just to get close to her, close enough to touch something she touched. Danger-creeps that went through our trash and stole our mail. A man once tried to lure Layla into his car as she crossed a road near campus. Another time someone broke into her dorm room and stole dirty clothes from her hamper.

I've gotten my own share of unwanted attention. I've been catfished more times than I can remember, approached for "opinion pieces" and college essays; I was even offered a creative arts scholarship, subject to lengthy interviews on the subject of Layla and her damn film. Whatever friendships I do have, I had to earn, and it took years to build trust. I have only been on a handful of dates, and the last time I kissed someone, the guy turned out to be (surprise!) a V-head. Shortly following our second "date," I got a news alert for a blog post outlining my date's experience of getting "close and personal" with "little Sophia Galich, all grown up now."

I can still taste the bile of disgust at the memory.

When I look at Arthur Sawyer, my dangercreep radar doesn't tingle. But I can't really trust myself, not fully.

"I really hope you're not one of those mega-fans who used to run surveillance on our house," I deadpan, watching his face for signs of deception.

"Is that what you think of me?" He chuckles softly, but his eyes are sad. "Some first impression I've made."

He looks like he wants to say something else, but then a pleasant mask slides over his features and he steps out of the way, leaving the honor of opening the bedroom door to me—and the cameras that follow my every move.

"All right, *mega-fan*," I tease darkly. "Try not to faint now."

I feel it the moment I open the door, before I even enter my old bedroom. The unnatural weight of her eyes lands on me before I even see her up there, spread out against the wall.

Her presence knocks the air out of my lungs.

It's Vermillion.

She's been waiting patiently all these years for my return.

Hell.

I didn't sign up for this.

Vermillion wasn't real, my sister created her. But . . .

Wait. *Wait.*

I blink and realize it's only a painting.

As air flows back into my lungs, I'm relieved that Miriam didn't get to film my face a moment ago when it was contorted in mortal panic.

I think the cameras here can only see my back. I hope.

I brave another look.

I definitely don't remember a life-sized portrait of Adrianna Kashoroff over my bed.

Her ancient blue eyes follow me as I enter the room.

It takes me a second to notice the motion activated camera trained directly on my face. I was set up. They totally saw my face. They knew I'd react this way. They were ready and waiting to film my fright. And suddenly, a different feeling surges through me: white-hot rage.

Six

I n the absence of Erasmus Sawyer, I turn on his son.

My twisted expression wipes the tentative smile from Arthur's face.

"Is this what it's going to be like?" I face him, forgetting about Miriam lurking in the corridor and the motion cameras in the room.

He flinches.

"Cheap shots? Scaring me shitless around every corner because it looks good on camera? What a sick, disgusting thing to do!"

The irony of my indignation is not lost on me. With *Vermillion*, Layla did exactly that—scared me shitless when I was just a child and filmed my reactions, over and over again. I was too young and too obsessed with her to understand what she was doing.

Arthur's arms fly up, but he has the decency not to mollify me with false declarations of innocence.

"It's just a portrait," he says, eyes flitting to the painting before returning to me. "The owner of the house recently bought it at some auction. My dad thought it'd be a cool idea to display it. He says you used to be a local history buff. I'm sorry it scared you. Now that I look at it, it *is* kind of freaky."

Maybe he's just a well-trained actor, but I can't help but soften in response. He's totally placating me, but I blush and move sideways, hoping my hair conceals most of the red on my cheeks.

"I—I'm sorry I shouted," I squeeze out. "It caught me off guard. I thought it was . . ."

What?

The entity from Layla's movie?

The stuff of my red-tinged nightmares?

A ghost that doesn't exist outside of my sister's disturbing work of art and her fans' collective imagination?

I never finish the sentence, and Arthur doesn't push it. Instead, he does something unexpected. He approaches the bed in three quick steps, balances atop the frame, and reaches for the portrait. Given the one-sidedness of his rushed effort, it takes him several attempts to lift the framed canvas off its hook, and when he does . . .

Everything slows down. My hands fly to my face as Adrianna Kashoroff plonks facedown on the bed. I let out a shocked squeak, which would be funny if the situation wasn't so bizarre.

"What are you doing?" I ask, my voice raw.

"Removing it from your room," Arthur says as he maneuvers the painting off the bed and then stands it up in front of him. The picture's upside down, Adrianna's high chignon reaching for the floor. With the painting almost the same height as Arthur, all I can see is the top half of his head and the two sets of fingers curled around the sides of the frame.

"A little help?" His voice comes from behind the canvas.

I come over, and we engage in a weird dance of gripping and twisting, our hands touching and brushing repeatedly, until we end up carrying the painting like paramedics toting a stretcher.

I notice a set of hinges on my side of the frame. "I think there's supposed to be a second painting," I tell Arthur, indicating my discovery. "Like a diptych."

But he just frowns and shrugs in response.

At first, I think his plan is to lean the painting against the wall somewhere in my room, but it turns out Arthur is a go-all-the-way, do-the-job-right kind of guy. Together, we carry the portrait toward the shared bathroom, which leads to the bedroom adjacent to mine.

Layla's old room.

There, a camera mounted into the wall immediately comes to life, its bottomless black eye focused on me and my partner in crime. I do my best to ignore it as Arthur and I leave the painting propped against the wardrobe. I can easily imagine Adrianna Kashoroff's artfully thin brows quirking in response to our efforts.

I hope that if this painting is haunted by her restless spirit, she at least has a sense of humor.

"There. Now you can sleep without being watched by a creepy ballerina," Arthur says as he catches my eye and gives me another earnest smile. Despite myself, I smile back.

There's this disarming, earnest quality about him, but as my experience has proved again and again, anyone too interested in my sister and her movie has an agenda when it comes to me.

"You're very proactive," I let out.

"It's actually part of my job on set—to make you comfortable," he says.

His quasi-professional tone sobers me up. It reminds me that I have a job to do too. The photo of Layla entering Cashore House burns in my memory, the desperation on her face imprinted all over me.

And if I'm indeed right and someone took my sister, Cashore might hold the clues as to where she is now. Being here might reveal some crucial detail, an important clue the police have missed because they didn't even realize it *was* a clue. But I know what to look for, or so I tell myself. And who knows, if all else fails, maybe the documentary will help flush out Layla's kidnapper.

With Adrianna's portrait out of my hands, I take in Layla's old room, resurrected from its lonely slumber and cleaned up for the occasion. Unlike some other places in the house, particularly the west wing, this room has no distinctive scent, yet to me, it's fragrant with anticipation—ink and leather and musk. A confusing scent that sends ripples all over my skin. Did Layla come to this room the night of her disappearance? Did she go to the forbidden west wing? I wish I could retrace her steps. I wonder if the house itself knows what happened to my sister.

"Everything's been arranged to look exactly as it was back when you and Layla lived here," Arthur says, watching me as I study the space.

"Except for that painting," I say.

"Except for the painting," he replies, with a guilty smirk.

"What's your dad's angle here exactly?" I ask him point-blank. "I mean, is he just curious about how the movie was made? Is it, like, a tribute to Layla?"

Arthur's response isn't going to change anything, not at this stage, but still, I'd like to know what Erasmus hopes to achieve. He's been infuriatingly secretive whenever I've broached the subject, telling me he'd like it all to be a surprise. He did mention reenactments, but that's all I know.

"He'll explain it all over dinner tonight," Arthur says cryptically. My earlier suspicion returns, like a crawling thing, its skin cold and slimy. Oblivious to my darkening feelings, he adds, "We're gathering downstairs at eight thirty to celebrate the start of filming. Get ready for some grand posturing and boring speeches. Dad hasn't made a new film in ages, so this is a big deal for him. He was so worried about receiving your parents' consent—it was a big relief when those signatures came through."

"Sounds good!" I say quickly, not wanting to linger on those signatures I forged. "I guess I better get ready." My cheeks flush slightly again. I'm only a few months away from becoming a legal adult. And I couldn't risk them getting in the way. My parents did their best trying to protect me from the media after Layla's disappearance. As a family, we've kept a united front, never even granted a single interview. Until this documentary. I'll deal with my parents' disapproval when the time comes. For now, I need to focus on the task at hand.

"I'll leave you to it," Arthur says.

Rather than retracing the roundabout path via the bathroom and my room, Arthur reaches for the door that will take him straight to the hallway. But brief confusion passes over his face as he grasps the handle and finds it locked. "Oh, right . . ." he says.

I trail after him as he goes back the long way after all. Miriam perks up.

"The issue of privacy has likely crossed your mind, with the cameras everywhere," Arthur says, pausing in his retreat, his words falling halfway between a question and a statement. "Obviously, bathrooms are no-camera zones. But that corner over there is your room's only blind spot." He points at the space where the monstrous wardrobe doesn't quite fill its designated corner, leaving a tight spot between its side and the wall, barely enough for a slender person to slide through. "I thought you might want to know."

"Thanks," I reply. "I'll make sure to squeeze in there if I want some privacy."

Arthur snorts at that. Once the door shuts behind him, I exhale some of my tension. The whirring of the motion cameras is subtle but consistent as I move around. This room is familiar, and yet alien, like I've been here before but in a dream. I tend to overuse the word *haunted* in my head, but it's the only one that truly works when I attempt to describe how this house, how this room, feels to me. Our memories can be a frightening place, and Cashore House is one such place for me. Here, my past and present seem to coexist on the same plane of reality, and I'm trapped in between.

Even with the walls between us, the eyes of Adrianna Kashoroff follow me as I unzip my suitcase and extract one of the evening dresses I've brought with me. A pair of ballet shoes, black and sleek, peek at me from the depths of the folded clothes. I don't really know why I brought the shoes here. My ballet days are far behind me, and the only tangible reminder of my dancing past is the deep-seated pain that lives in my right ankle, a physical memory of a terrible accident that happened years ago, in this very house.

I shove the shoes deeper into the suitcase.

It's only after I take a quick shower and get dressed for dinner that I have a moment to check my messages.

The most recent are from my friends, as expected, accompanied by selfies and photos of the lake house, preceded by a message from Mom asking how I'm settling in. I've been diligently forwarding my friends' snaps to my parents, carefully choosing the photos where nature takes center stage and people are blurry figures jumping into water from a distance. Then, I notice one more unread message on the app.

in the end of the Path

It's not even a proper message, a fragment more like. To anyone else it'd appear truncated into near incomprehension, but to me it's frighteningly meaningful.

Because the sender is my sister.

Seven

in the end of the Path

I stare at the words.

Layla's name stares back at me from the screen.

Her avatar is a still frame of Vermillion's face, all snarl and black eyes. One of those rare moments the entity shows herself to viewers.

The online status indicator beside Layla's profile is lit up.

My heartbeat hammers in my ears. I imagine somewhere out there—maybe not too far from me at all—Layla is staring intently at her phone, waiting for my reply with bated breath, our long-played roles reversed. The green online symbol is like a lifeline to me, because if Layla is indeed back, if she's alive and well, I don't have to go through with Erasmus's documentary, any of this. I can go back home and live my life for *me*.

Frantic, I locate the number for the lead detective assigned to

Layla's case. I have to call him. Now, while the signal is still there. If they work fast, maybe they can trace the line back to Layla's location. Shaking, my finger hovers over the number that I've used and abused in the past.

But instead, I scramble for the video call next to my sister's name. It's an instinct that overpowers logic. Before fully realizing what I'm doing, I move toward the blind spot between the wardrobe and the wall. I pack myself into the tight space, trying to ignore its dank, dusty smell. The phone rings as it attempts to connect. I imagine I hear the sound reverberating through the house. My skin is all shivers and ripples. I expect to hear Layla's familiar away message—"you know what to do". The message I've heard too many times to count, my sister's voice unchanged, sounding so close, like she's murmuring in my ear. But instead the ringing continues until there's a distant click, followed by silence.

Did someone just pick up? My breath hitches, my fingers are coated with sweat, the phone is slipping away. I grip it tighter.

"Layla? Are you there?" I speak into the cold, waiting silence.

It might be my heart thudding in my ears, but I imagine hearing someone breathing in the background, the eerie sound sends my pulse racing.

My hope darkens around the edges, and sickness roils in my chest. I don't even know if the damn phone is still in Layla's possession. Someone could've hacked her WhatsApp.

"Who is this?" I demand, imagining I'm talking to Layla's abductor. "What have you done with my sister?"

The line goes dead.

Layla's online indicator vanishes—if it was ever lit up in the first place. My perception has been twisted by grief and by hope in the past—I don't fully trust myself.

"Shit!" I hiss, frustrated with myself and with this entire damn situation. I've lost my chance to contact the police.

But . . . they've never been able to trace Layla's number, or extract anything useful from its continued existence. And they didn't believe me about the photo either. Why would things be different now?

The lead detective always has a "reasonable" explanation where Layla's phone is concerned. He'd probably say the message I received today was a glitch, or a delayed delivery, something years old and unimportant. And then he'd contact my parents, and that would mean the end of my deception. I'd have to come clean about where I am and what I'm doing. No, I decide, I definitely made the right call. I have to believe that.

My sister's phone has been in limbo since her disappearance. The PI our parents hired suggested they maintain the account because Layla might try to use it again. At the time, I thought it was just something he said to keep their hope alive. But it gave me a connection to my sister, even if it was one-sided. Whenever I press the call button, I can hear her voice, even if only for an instant, her pre-recorded response always the same: *You know what to do.*

For a while I continued messaging Layla. Her unresponsiveness made her into a perfect listener. At times, I think I forgot that there might be a real person on the other side of our unbalanced exchange, and I treated her like some made-up entity, a sympathetic ear, an imaginary friend: Dear Diary, Dear Layla.

The grandfather clock in Layla's old room emits a low, reverberating chime.

A faint double knock on my door pulls me from my conflicted thoughts.

"Sophia? You coming to dinner?" Arthur's voice drifts in.

I leave my hiding place and shake the dust off my dress as best I can.

I stuff my phone into a sequined clutch bag that used to be Layla's. My fingers grasp the bag like it's precious, like it contains a lifeline—hers—my only connection to my sister and the resolution of this mystery I'm forcing myself to face.

I relax my shoulders and smooth my features into what I hope looks somewhat normal and not like I'm hiding something. I can imagine how ecstatic Erasmus would be if he knew about the message I'd just received; he would probably think it's a sign that we're on the right track, that my being here is serendipitous, and Layla is giving us her blessing. But this message feels like it's mine and only mine. I'm not going to share it with Erasmus or anyone.

When I step into the corridor, I take in Arthur's appearance. His hair is smoothed down, a few wavy strands falling across his forehead in a kind of adorable way. He shed his torn jeans and band tee in favor of black trousers and a dark silver, silky button-down shirt. The top button is loose, giving me an extended view of his neck, which appears tense.

He's taking me in too, but his staring feels a little bit less obvious than mine. I wonder what he's thinking, how he's seeing me. I realize I'd like for him to like me, but it's a fleeting thought, quickly overwhelmed by my earlier suspicions and by the enormity of my task ahead.

"Are you okay?" Arthur asks.

I'm still shaky from before, and it shows. "I'm fine," I say, feeling anything but fine. "It's just this place. Too many memories."

"Some food might help?" he says.

"Lead the way." My fingers dig into the clutch bag.

We proceed downstairs to where a long table is set, and a luxurious dinner awaits us. The only problem is, we're not eating in the dining room.

I tense up seeing where we're eating. If I wasn't certain that Erasmus had a hidden agenda before, I am now. In having the dinner table set here, in Cashore's cramped secondary reception room, where child-me had her first encounter with Vermillion, under the omnipresent scrutiny of Layla's camera, he's clearly setting me up. But for what?

Arthur's hand is soft on my elbow as he leads me toward the table, but I take a halting step. I need to slow things down, to be thorough as I take in this space. I stop and whisper to Arthur, "I'll join you in a second."

Suddenly, thunder cracks, and it's like a jolt to my heart. My skin erupts in goose flesh. I smell a whiff of rain. I look around, but I can't tell if anyone else noticed or if it's just me, if simply being here, in this room, has transported me into the labyrinth of my memories.

I'm outside, in the rain, looking into this very room. I see Vermillion.

But what I see of her is distorted by the mullioned glass and the rivulets of water. I know that this ghost is Layla's trick, one of many, but terror is already unfurling within me like embers trapped under my skin.

As if called forth by my curious gaze, more of Vermillion descends from the ceiling. Headfirst, matted hair hanging long, like a demonic Rapunzel. Her blood-coated fingers strain and push against the ceiling, as if she's climbing up out of a grave.

She flips in the air and floats toward me until only the thin glass separates us. She bangs her bloody fists against the window, but it doesn't give. The house is her prison. Her mouth moves, but the house devours her words like hungry earth soaking up rainwater. Vermillion's black eyes, opened so wide they seem to not have eyelids, sear themselves into my memory.

I look up. The spot on the ceiling from which Layla had suspended that terrifying dummy is now occupied by a crystal chandelier of gargantuan proportions.

As I slowly approach the table, I set my unease aside. The air itself is alive with excitement. And soon, my suspicions and fears are nothing but dark ice melting. As for Layla's incomplete message . . . I decide to take it as a sign. A good omen. Perhaps my sister wants to be found. If she texted me once, it's bound to happen again. I just have to wait for the next clue. That is, if it is indeed Layla behind the mysterious text. I want to believe it so badly. But the realistic pessimist in me suspects that if it's not a glitch, then it might be Layla's kidnapper.

I feel watched, studied. But when I scan the faces of the people seated at the dinner table, no one makes my suspicions rise.

My stomach whines, and I realize I've had nothing to eat since morning as I approach the table and take my assigned seat next to Erasmus—the chandelier behind me, over me. My eyes seek out the waiting staff; their crisp shirts match the white of the tablecloth.

I flinch when someone leans over my shoulder, hair brushing against my cheek. But it's just a waiter filling a crystal flute next to my plate with sparkling wine. I reach for the flute and slowly bring it to my lips for a nervous swig. Before taking another sip,

I notice that no one else is drinking. I set the glass down. Though Miriam and other crew members are seated at the table, those motion-operated cameras are everywhere, always rolling, documenting my every move, misstep, and embarrassment.

It occurs to me that a recording might exist of me calling Layla and then shouting at her possible abductor—despite what Arthur said about the blind spot in my room. But there's no way there's a record of what I *saw* on my phone's screen, which comforts me.

"Arthur told me about your reaction to Adrianna's portrait. Sorry it disturbed you," Erasmus says. I turn to him, feeling the chandelier's presence behind me—not being able to keep an eye on it bothers me.

To the director's left, facing me across the table is Arthur, looking positively Byronic. Handsome but somewhat burdened, dark eyes red-rimmed, mouth pained.

"It just caught me off guard," I reply with a shrug, hyperaware of the chilling draft licking at my back, of the chandelier's soft chiming.

I meet Erasmus's eyes before adding, "I'm told the painting's courtesy of the house's owner?"

"That's right," Erasmus says, looking at me but kind of through me. "She's an amateur historian. Something of a von Hahn enthusiast. She's amassed quite a collection over the years. Supposedly, she's gotten ahold of the Baron's personal, annotated copy of the *Book of Ka'schor.* I couldn't convince her to loan it to me . . . yet." He grins.

The Book of Ka'schor rings some eerie bells. As an occultist, and a self-proclaimed magician, no wonder there is some book the Baron perused—come to think of it, did the book inspire the name of the Baron's house, or was it the other way around? And then there's Adrianna. Was "Kashoroff" a stage name she chose, or was it something she brought with her into immigration? I keep these questions to myself.

"Who is she exactly, this current owner?" I ask Erasmus, briefly glancing at Arthur to confirm he's definitely listening to this exchange while pretending to type on his phone. It's in the angle of his head, the curve of his lips—his attention is externally focused. Living in a faux haunted house with an unpredictable, aloof sister has made a body language expert out of me. With Layla, a particular turn of her head could mean the difference between a perfectly pleasant morning and a gloomy, anxious one. And I preferred to be emotionally prepared.

"She's a very private person. I hear she might be a distant relation of Adrianna herself," Erasmus says. "We've been communicating through an assistant. But regardless, it's been a most fruitful exchange, the *Book of Ka'schor* notwithstanding. She's been tracking a number of rare von Hahn items for years, and some of those can now be found on display, Adrianna's portrait included."

"Kudos to the owner, I guess," I say.

I wonder what other items have been added to the house decor, what other surprises are waiting for me, and if, unlike those elusive eight swan designs we could never locate, I'd recognize them for what they are before they have a chance to startle me.

The caterers begin serving the first course and Erasmus picks up his champagne flute and stands. All conversation dies down, and everyone reaches for their glass. Erasmus towers over us, his shadow looking too long and twisted in the fractured light of the chandelier.

"Five years ago, something remarkable took place in this house," Erasmus begins. "Tonight, we gather here to pay tribute to the genius of Layla Galich and to follow in her footsteps. Cashore House is ready, the actors are all here and . . ."

I brace with unease when, a vague smile dancing on his lips, he looks down at me and adds, "In no particular order, *V*'s key scenes will be reconstructed, with Sophia's reactions recorded anew. So, let's raise our glasses to celebrate our first night of filming *V: The Return*."

Amid glasses clinking and the film crew cheering, I hope no one notices me cringing. This whole "key scene reconstruction business" is not exactly news to me, but it doesn't mean I have to like it. I can't show my displeasure openly—the cameras are rolling and Erasmus—as I remind myself for the umpteenth time—is my ticket to the house. Which means I'll do whatever needs to be done, and suffer through it, within reason, to remain here for as long as I can. Or at least until I find my sister.

I dig into the first course, shrimp ceviche in a lemony marinade, while maintaining a neutral expression.

Once Erasmus is seated and picking up his fork, I say, "I thought the documentary was about trying to understand how Layla pulled off all those ghost tricks. I didn't realize your intent here was to frighten me and then film my reactions."

He looks at me, and, unlike earlier, this time I feel the full weight of his attention.

"When you were a child," he says, soft and somber. "Your unpracticed responses to the triggers your sister set up were a huge factor in *V* becoming the cultural icon it remains to this day. Just like then, you still have nothing to fear. We might have better special effects at our disposal, but no matter how realistic things might look, the only *real* thing will be your reactions. That's what I want to focus on."

I hate to admit that there's a certain brilliance to his plan. I haven't come across a documentary structured quite like it, involving original participants in simulated reenactments. And perhaps it's exactly what I need—to retrieve some lost memory that might help me reveal a clue as to Layla's current whereabouts. Besides, if Erasmus is really going to have me reenact all of *Vermillion*'s disordered scenes, the process will take me all around the house, giving me access to all the places my sister might have visited the last time she was here.

Erasmus doesn't need to know any of that.

"I'm not twelve years old. It won't be the same," I say to him, sounding more confident than I feel.

"Well, like I said, we've got better special effects this time," Erasmus assures me, like I give a damn about his special effects. "I don't want to give away too much, but I think you'll be pleasantly surprised. Besides . . . this is an old house. It's seen a lot of strange things, I'm sure. Perhaps us being here, filming something *real*, will trigger something even more . . . real?"

The last bit he says in a playful, casual way, but I don't buy it. I shiver in the breeze that keeps finding its way into the house, tinged with the brine and the salt of the rumbling ocean outside. There's something off about Erasmus's vibe. On the surface, he's legit, he says all the right things, but I can't shake off a feeling that there's more to it. He's a great indie director, with an impressive body of work, nominations, and awards, though nothing major. I didn't give much thought to his motivation for doing this before agreeing to be in his documentary. But it's too late to reconsider now. I'm here, in the house. I'm not going anywhere.

Before I can ask what the hell Erasmus means, a series of subtle cracks and groans reverberate through the air, each new wave of sound louder than the one that preceded it.

The light flickers.

Someone gasps.

Someone else whispers.

Everything slows down.

I meet Arthur's eyes in the dim light, but just like his father, he appears to look through me. Or, more correctly, over my shoulder and up.

He's looking at the ceiling. Something is happening, right behind me.

I imagine the grand chandelier behind me coming alive, dangling crystals merging, becoming skeletal limbs that reach for me. Its chimes the whispers of the dead.

I can't turn around.

I won't.

Never, ever look directly into the eyes of a ghost.

Because once you see it, once you see *her*, once you acknowledge her impossible existence, you can never unsee it.

And that's how she gets you.

I learned that lesson a long time ago. And it didn't matter that Layla assured me the ghost was never real. Vermillion was real enough for me, real enough to leave a scar.

Absently, I reach for the faint circle of half-moon scars around my wrist. I know it's all in my head, but my old scars feel inflamed now, itchy.

The ceiling cracks. A whisper of chimes follows.

A cloud of fine dust descends, covering my plate, my skin. My hands shake.

I drop my fork.

"Move!" Arthur shouts, but he sounds faraway. I feel as if I'm submerged in a tub full of water.

Erasmus isn't beside me anymore. But Arthur is. I missed the moment he rounded the table to get to me. He's looking right at me, gesturing wildly. His warm fingers close around my wrist. He pulls me toward the window, where the other diners already stand. I catch a glimpse of the ocean through the glass. It looks cold, vast, unknowable.

By the time my senses return, I see that the majestic chandelier is hanging askew, dangling by a lone wire.

And then, we all gasp as the wire snaps and the chandelier drops onto my chair, sending crystal shards everywhere and plunging the room into utter darkness.

Eight

Everyone retreats to their rooms to get cleaned up. Dinner is canceled, and my empty stomach won't stop complaining. Back in my bedroom, dizzy and a little bit sick from the glass of sparkling wine I downed earlier on an empty stomach, I can't stop messaging Layla. I hold my phone at an angle I hope won't reveal anything to the cameras.

Please let me know if you're getting these.

But none of these newer messages show up as "read." Another attempt at a call again triggers my sister's autoresponse. "You know what to do," Layla assures me. But do I?

A growl of frustration bursts from my chest and I fling the phone onto my bed and head for the shower.

In the bathroom, I stand facing the door to my sister's old room. My fingers wrap around the swan-shaped door handle. One turn would take me into Layla's domain, where Adrianna Kashoroff's piercing eyes would find me. I don't move. Invading my sister's territory twice in one day feels like too much. Even for me.

I enter the miniature shower cabin, forgoing the clawfoot tub. I'd have to be possessed to get into that antique monstrosity.

I don't feel the cut under my hair until I'm in the shower, hot water prickling my scalp. A tiny crystal shard clangs against the tiles by my feet. Without thinking, I nudge it toward the drain with my bare foot. The house might have century-old bones, but its guts are fairly modern, water pipes included.

I don't hear the knocking until I emerge from the bathroom, slightly dizzy, dressed in pajamas and towel-drying my hair. I open the door to find Arthur. He balances a covered plate and a steaming mug of tea on a silver tray.

"Your dinner," he announces, with a crooked half-smile. "Our caterer is pretty devastated about earlier. He's been busy prepping these meal replacements."

I consider accepting the tray from his hands but change my mind—in my shaky state, dinner will likely end up scattered on the floor. I move out of Arthur's way and let him into my room.

He leaves the tray on top of the vanity and turns to face me, looking like he wants to say something. He's still wearing his dinner attire, but his sleeves are rolled up, showing the beginning of a tattoo that climbs up the inner side of his left arm. I stare at it for too long, unable to make out what it is, but too shy to ask. Given its location, it feels like it's a private one.

"Do I have to tip you?" I deadpan. Arthur's presence in my space makes me nervous, and sarcasm is my best defense.

"The delivery service is complimentary," he deadpans back, but I catch a playful spark in his eyes.

"Thanks then . . . I like the personal touch," I add, noticing a delicate stem dotted with sweet alyssum flowers arranged on the tray. The flowers appear freshly cut—but it's more likely the floral addition was the caterer's, accompanying every meal sent to the rooms tonight.

"Have you already had dinner?" I ask, meeting Arthur's eyes.

"Yeah, kind of." He fidgets with his rolled sleeves until they come down, covering his forearms. "How are you doing?"

"Not too bad, I guess." A half-lie. "Considering I was nearly killed by a chandelier and had a shard of crystal embedded in my skull."

I regret saying it at once, because Arthur immediately looks alarmed. "Do you need to see a doctor?" He moves toward me, but recalibrates almost instantly and stays put, studying me.

"It's fine. Just a scratch. I'll survive."

I give him the best smile I can manage and transfer my dinner tray to the bed. Arthur must take my casual act as an invitation to stay. He maneuvers the room's only chair, velveteen stuffed, out of its corner, so it faces the bed. I don't mind the company, though the presence of my phone next to the pillow reminds me of Layla again. There's a permanent quiver in my gut. Layla's message feels like too heavy a secret to keep, but I must. I can't trust anyone but myself. Especially, considering the reason we are here, at Cashore. Arthur, his father, everyone involved in the making of this documentary is potentially a V-head in disguise.

The tea, too hot to drink just yet, smells divinely of peppermint and lavender. I remove the plate's cover to reveal a roast chicken sandwich. I dig in. The sandwich tastes *fancy*. I overheard a crewman say Erasmus contracted some posh catering company worthy of the Baron's famous extravagance. I'm not sure grapes and chopped celery belong in a chicken sandwich, but it's food, and I'm hungry.

"So . . ." I meet Arthur's eyes. "Was that whole chandelier thing a setup? One of your dad's planned scene reenactments?" I ask casually.

"Of course not!" Arthur replies. "Dad would never endanger his crew and talent like that."

He sounds like he means it. I decide to trust him, but I still harbor an ember of suspicion where Erasmus is concerned. It was sheer luck that no one got seriously injured tonight. But the emotional toll it had on all of us has yet to be determined. I wonder if Erasmus is superstitious. And if yes, does he see the chandelier as a sinister omen, or an encouraging sign?

"Besides, what scene would that be exactly?" Arthur asks.

"Well, that particular spot on the ceiling does have a special meaning in *Vermillion*."

A distant shiver licks at my skin. The memory of Vermillion's upside-down entrance in that scene all these years ago still gets me anxious.

Arthur winces. Or maybe it's just the play of light as the overhead lamp flickers, making a quick shadow pass over his face. The freaky chandelier incident aside, Cashore House's wiring is in pretty good shape, if memory serves, but there's always been an occasional current fluctuation—a feature Layla incorporated into her film. If I were the superstitious type, I'd associate the flickering light with me saying the word *vermillion* aloud just now, and many of Layla's fans would agree. Over the years that followed the film's release, my sister's spooky creation bred its own universe of superstitions. CrimsonDreadNet is full of rules and lore. There are those who believe in the Seven Signs woven into the footage of Layla's movie, and there is a school of thought that insists on the old-as-dirt conjuring rule—say Vermillion's name three times and you will summon the entity. I'm not a believer—a V-liever—but I am something of an expert on *Vermillion* lore.

"You know, if something, anything at all, makes you uncomfortable," Arthur says, "you just have to say so. Without you, Dad can't do any of this, and he'll do anything in his power to ensure that you're happy. It's my job to hold him to his word."

"It's okay. No complaints at this point, except for nearly being killed by a chandelier." I force a laugh. "But I admit I'm curious to see Erasmus's special effects. That's the question, isn't it? Can he make Vermillion look *real*."

There's a sinking feeling in my stomach as I say this. I was going for a light, teasing tone, playing along with the cameras that I know are rolling, but just as I say the accursed V-word again, the lights in the room go out completely.

When the lights return, Arthur is as pale as the comforter on my bed.

"It's all fake, anyway, right? Always was," I add with another nervous laugh.

Arthur nods, but the frown between his eyebrows taints any potential levity. I suspect that the real reason he came into my room tonight hasn't been broached. But I can't help him find his courage, or whatever it is he needs. That's not what I'm here for.

Nine

Alone at last, I crawl under the blankets.

This queen-sized bed is new and a far cry from the narrow one I remember from my childhood.

Eyes open, I listen to the subdued roar of the ocean. It permeates the house, my room. If I close my eyes and focus on the sound, I can almost sense its vibrations on the surface of my skin. Tonight, Cashore is full of all kinds of jarring noises. Fragments of conversations. Sporadic bursts of laughter. Footsteps thumping against the floor. Someone swearing.

When was the last time these walls hosted so many guests at once? I imagine the days when the Baron and his ethereal beloved threw their lavish parties. I bet the house felt different then, more alive.

There's a certain sadness to it now, like a fire diminished.

The room is never completely still, shadows moving, coalescing, dissipating. I try not to look too closely. Try not to imagine that there's a shadow shaped like a hand, fingers rippling like smoke, reaching through the door from the corridor and into my room.

I must have drifted off at some stage, but I wake to a splinter of a dream in which both bathroom doors are cracked open, creating a corridor between my room and my sister's, and there are noises coming from the adjoining room.

It takes me a moment to realize that I'm awake now, and still hearing the noises.

I hear a suppressed cough. An uneven release of a held breath . . . things you don't want to hear in the dead of the night, coming from the next room over—a room that's supposed to be empty and locked.

Flat on my back, blanket twisted around me, I don't dare move.

The lighthouse beam draws a harsh line across my face through the window, and I can't help but be freaked-out. In Layla's movie, a moving path of light is an omen, an invitation.

I turn my head sideways to find the bathroom door wide open, but I remember leaving it closed. Right now, there's nothing standing between me and whoever, *whatever*, is currently in Layla's old bedroom.

My mind races. Is this one of Erasmus's reenactments?

But which of *Vermillion*'s key moments is this supposed to be? The awakening? The visit to the Baron's Preparation Room?

Deep, ragged breaths drift from Layla's old room, sounding closer and closer.

No, no, *no*, this is real. Something is truly happening, only it has nothing to do with Erasmus and his documentary.

It's this freaking haunted house.

I may not believe in ghosts, but my memories are possessed by what happened here five years ago.

I'm twelve years old again. I'm lying completely still. Because staying still is important. When ghosts are getting to know you, they could be skittish at first, the smallest of movements might spook them. Layla points her camcorder at me: if I look paralyzed with fear, it's likely viewers will be too. Layla explained it all to me, but I was only twelve.

I remain motionless, but secretly I watch my sister. She seems satisfied with my performance. Even with my entire child body poisoning itself with terror, I must look peaceful, deadly calm. Layla calls me her sleeping little angel.

But I'm not little anymore. And I'm no angel.

I try moving, but my limbs are deadweights against the bed. Worse, I feel like I'm being swallowed whole into the mattress. I know what comes next. Vermillion will come, she will lean over me and shove me into the foam, and no one will hear me scream.

I'm falling.

The white ceiling flies upward, and I'm at the bottom of a dried-out well, rocks digging into my back. I can't breathe.

I breathe.

I force a blink, and the effort leaves my eyes stuck half-open, retinas starting to burn.

I'm just in my bed. I'm in my bed, I repeat in my head, trying to jolt myself out of this state. In the end, it's the uninvited guest next door who helps me snap out of it.

I hear the phantom in Layla's bedroom open a drawer, then close it, then exhale, fast and annoyed, her frustration palpable. My breathing quickens.

"Damn it!" the presence next door says, irritated. "Where is it?"

I exhale.

But that voice . . . it belongs to my sister.

How?

I brace for the inevitable. A tearful reunion? A confrontation? It's been two years. Has she been here, in the house, all this time?

Unless, Erasmus had this planned out all along.

I try to say something, *anything*, but only a pitiful rattle issues from my throat. And then, from a distance, from the thick, thick coiling fog that numbs the edges of consciousness, understanding comes. I'm still dreaming. That's why I can't move.

My sister's not really there.

And just when I almost believe my theory, the invisible visitor speaks again.

"You shouldn't have taken it, Sophia. Where is it? You have to give it back," Layla mutters, slipping in and out of the fake accent she'd put on whenever she was in front of the camera.

Straining to break the hold of fear that's flattening me against the bed, I lift my head and peer into the dark sliver of the bathroom. I want to say to this dream-version of Layla that I have nothing of hers. It's been a long time since I last found my way into her room and went through her stuff, looking for her secrets. What is she looking for now? What does she want?

And there's more, so much more I want to ask her, as if this dream-Layla would know what's really happened to my sister, where is she now, and how I can save her.

My fingers are all pins and needles as sleep lets me go slowly, freeing one piece of me at a time. My voice returns. "I . . . I . . ."

In her old bedroom, Layla's search turns violent. Drawers fly and crash to the floor. Layla screams, swearing and cursing. She's a poltergeist, unleashed.

I'm dreaming. I know I'm dreaming.

I'm already collapsing back into sleep, the non-lucid kind. The mattress is just a mattress, I tell myself. My missing sister is not in the next room.

I'm not in Layla's horror movie anymore.

I'm just in an old house built dangerously into a cliff. I repeat these statements in my mind until I believe them—a therapeutic method to deal with lingering trauma that I mastered in a psychologist's office over the years.

I'm not a helpless kid anymore.

I'm strong, and I'm ready.

I know how to defeat these ghosts.

With a jolt, I sit up in bed at the exact same moment a powerful draft slams the bathroom door shut.

Ten

I lie awake in my tousled bed until a quarter past four.

Having Layla, even just her disembodied voice, direct my nightmare with a steady hand has left me aching. My joints and muscles strain as I leave the bed and change into a pair of clean jeans and a sweater. As a child I remember how Cashore House always felt cold. Apparently, that hasn't changed.

I check my phone. The latest string of messages addressed to my sister remain unread. Looking now at all the words I wrote, I can see how they grew more and more desperate each time I hit "send." I'd begin doubting my sanity if not for Layla's incomplete message. I can still see it, burned into the screen. But even that feels more like a twisted dream than something real right now.

I stand by the window, my bare feet curling against the cold floor. My eyes trace the lighthouse's path over the water. I wonder how cold the ocean is. I could go down to the beach and see for myself—fifty-three mist-strewn stairs run between Cashore's clifftop seat and the shore, a semi-secret passage cut into the rock, partially concealed by white bushes of sweet-scented alyssums—but sunrise is still over an hour away.

So instead of venturing out, I decide to explore the house. On my own terms.

I don't know what I hope to find, but I'll know a clue when I see it. Something that meant nothing to the police when they searched the house, but that would have a hidden meaning for me.

I'm all too aware that the motion-activated cameras are following my progress, but I leave my room anyway. I'm used to feeling watched in this house, always. The soft rubber soles of my tennis shoes land silently against the lush rug that runs the length of the corridor. I creep around the second floor, studying the doors and the corners. Most of the rooms are occupied, by people or equipment, which complicates my search. And then I hear sounds coming from downstairs, a suppressed cough, a stuffy inhale. Maybe it's Erasmus, unable to leave his own set? I don't want to find out. The director is hiding something, I can feel it. But so am I, so perhaps that makes us even.

The air is stale, but other than the eucalyptus scent of cleaning supplies, it's deprived of any of the smells I associate with old houses—and this old house in particular. I feel a special kind of gratitude to the universe that my bedroom is in the east wing. Because when I was a kid, the west wing always made me feel . . .

Let me start again.

Cashore's west wing has always been haunted by a smell. Ever-elusive, it moved and expanded, never the same scent twice, richly textured in one inhale and just a phantom of a presence in another. It wasn't unpleasant, not exactly. It smelled like anticipation and restlessness, of sweat and . . . desire. Though I didn't know the word for it then. I couldn't name it until much later, when I was older. And there was music too, a melody it seemed only I could hear, that drifted from the west and lured me in. But back then, that pervasive smell of the west wing, accompanied by that odd, syncopated sound, made me want to put on my ballet shoes and dance until my feet bled.

The smell didn't evaporate as Mom and Dad's restoration efforts progressed. In fact, it grew more powerful as the works neared completion, as the collapsed patio where Adrianna met her untimely end decades ago was resurrected to its former glory. And the weirdest thing? Just like that uneven, haunting melody that only my ears could perceive, I was the only one who could ever detect that smell. My parents, the construction workers they employed, even Layla seemed oblivious to it.

I've never encountered that smell anywhere else in the house, not in the Baron's Preparation Room—arguably Cashore House's most unsettling space—and not even in Adrianna's studio upstairs, where *Vermillion*'s longest sequence, the Dance of the Unquiet Spirits, ended with a bloody accident. So, yes, I felt grateful to the universe that my bedroom is in the east wing, and that I don't have to breathe in or listen to the west wing's restless ghosts.

That's not to say the east wing wasn't spooky, because it was, it is. In fact, I think I'm hearing that melody now, a ghostly whisper from my past. I shiver and listen, trying to determine the source of that music—moody, electronic, syncopated by an uneven drumbeat. Similar to the one from my memory, but not exactly the same. Following the sound, I end up in front of a door at the far end of the corridor. The door is open just a crack. I don't know who's staying in this room, but I have my suspicions.

I knock twice, and the door opens without so much as a creak.

Arthur sits on the floor, blanket thrown against his shoulders, his back to me, bent over a laptop.

I freeze. On the laptop's screen, to the soundtrack of that dark electronic rhythm, one of *Vermillion*'s spookiest sequences unfolds. How could I forget that melody, that unsettling sound my sister used to enhance the striking visuals of her film?

I've seen Layla's film too many times to count, an assembly of unsettling scenes sewn together with a ghostly thread. I know this footage's every twist and turn, can quote its dialogue and voice-over in my sleep. But the thing is, every time I see *Vermillion*, it's a revelation.

On Arthur's laptop screen, twelve-year-old me, wispy and

stick-legged, is trapped in an endless pirouette. In twisting wisps, white smoke rises from the spot where my weight-bearing right foot drills into the floor in an unnaturally long rotation. The smoke is a clever special effect; I remember Layla explaining it was dry ice hidden in the wooden floors. But I don't remember seeing much of anything. I was fully in the moment, not paying attention to where I was going . . .

Case in point, coming out of that impossible spin, child-me staggers but quickly regains her footing. I swirl across the room, readying for an arabesque. I wince just watching her—*me*. I know what's coming. The unfortunate sissonne that landed me on a rotted plank as the wood disintegrated under my feet.

I hold my breath, momentarily lost in the past. After filming this dance sequence, which ended abruptly with me falling through the unstable floors of Cashore House's west wing, both Layla and I were grounded for two weeks. While I spent that time healing my damaged right ankle, the punishment affected Layla severely. For the duration of the grounding, Dad confiscated her camcorder, her phone, and her laptop.

Meanwhile on Arthur's screen, the music builds to a frantic crescendo. The *Vermillion*-version of me flies up, up, up the Escher-worthy stairs—the camera glides, turning upside down, then back—moving along the corridor, toward my fate.

I release a shuddering breath, something between a whimper and a growl.

Arthur flinches. "What the——" he cries out, turning to find me gawking over his shoulder.

"I'm so sorry!" I let out a panicked whisper. "I heard the music and followed it here—I didn't mean to sneak up on you."

Already regaining his composure, he hits the pause button on the footage. The last moment of the damn movie I see before the laptop's lid comes down is a shot of me, airborne in a split leap, Vermillion's sharp-angled face protruding from the flowery wallpaper, black eyes watching me.

"It's okay." Arthur's so calm, it's hard to believe he was freaked-out at seeing me. "Did the sound wake you? I tried to be quiet . . ."

"Not exactly," I say. "I rarely sleep the first night in a new place anyway."

"New?" He smiles.

"It's been years, so it *feels* new."

"Do you want some coffee?" He points at a large, family-sized thermos next to him on the floor. "You can use the lid as a cup—it's clean."

The moment he mentions coffee, I pick up on its scent in the room.

"Have you been caffeinating while staring at the screen all night?" I ask, taking a seat next to him. This close, with our knees almost touching, the stubble on his cheeks and his red-rimmed eyes are more pronounced. He looked Byronic before, now he just looks tired.

I reach for the thermos. As advertised, the lid is clean and makes a perfect cup, which I eagerly fill with still-hot coffee. The first sip is divine; I luxuriate in its bitterness on my tongue.

"Can't sleep," Arthur explains. "Insomniac." He gestures at his head, as if it's in there that his adolescent insomnia lies, coiled like a poisonous snake at the bottom of a well.

"Watching horror movies all night will only make it worse, you know," I observe.

"Nah, my particular case is yet unknown to mainstream science. Nothing can make it worse—or better. It just is."

It's hard to tell if he's joking or if he's referring to an actual diagnosis.

My eyes are drawn to the laptop again. Even with it closed I don't feel completely safe nor distanced from what's captured on its frozen screen.

I shudder.

Arthur watches me with unrestrained interest. "I can't imagine your sister's movie still has much of an effect on you. You must've seen it thousands of times."

I have. But there's a disconnect between what I remember and what Layla's footage shows. Some scenes are set up, with Layla giving me instructions, like "do some ballet moves" or "stare at this corner like something in there is staring back." Sometimes, she'd use props or special effects. Though most scenes are improvised—I remember how Layla would grab her camcorder and start filming me and the space around me, seemingly at random.

It doesn't help that the film is not put together in a linear fashion. While the dancing sequence, with its dramatic finale, is the film's penultimate scene, chronologically it had actually taken place early on, and was among the first vignettes Layla had filmed. Those watching closely will notice me doing a poor job concealing a limp in many of the scenes. The trivial reason is that my damaged ankle was still healing after that catastrophically bad landing.

I give Arthur a shrug in response. "Yeah . . . is it weird that I actually can't stand horror movies?"

He snorts. "Yeah, it *is* kind of weird. I've always just assumed that since you got to be a part of something huge like your sister's movie, you'd be obsessed with the genre as a whole—or completely unaffected by it."

"I've always found horror movies silly. Jump scares and all."

"I hate jump scares, too," he admits. "But I do like to watch horror when I'm feeling down. There's something morbidly attractive about people having a way worse day than I am."

A laugh escapes my lips. "That's an interesting way to look at it. Does this mean you're super down right now, since you're glued to the screen at this ungodly hour?"

He gives me a sideways look. "It's different with *V*. Watching it has nothing to do with how I'm feeling."

"Why are you watching it then?" I ask. "Hoping for an 'encounter'?"

"Yes and no." Arthur lets out a tired laugh. "My relationship with *V* is . . . complicated."

His words trigger alarms in my brain, but I don't understand what it is exactly that I find unsettling.

Then I realize: It's his use of the V-word.

Last night when the lights went out in my room, I thought I saw Arthur flinch as I uttered the word myself, but I wrote it off as just a play of light. Now I backtrack. Have I heard Arthur actually say 'Vermillion' aloud? Great. I already suspected he was a Layla fanboy, a V-head. What scares me is that I don't know the extent of his obsession, and I'm going to be trapped in Cashore House with this guy for days, possibly weeks.

There's only one way to know for sure if his V-word avoidance is a fluke or something more sinister.

"I guess *Vermillion* means different things to different people," I say pointedly, eyes trained on his face.

With clockwork precision, he shivers at *Vermillion*. It's a tiny movement, but I've got my answer.

I exhale, take a big sip of the cooling coffee and stand up. I have one rule when it comes to Layla's superfans: do not engage. It's a pity about Arthur Sawyer though. It would have been nice to have someone my own age to talk to. Plus, despite what I saw just now, catching him staring at the screen like his life depends on it, he just doesn't strike me like a basement-dwelling V-head, studying *Vermillion* frame by frame, occupied with finding Layla's hidden messages.

"Before you go . . ." he begins to say, and it's his breathless tone that prevents me from leaving. It's like a beautiful hook, deadly sharp, hidden in something soft. "I'm sorry if something I said creeped you out. I've always admired your sister's film— from a distance. But then I received the First Sign. Ever since then, I've known there's more to it, that *V* is not just a film."

"The First Sign?" I squeeze the coffee cup with both hands, letting its dying warmth ground me. "You're on the Path then?"

A strange sense of déjà vu passes through me.

When CrimsonDreadNet began, V-heads used the online forum to report their strange experiences after watching Layla's film. What eventually became clear was that some of these experiences tended to be the same among the viewers, regardless of who or where they were. Was it collective psychosis? A shared delusion? Or was it that Layla's film was conjuring up some universal reactions among its fans? Somehow, these experiences evolved into Seven Signs, and the Path was born.

The way I understand it, *Vermillion*'s Seven Signs is a game, of sorts. The Path has seven turns, each corresponding to a sign linked to the film. Once all Seven Signs are received, seven turns of the Path cleared, Vermillion appears. It's like an extended, overcomplicated version of Bloody Mary, but it all depends on getting the Signs right.

If all this sounds too esoteric and weird, it's because it is. *Vermillion* is like a religion for some people. Not everything about its lore can be understood logically; some things must be believed.

Layla's text message yesterday cited the Path.

I feel like I'm on the verge of something, a hidden pattern about to reveal itself.

Arthur nods, and though everything about him in this moment seems unsettling, there's also this undeniable glint of hope in his eyes, a hint of wistfulness. He reminds me of myself five years ago, a determined kid, swirling through this house in a series of twisted ballet moves until my feet blistered and bled through my shoes.

"It all started after I had that dream—the one with Layla. The invitation," Arthur says, in a near whisper.

"What?" A touch of frost moves over my skin. The déjà vu returns, stronger and more persistent this time.

"I wasn't sure what it was at first but then . . . I knew it wasn't a regular dream when it didn't fade in the morning. On the contrary, every time I thought about it, more details emerged. It was my First Sign," Arthur says.

I barely hear him amid the blood drumming in my head, tinting my vision red.

"Layla, the Director, appears in a dream," Arthur goes on, encouraged by my stunned silence. "She's off camera, not seen but felt. She's looking for *something*, and by doing so she invites you to join in the search—to start on the Path. I'm not supposed to be telling you this, but . . . it's only the First Sign, there are public accounts of people trying to invoke it. Hopefully this won't get me in trouble . . ."

The air's too thick. Toxic fog crawls in, twisting my vision. Last night's ghoulish dream floods my mind. I'd forgotten some details, but I remember it all now. The sounds coming from the empty room. Layla's voice.

God.

Arthur's right. I've read that before: You can't start on the Path yourself; you need to be invited first. I came across accounts of V-heads who tried to induce their own Path experience, by watching the film thirteen times back-to-back without breaks, or by repeating phrases from the spooky voice-over Layla narrated like an incantation. But those accounts always ended the same, with V-heads acknowledging they had failed.

"The invitation comes to you in a dream?" My voice is unrecognizable, hoarse and weak.

Arthur nods. "Are you feeling okay? You look . . ."

I miss the rest of the question.

Despite my plan to think like a V-head in my search for Layla, I've become too numb to the *Vermillion* lore over the years. It's no wonder it didn't even occur to me to associate my last night dream of Layla with the Path. Why would I? I've never believed that the Path was a real thing, that people could actually follow it objectively rather than twisting random observations and coincidences into a semblance of order. How can V-heads even be trusted? They try to impress on another with their "authentic" experiences, claiming some kind of communion with Layla's art, all the while creeping on my sister and me in real life?

I've dreamed of Cashore House many times before, but almost never of my sister. And those rare dreams featuring Layla have never felt like anything more than my brain trying to make sense of things, sewing bits of emotions and memories together. Sometimes, a dream is just a dream.

But the dream I had last night was different. It felt *real*. Too real. Like Layla was actually there, close by, felt and heard but not seen. She was looking for something, while accusing me of taking something—from her? Could that dream be my invitation to walk the Path? No, no, no . . . It's against my nature to believe in these things, to see *Vermillion* as anything more than my clever sister's creative project, no matter how eerie and disturbing.

To actually believe in the Signs and the Path would also mean everything else about the movie and my time in this house five years ago was real too.

"I—" I'm not sure what I want to say. My heart is shuddering like it's about to explode. My hands are frozen around the thermos lid. "I need to go."

I miss Arthur's response because I'm already rushing out of his room.

It's only after I make it back to my icebox of a bedroom and shut the rattling door behind me that I realize I'm still clutching the lid of Arthur's thermos in my hand.

I drink what's left of the coffee in one semiconscious gulp and set the lid aside.

I grip my phone so hard my fingers begin to hurt, but I barely register the discomfort.

I remind myself to think like a fan. I will pretend to believe in the Path and the Seven Signs, even if it goes against everything I know.

Even if the possibility of having already received my First Sign fills me with bloodcurdling dread.

Without giving myself a chance to back down, I type a message to Layla.

I'm on the Path. I'm on my way. I'm coming to get you.

I hit send.

Eleven

The sun rises, but instead of bringing warmth, the temperature plummets. Shivering, I curse past me for not packing more substantial warm clothes.

Climbing into bed, I fashion the blankets into a tight-fitting cocoon. But even as I begin defrosting, the shivering doesn't subside. My heightened agitation takes control of my muscles, this fight-or-flight state becoming the norm. Haunted houses are ill-advised for those of nervous constitution.

But as long as I'm still able to function in my self-appointed detective role, I'll keep searching for my sister. Once I find her, I'll have the rest of my life to calm down.

I think again about the dream I've had, of hearing Layla, of not seeing her. There's a heaviness in my chest, a clot of fear that slowly grows. Am I really on the Path? But what does it even mean?

There are rules surrounding the Signs and the Path, but much of this lore is not openly talked about. Arthur's hesitance this morning reflects what I've read online. V-heads are notoriously secretive when it comes to the Path; they discuss the Signs in the general way, but specifics are not easily found. There are sections of CrimsonDreadNet that are closed, locked away, even to those with valid login credentials. God forbid the uninitiated get a hold of this sacred *Vermillion* lore.

But aside from going back to Arthur and begging him for more information, CrimsonDreadNet is my best bet. Perhaps my only bet. As much as I hate the V-head community, I admit they've been helpful in the past.

Positioning my laptop's screen away from the cameras, I disappear into the deepest recesses of the Internet, where the strangest *Vermillion* lore lives. It's time to try and get some help from people who treat Layla's film as nonfiction.

I type CrimsonDreadNet into the search engine and skim the results—the site is always on the move, tweaking its domain regularly, making it impossible to bookmark. Some days, I can't find the site at all. It's not exactly dark web—you don't need a special browser to access it—but it's bizarre and almost sentient in the way it behaves. If I believed in the supernatural, I'd say that photo of Layla entering Cashore was something the site conjured up itself. But a ghost in the machine would be a convenient explanation, one that excuses the ones truly guilty.

As I search, I forbid my eyes from wandering too far down the list of results. I know what's there. Annoyance and heartache. The bane of my existence: the buzzy listicles written by mindless bots.

TEN TEEN HORROR MOVIES TO KEEP YOU UP AT NIGHT.

CREEPY KIDS FROM HORROR FLICKS: WHERE ARE THEY NOW?

And my personal favorite:

YOU WON'T BELIEVE WHAT THAT KID FROM VERMILLION LOOKS LIKE NOW!

Basically, cutting-edge reporting accompanied by some god-awful snaps of me. Usually, I'm captured biting into a burger or, worse, baring my teeth at the camera like I'm demonically possessed.

Resisting the magnetic pull of clickbait, I finally bring up what I'm looking for, its link long and convoluted.

WELCOME TO CRIMSONDREADNET.

The familiar Gothic letters claim half the screen, red against black. The sign-in window is nestled underneath. I type in my credentials—*@BloodRedkNight13*, my sarcastic username takes on a new meaning now.

I'm in. The glittering catacombs haunted by real-life *Vermillion* horror stories await.

This site is the living testament that Layla mattered and continues to matter to thousands, tens of thousands of people. They're all obsessed with my sister, her creation, this house. With me. Like Arthur Sawyer, they all *believe* there's a Path and that there's a dead woman in a filthy red dress waiting for them at its end. Why can't I be more like them? Why am I tormented by this terrible doubt and skepticism? I have so many questions about all of it, like what actually *happens* at the end of the Path, after Vermillion shows her face? Surely, encountering the terrifying ghost from my sister's movie can't be a good thing . . . but the fan community keeps that information close to heart. Would Arthur know? Would he tell me if I asked?

While not as bad as the horrible listicles, CrimsonDreadNet presents many temptations. I must fight this powerful pull to go to my most visited thread: **__LaylaGalichIsAlive.** I checked the thread yesterday, before embarking on my trip to Livadia, and I know I'll go back to it soon, but right now I need to focus on something else.

__OnThePath

It's the only section of the forum that requires a passcode to be unlocked and access the inner sanctum.

In the past, no matter what connections I've pulled and what codes I've used, I could never enter **__OnThePath**, which, as the name suggests, is exclusively for those actively tracking the Seven Signs.

I've never attempted to walk the Path in earnest before, being the skeptic that I am, but I've definitely tried to fake my way into this secret sub-forum many times in the past.

If I'm right and my fever dream last night is my invitation to the Path, this time I won't be faking it. I'm going to be let in.

I click on the link. The familiar window pops up.

__OnThePath: What Does the Director Say When She Invites You?

The question's always been the same. And I've tried *everything* before, from creepy *Vermillion* quotes to enigmatic things Layla uttered during her rare interviews. I've even tried private things that only Layla and I would know, but nothing's ever worked. A single wrong answer gets you locked out of the entire forum for a week.

This morning, instead of triggering frustration, the familiar question takes me back to my lucid dream. To the words I heard, or thought I heard, coming from Layla's old bedroom while I sweated fearfully in my bed. Does the Director's wording need to be reproduced verbatim, or is it the general meaning that matters? And how does this website even decide who gets it right? How does it know?

Think, Sophia, think.

I close my eyes, tuning out the increasing noises of the house waking up. My heartbeat slows down and I almost feel Cashore zeroing in on me, its attention like a magnifying glass hovering over a peculiar bug. It waits for me to play my next card. It holds its stuffy breath.

In my dream, Layla was searching for something. Upset, she rifled through things in the adjacent bedroom, muttering questions and accusing me of taking something that wasn't mine, which she wanted back. My sister's always been a big cusser, her wicked tongue's never held back any F-bombs, but this time she was actually quite subdued in that regard. I shut my eyes tighter, searching for Layla's exact words in the bubbling brew of my memories.

Finally, I get it. I think. I hope. The memory is slippery, but I catch it and hold on.

"Damn it. Where is it? You have to give it back." I hit enter.

I don't dare blink.

After many unsuccessful login attempts in the past, I'm used to the black lock out screen.

So, when instead of reverting to black, the screen flickers and then there's a wall of blood cascading down, Vermillion's pixelated face, all snarl and dead eyes, flashing on the screen for a fraction of a second, I know I've finally done something right.

The page reloads, and I'm in.

A message pops up at the top of the screen.

Welcome, @BloodRedkNight13
Travel well along the Path, and let your nights be ruled by fright and flitting shadows.

My heartbeat rises. The message disappears, leaving me with nothing but a numbered list of seven threads. My fingers are slippery against the keyboard when I click on the first thread from the top, **First Sign**. It contains potentially thousands of posts, a record of fans starting their journeys on the Path, recounting their special moment of receiving the invitation from Layla, the Director. One of the latest additions is an entry from @MidnightFable1-85-1:

In my dream vision, LG was exactly like I remember her, but her eyes stayed closed the entire time. I think she could still see me though. One doesn't always need eyes to see. She offered me a hand. When I reached for it, LG disappeared in red smoke. Afterward, I cried so much. But I'm happy too. I'm walking, folks. I'm moving toward her. I'm not scared of what awaits in the end.

I skim through dozens of similar, nearly identical entries, confirming a gut feeling I've had that my own "First Sign" was an anomaly. I didn't even *see* Layla in my "dream vision," only heard her. Can I really say I was *invited* to walk the Path if all Layla did was accuse me of taking something that wasn't mine? But my encounter must've sounded convincing enough to whoever or *whatever* decides who gets to enter this forum.

I wonder if there are many answers, or only one. Or maybe it's not the answer that matters but intent, one's drive.

I wonder if I scroll back through thousands of posts on this thread, will I be able to recognize Arthur's contribution? He made no mention of CrimsonDreadNet this morning, but V-heads' awareness of the website's existence can be assumed. And what about Erasmus? For all I know, he is @MidnightFable1-85-1. In fact, anyone currently in the house, including members of the crew, can be V-heads. The thought of being surrounded by people obsessed with my sister and her movie sends an icy shiver down my back. As I turn my attention back to CrimsonDreadNet, I see the usernames and the posts in a twisted new light.

While it's tempting to read through the entire **First Sign** thread, it's not the First Sign that I need to concern myself with anymore, it's the second and what lies beyond. But when I click on the **Second Sign** thread, I get redirected back to the first one.

Only after angrily clicking again and again, each time ending up where I've started, I notice a little disclaimer at the top of the **First Sign** thread:

Share your encounter to unlock the next level.

I frown, biting my lower lip.

Reluctantly, and in as few words as I can manage, I type up my "encounter" and hit enter. I could lie, but I choose not to.

There's a certain superstition where CrimsonDreadNet is concerned, and it affects even levelheaded me. If my past experiences are anything to go by, this website knows when you lie.

Having added my own experience to thousands of other **First Sign** entries, I refresh the page.

The second thread of **__OnThePath** becomes unlocked, and it offers me a riddle.

Second Sign:

I am the past, returning

I come in disguise—will you recognize me?

Before I can take a snap of the creepy message with my phone, the words fade away, leaving me wondering if it was ever there to begin with.

PART TWO

The Path

Twelve

The past, returning. In disguise.

My brain is working hard, my vision blurs. It makes sense that the Path is paved with creepy hints. Hell, V-heads call *Vermillion* a puzzle. But what does it even mean that the Second Sign comes "in disguise"? I need to go out and search the house, go room by room, dusty corner by dusty corner, until something sticks out.

A door slams somewhere in the house, followed by the rapid patter of busy steps. Despite the early hour, Cashore is coming alive. My initial impulse to march out there, hoping that it'll propel me further down the Path, is dampened by my reluctance to face Erasmus or the crew. I haven't thought this through. I can never really be alone in Cashore. And while the company of the living keeps the skulking ghosts of my memory at a distance, it's not the best setup while trying to unravel a personal mystery.

I'm grimacing at my laptop, irrationally bracing for something to jump out at me, when someone knocks on my door.

I flinch.

Another knock sounds from farther down the corridor. "We're gathering downstairs in thirty! Last chance to grab breakfast!" Someone's going around, waking up the late risers. This interruption is annoying but unavoidable. I'm not on vacation, and my time is not entirely my own. I was lucky to get this hour of research in, but now it's time to face the day.

I log out of CrimsonDreadNet and erase my browsing history. One can never be too careful.

I leave the bedroom, greeting the crew members with polite nods as I pass them on my way down. I ignore their curious stares, trying not to dwell too much on my earlier suspicions about every single one of them. But I feel like they are all watching me, seeing right through me. The distant clanging of plates and the scents of food drifting from downstairs hijack my attention.

I don't run into Arthur, which is something I'm both relieved and disappointed about. We have things to discuss. Or more like, I have questions for him. He's on the Path, and he really seems to believe in the supernatural. I wonder what his take is on Layla's unexplained vanishing. And what if I'm not the only one who was stalking the **__LaylaGalichIsAlive** thread when that photo of Layla entering Cashore made a brief appearance? Except for my own attempt to convince the police of what I saw, no one else came forward—as far as I know. Where Arthur Sawyer is concerned, suspicion and curiosity wage a war inside my head.

I wonder how many Signs he's already received, how far down the Path he's progressed, and what he hopes to achieve.

As I follow the scents to the dining room, I pass by the site of yesterday's dinner fiasco. If my bedroom is chilly, this space is now arctic. Sunlight streaming through the mullioned windows might as well be a movie prop.

Aside from the rough-edged cavity in the ceiling and wires sticking out, all signs of the chandelier's desolation are gone. But despite the clean-up, my twisted imagination keeps seeing dirty strands of hair hanging from the hole above.

I don't linger.

In the dining room I find Miriam and two others finishing their breakfast. I might have seen them yesterday at dinner, but it's not like I was paying attention amid the falling chandelier and the ensuing chaos.

When I greet the trio at the table, my voice is a little hoarse, unfamiliar. Miriam meets my eyes and smiles in a way that implies we're friends or perhaps there's a shared secret between us. But that would be a stretch. We've barely exchanged two words since meeting for the first time yesterday.

The conversation at the table stops, and I sense all eyes on me as I head for the impressive-looking buffet-style spread. With all his secretiveness and general weirdness, I've got to give it to Erasmus. He didn't skimp on catering. Eggs are: scrambled, poached, fried. Your pick. Fresh fruit slices are lovingly arranged in concentric circles. Bread is fresh, artisanal looking. A selection of freshly squeezed juices in jars sweating with condensation. This contemporary breakfast selection is somehow mismatched with Cashore's antique vibe, with its herringbone wooden floors and mullioned windows that bathe the room in subdued light. I imagine the house is used to Vienna rolls and black caviar, something extravagant and ridiculously expensive.

The ocean's deep boom is more pronounced today, adding to the eclectic ambience. With an inner shudder, I recall the silvery dust veiling the table, covering the food, coating my hands. The chandelier collapse etched in my memory.

I drop a slice of bread into the toaster and grab a clean plate. Despite everything, my appetite is intact.

Taking a seat at the table, I face Miriam and the others, feeling like a job applicant about to be peppered with questions. As if sensing my nervousness, Miriam gives me a close-lipped smile again. Her aviators are folded over the collar of her button-down. Without her mirrored lenses, she seems younger than the late thirties I assumed she was. Less enigmatic, more approachable. I struggle to reconcile this relaxed, kind-eyed woman with my initial impression of her, tirelessly wielding her camera.

Lost in my own head, I almost miss when Miriam introduces her colleagues. A forty-something man called Ivor to Miriam's right is a sound engineer, and the young woman next to him is Raina, a makeup artist. Raina doesn't look that much older than me. Ivor is pinkish white, and Raina is dark-complexioned, with deep brown eyes that study me for a moment too long.

"Today, I'll be fitting you with a roaming mic," Ivor says to me in lieu of a greeting. "It's a really sensitive one, captures even whispers. Maybe it'll even catch things that are not really there." He smiles mysteriously.

"I look forward to it," I say to Ivor, though it's the opposite of how I feel.

I savor the eggs on toast that I've assembled on my plate as I turn to Raina. She looks like she wants to say something, but instead she just stares.

"I hope there's nothing wrong with my face," I say between bites of food.

Raina flinches, a full-body movement that looks painful. Whoa, I spooked her good.

"I'm sorry," I say, with a small laugh. "It's just you've been quietly staring at me."

"Oh, sorry!" She blinks, long, forced blinks, like she's waking up, exiling sleep from her eyes. "It's really cool to meet you officially. We didn't really have a chance to socialize last night. I was looking forward to this, meeting you, I mean . . . I'm being weird. Sorry!" She has a soft Slavic accent, maybe Bulgarian or Serbian. I can't place it.

She turns red. I can almost *sense* her embarrassment, an emanation of pulsing heat from her skin. I don't quite know what to make of her. Is she just nervous in general, or is my presence making her flustered? This whole house feels like a powder keg, and I'm the spark.

I decide not to read too much into her reaction, but the idea of facing the many unknowns of Erasmus's crew bothers me.

When the police opened Layla's dorm room, they found the walls painted with blood. My sister's blood. It was used to draw occult symbols and diagrams. At least, judging from its amount, Layla didn't lose enough blood to endanger her life.

It was never established whether someone else was in the room with Layla that night. But even if police couldn't locate enough useful DNA evidence to identify suspects, there's a possibility someone attacked Layla. Blood was spilled. And then she ran, got into that mysterious car, and drove all the way to Cashore. Was she alone? Was she pursued? Her digital trail that night is inconsistent, full of gaps.

I struggle to arrange my face into what I hope is a neutral mask. Raina doesn't look like she could hurt someone.

"Good thing that *Vermillion* has brought us together," I say, to soothe the nervous makeup artist.

But my dispassionate statement has the exact opposite effect.

Raina gasps while Ivor swears—"Forfusake!"—and looks away. Only Miriam seems unaffected, at least to the naked eye.

"What?" My shoulders rise in a questioning shrug, but I think I already know the answer.

"We've been banned from saying that word, at least while we're on set," Miriam explains. Her eyebrows arch.

"Seriously?" I roll my eyes and shake my head. "You can't possibly believe in that nonsense?"

"I certainly don't," Miriam says. "But after the chandelier fell last night, many of us have been converted. This place can be very convincing."

I don't know what to say.

Ivor is first to leave, but not before filling up a gigantic travel mug with coffee. No milk, no sugar. With him gone, the balance in the room shifts. Raina keeps shooting me agitated looks, while Miriam's eyes grow steely, lips tightening into a determined line.

I don't see Erasmus, but I know he's nearby when his booming voice summons everyone to his side. I finish my breakfast in a hurry and follow Miriam and Raina out of the dining room.

In the bright light of day, it feels odd to be back here, in the house.

Even though all my memories of this place are steeped in darkness, I know logically that Cashore doesn't cease to exist while the sun is high.

It's also a little bit awkward to inhabit this glamorous space while wearing my jeans-and-sweater ensemble. But then, none of us really belong here, in this extravagant home imbued with glittering, morbid history. We should be smothered in embroidered silks, sporting shoes handcrafted by Italian masters, not denim and sneakers.

"Okay, folks, welcome again . . ." Erasmus launches into it the moment I join the half-moon shaped gathering formed around him. He glances at the crystal lamp, wagging a finger at it. The theatrics earn him some giggles from the crowd.

"Last night was quite something, wasn't it?" he goes on, without skipping a beat. "Some of you already know this, but I'll repeat so that everyone's on the same page: Not to anger the spirits, let's refrain from saying the V-word for the duration of the shoot. Okay. That out of the way, we have lots to get through today . . ."

I spot Arthur behind his father, his back resting against the wall, eyes half closed. Since I saw him earlier, he's changed into black cargo pants and a dark gray t-shirt. His hair appears freshly washed. I can't see his eyes well from where I stand, but his overall demeanor is subdued. I wonder if he got any sleep at all.

As if he can sense me watching, his eyes open fully and he turns his head a fraction, facing me from across the grand room. For no reason at all, I panic. My heart comes alive in my chest. I start to raise my hand to wave at him when the crowd shifts, hiding Arthur from view.

I exhale the tension and repurpose my half-raised hand to scratch a nonexistent itch.

When Erasmus concludes his morning oration, he finds me in the crowd. He approaches, with Arthur in tow.

"How did you sleep, Sophia?" the director asks. An innocent enough question, but the hidden gleam of Erasmus's eyes tells a different story. I bet he hopes, desperately so, to hear something revelatory, anything that could feed into his documentary.

Perfectly attuned with Erasmus, Miriam appears from the dissipating crowd and props up the camera, its cold eye trained on me.

"Exactly as expected," I say, with a well-practiced smirk. "Fitfully and blanketed by ghosts."

Arthur snorts at that but is quick to hide his grin. His father is not in a joking mood this morning. Erasmus's frown lines deepen in the weak morning light, and the dark crimson circles around his eyes rival those of his son's. The director's black beard is shot through with silver gray, something I failed to notice last night.

"I've always found that, ironically, those with a guilty conscience get the best sleep," Erasmus says. It takes me a moment to realize he's making a joke. "But it's good you got some rest. Cashore's ghosts weren't kind to me last night." He rubs his eyes and pushes his curling hair away from his forehead as part of the same gesture.

Arthur avoids my scrutiny when I try to catch his gaze. It's anyone's guess whether Erasmus is being metaphorical or referring to actual ghosts. I'm willing to suspend belief as far as the Path is concerned (*anything* to find Laylà), but I draw my personal line at the actual existence of ghosts. I know too well that all those sinister encounters, no matter how real they felt to me while filming *Vermillion*, were staged by my sister.

"But we've got work to do." Erasmus snaps out of his melancholy mood. "Arthur, will you take Sophia to wardrobe?" He turns to me then, adding, "There may not be a script, but I do have an idea of order." He taps a finger against his forehead. "And I think it's best to get right into the thick of it instead of dillydallying. Today we'll do the Baron's Preparation Room scene."

My blood chills. I feel it, like the first gust of wind before a hurricane—something is coming. And in my head, I hear Layla's voice, repeating her prerecorded message over and over again. *You know what to do.*

Thirteen

"How many Signs have you got so far? I mean, how far along the Path . . ." I ask Arthur once it's just him and me, on the move. He's taking me to wardrobe, while Erasmus stays back, to discuss "angles" with Miriam. Judging by the parting look Erasmus gives me, *angles* is code for *we need to talk about Sophia.*

"Not here," Arthur whispers, looking sharply at the motion activated cameras which follow us from their high perch near the ceiling.

I can't decide if he's terrified or angry. Either way, his mild-mannered mask is slipping.

Cashore is full of activity, of people in constant motion. Everyone's carrying something, rushing somewhere, but my own movement feels unnaturally slow. Like I'm trudging through a swamp. I sink deeper and deeper with each step. What awaits me today in the Baron's Preparation Room? I'm not sure I want to find out.

I'm almost grateful when we reach the wardrobe station.

Wardrobe is set up in a rectangular space without windows at the very end of the corridor. Once upon a time, this must've been a storage room. Now this half-room is filled with clothing racks, the movable kind. In the mix of clothes and fabrics, I notice a hint of bright red, but before I can take a closer look, someone moves the racks around, and the red disappears.

These are outfits, disguises. Could that have something to do with the riddle associated with the Second Sign? I wish Arthur was in a more talkative mood when it came to *Vermillion* lore.

A tiny changing room is set up nearby, with a makeup station next to it.

"Sophia, meet Serge, our wardrobe tsar. He must've worked on all of Dad's movies," Arthur says, introducing me to a reedy guy with the most beautiful shoulder-length hair I've ever seen. We're talking natural-looking waves.

I shake Serge's hand, as he corrects Arthur, "All but one. Don't forget how I got fired from *The Trench.*"

"What happened?" I ask, genuinely curious.

"Oh, I just dared to have an opinion, my dear," Serge replies, with an easygoing smile. "But you know how tyrannical directors can be. It's their *very* specific way, or the unemployment highway."

Serge seems nice enough, but I choose to politely smile at his comments and otherwise not engage. My only experience with "directors" prior to Erasmus comes from collaborating with my sister. I doubt that can be used as any measurement of a normal experience. My sister was not a normal girl. And I say that with love.

"But here comes the fun part," Serge says, switching effortlessly into business mode. "I've got some very special things for you to wear for the shoot."

He gestures at the nearest clothing rack, heavy with an assortment of elaborate, old-fashioned looking attire.

"I wasn't aware I'd be playing dress-up." I look between Serge and Arthur. The latter gives me an innocent shrug, while the former is all action. Serge fetches one of the outfits from the rack and hands it to me.

"Don't knock it till you've tried it. On, that is. I guarantee you'll be transformed."

If Serge thinks his promise of transformation will relax or excite me, he's dead wrong. But I accept the outfit, and as I do, an unpleasant shiver crawls down my spine.

Serge's efforts result in me wearing what can only be described as a bride-of-Dracula nightgown. I'm barefoot, the chill from the floor seeping into my soles. The gown's frilly lace chokes my neck, while the hem trails behind me.

I can guess what Serge is going for with this clothing choice: something not quite alive.

Raina proceeds to cover my face and neck with pale, translucent foundation, clearly unsuitable to my skin tone. When I say something, Raina politely cites Erasmus's orders. Her nervousness at breakfast has given way to steely-eyed professionalism. She maneuvers the makeup brush like a knight wielding a sword, all practiced precision and zero hesitation. With Raina painting my face and Serge poking me with tiny safety pins, I feel like a cursed doll, dressed up, made up, ready to enter some macabre game. Which is exactly what I am, I suppose.

Whatever Erasmus has in store for me today is clearly setting me up for a visual shocker.

But I remind myself that I must focus on the Second Sign. While ghosts are not real, my sister's absence is, and her return might depend on me deciphering the Signs as a V-head would.

The Preparation Room played such a pivotal role in *Vermillion*, being granted access to this space now means I can snoop around, regardless of whether I believe in the Signs and the Path.

Still, once Serge and Raina release me, it's difficult to think about anything else but the effect my new look has on people. The crew members in the corridor, Miriam among them, react with gasps and sharp intakes of breath. I must look quite impressive. Transformed.

Arthur does a double take when he sees me gliding toward him, resplendent in my nightgown.

"You look incredible," he says, looking me up and down. He blushes, which makes me react in kind. But I suspect Raina's funeral makeup conceals my blush quite well.

"You have weird tastes," I tell him, secretly pleased.

Whatever Arthur is going to say to me next is interrupted when Erasmus joins us. The director doesn't react to my transformation at all.

Erasmus leads me down the corridor, toward the Baron's Preparation Room. I want to look at Arthur over my shoulder, to see if he's following us, but the gown's collar prevents my head from moving much.

I keep looking straight ahead until our short procession stops before a familiar door. Back when I lived at Cashore with Layla, the Baron's Preparation Room was concealed, hidden behind a layer of wallpaper. My sister claimed to have found the room by accident. I had no reason not to believe her.

If Erasmus is hoping for authenticity in his reenactments, for this particular scene we'd have to wait for nightfall. The moment I think that, it starts to rain, and the light all but vanishes. This uncharacteristically gloomy weather belongs in Washington or the Scottish moors, not in sunny California. The effect is striking. It's nearly as dark now as it was five years ago when I returned to the Baron's Preparation Room to appease my camera-wielding sister. The only difference is that now, this daytime darkness carries a hint of purple, courtesy of Cashore's tinted windows.

"Here, take this." Arthur appears in my line of vision and offers me an antique-looking flashlight, which I accept. His fingers, warm and soft, leave my skin burning.

The flashlight's bulls-eye glass lens that bulges from the metallic tube is something out of a Jules Verne book. Flipping the switch on creates a weak circle of light on the wall.

"I'd save it for when you need it. It's a real deal, from the Baron's era, and its light doesn't last long," Arthur says.

I aim the flashlight at his face before clicking it off.

"What do you want me to do?" I turn to Erasmus, who's been listening to our exchange. I hope my confident tone is convincing because my bravado is entirely put on. I'm trembling inside.

"Just act natural," he says. "I want this scene to be true to the original, to capture your unpracticed reaction."

His response doesn't exactly fill me with confidence, but my interactions with Erasmus so far are a step up from the way Layla behaved as a director. My sister usually wouldn't say a word before filming, most scenes starting as if of their own accord, usually at nightfall. Afterward though, Layla would be full of explanations and words of encouragement.

A woman I haven't met approaches the closed door of the Preparation Room, shoving a clapperboard in front of Miriam's camera.

The sound of the clapperboard slamming is like that of a guillotine's blade. But instead of someone's head rolling away, it's my heart that feels like it's escaping from my chest.

"*V. The Return*. Prep Room scene. Take one!" the woman with the clapperboard announces.

And so it begins.

I reach for the closed door with my free hand, while my other hand grips the flashlight like my life depends on it.

When I hesitantly touch the swan-shaped handle, it's clear that the door is unlocked. I press it lightly and it slides inward, spilling me into the Baron's Preparation Room.

Fourteen

A vacuum forms around me. Everything else disappears.

The floor is ice against the bare soles of my feet. All I hear is my own erratic breathing.

Calm down, calm down, calm down.

I take a deep breath in, then slowly release it.

Erasmus and his crew do not follow me into the Preparation Room. I know there are hidden cameras, fastened to the walls, hiding in the corners, but I feel like I'm all alone, free to do as my instincts tell me. Too bad those instincts scream at me to close my eyes, turn around, and run.

I draw another deep breath and hold it until my lungs scream to let go.

It's stuffy in here, and dark—darker than in the corridor. I let my eyes adjust until I distinguish shapes, then textured shadows.

This is it, my chance to uncover the Second Sign, and that matters to me more than Erasmus's plan. But I have no idea what shape this Sign will take.

Switched on, the flashlight reveals the room in patches of wavering light.

The Baron's various disguises greet me in the form of dust-covered items laid out in neat rows. This condensed version of a theatrical green room is exactly as I remember it. But . . . I'm not sure I can tell the difference between my actual memories and whatever imagery's been drilled into my head by Layla's flick. It's all jumbled up in my mind.

I can't bring myself to touch anything in this room.

As a child these objects terrified me. I thought they were real body parts. Eyes. Noses. Swathes of flayed skin, still covered in hair. My mind then busied with conjuring horrifying backstories to explain the purpose of this room. The Baron as the leader of a cult that trapped innocent souls and tormented them by cutting off one bodily protrusion at a time. Was Adrianna complicit in these dark deeds? It was difficult to imagine the ballerina as a blood-hungry monster, but looks can be misleading.

Looking now at these odd items, I see them for what they are: pieces of plastic. Bottles of what I suspect are glue, brushes, and scissors and whatever else an actor needs for transformation.

Disguises.

My attention turns to the walls: Each is covered by a curtain. I know what's behind them. I reach and pull the nearest one free. It slides to the floor in a cloud of dust. When the veil of dust settles, a sound of shock tears from my lips.

A ghoul stares back at me.

I understand now why Raina wouldn't let me see myself in a mirror earlier.

Erasmus said so himself, he wanted to capture my authentic reaction in this dusty, old room. Hence, the outfit.

Aiming the flashlight's shaky beam at the mirror, I hold back a grimace.

The gown's ivory hue combined with Raina's funeral makeup turns my skin sickly pale, my eyes bottomless black.

I move my head from side to side, up and down, and my undead doppelgänger imitates me perfectly. I exhale, watching my breath cloud in the mirror.

Back when I lived in this house as a child, my fears and terrors were externally facing. Layla's haunting creation came from *elsewhere*. I was never the source of fright. Seeing myself now, wearing this burial attire, I look dead, and I'm afraid of myself.

I loosen the rest of the curtains and pull them down one by one, using too much force, so that some of the fabric tears. The result is a house of mirrors, with endless corridors and countless copies of my funeral self. I bet Layla knew back then the true meaning of this room, though it took me years to realize. The

Baron's Preparation Room is a psychomanteum—a special space designed for communicating with the other side. I know this now. But it still doesn't explain the assortment of theatrical disguises, or how the Second Sign fits into any of it.

I ignore my own movement in the mirrors as I search among the items on display for a certain pair of rectangular glasses. Here they are, between a curling red beard and a grotesque mask of a plague doctor. I wonder if these glasses are the same ones that Layla wore while she danced for me, swaying in the flashlight's shaky beam. Might as well give Erasmus and everyone a show.

I pick up the glasses and put them on. The room swims. Were these prescription lenses back then too? I don't remember.

Hissing emanates from behind me, and I freeze.

With the stiff, oversized collar restricting my neck, I slowly turn. I half expect to see a bunch of snakes writhing on the floor, but the sound accompanies white smoke that begins filling the room.

Dry ice. That's how Layla did it, shrouding all my direct encounters with Vermillion in mysterious smoke. As if whenever the red ghoul crossed into our world, she brought the remnants of the underworld with her. But no matter how real it looked, I knew it was fake. I knew it then, and I know it now. *Dry ice. Dry ice. Dry ice.* I hold onto this rational thought like a life preserver.

Where has Erasmus hidden the dry ice in this room? The smoke seems to be coming from the ceiling and the floor at the same time. My heart slams against my chest, fear overpowering logic.

When she appears in the doorframe, a column of red, encased in smoke, my heavy breathing intensifies. I bite my lower lip and taste blood.

Can she smell it, like a shark in the water?

I stand still in fright as the room continues to fill with thick, vision-distorting smoke. I tear off the glasses from my face.

Vermillion blocks the doorway. An unmoving red figure clouded in unnatural fog. The monster of my childhood has finally come for me. Layla's horrifying dummy. She looks so real!

I watch her, she watches me. It's the moment I've been both waiting for and fearing all this time.

We are both reflected in the mirrors, red ghost and white ghost, multiplied a thousand times.

Up close, if not for her statue-like stillness, she appears like a real person. Her hair is long, matted in parts, covering most of her face. Water drips down her dirty red dress clinging to her emaciated figure, and a small puddle forms around her filthy, bare feet. And yet, she looks different from how I remember her. Something about her appearance is off.

She's not real. Of course not. She can't be. Erasmus has mentioned better special effects, so this must be it. A superior dummy.

My fright paralysis wears off.

But then, jerkily, the dummy moves.

I flinch as I step back, feet trapped in my trailing gown. My hands are like wings of a spooked bird.

Is this the Sign I've been waiting for, my Second Sign? Vermillion returning from the past to shepherd me to where my sister is being kept?

Fighting down my fear, I take a step toward her.

She takes a step back, moving from the room's doorway into the corridor. Odd.

Using the momentum of my bravery, I chase after her. And she turns and leaves the room in a smooth rush of feet. This feels like a dream, but I can't wake up.

Something's terribly wrong. The real Vermillion would never do this. Layla's Vermillion chased me, she didn't run away.

Fighting against my restrictive gown, I scramble out of the Preparation Room. There is no Erasmus waiting, no Arthur or Miriam. Everyone's vanished, leaving me alone with this skittish ghost who's galloping away, putting distance between us. If it is some animatronic dummy, the way it moves is the realest thing ever. I don't see any cables, no indication that it's being operated remotely.

I give chase, cornering her at the blocked entrance to Cashore's west wing. For a ghost that lives here, she's certainly not aware of her surroundings.

I reach for her but stop before I can touch her. "What are you?" I ask.

Can she even hear me? Am I imagining her, conjuring her up somehow? Any moment I expect her to melt away, vanish into the ether, but she remains solid and very much real.

When I was a child, my encounters with Vermillion were dream-like, shrouded in fog. I never believed she was *real*, not in the sense of flesh and bones. But she wasn't completely ethereal either. Layla never revealed exactly how she did it, but I thought she created Vermillion by running wires through an old manne-quin. Only filming at night and in poorly lit areas of the house made this horrifying dummy more real and way scarier than it would be in the unforgiving light of day.

This Vermillion is something else entirely. Her chest rises and falls rapidly. I hear her breathing, smell her sweat. When she tries wiggling out of my reach, I grab onto the sleeve of her rotten dress. She tries to jerk away, and the sound of fabric tearing is definitely real.

"What the . . ." I say, staring at the torn piece of red dress in my hand, then at Vermillion's face, half concealed by unruly hair.

The cornered ghost looks me straight in the eye and smirks.

"And scene!" Erasmus declares somewhere behind me.

There's a scattering of applause, along with the movement of many feet against the floor.

"Serge is going to be pissed about the dress. It's antique, you know," fake-Vermillion says, as she pushes her hair from her face.

Fifteen

'm back in my room and so angry I could punch a wall.

My right hand gathers into a fist, but the prospect of breaking something stops me from the actual act. Any kind of injury could put an untimely end to my visit, and no matter how furious I am, I'm not ready to go home yet. Far from it.

I kick the bed instead; the impact reverberates through my bones.

I feel tricked, yes, but there's more to this fury strumming through my veins. I was hoping to . . . see a real ghost.

The realization comes to me as a shock, but here it is: There's a tiny part of me that's willing to consider a supernatural explanation for Layla's disappearance. But then, even the most rational of us crave the irrational at times. Even my atheist mom confessed to me once that she had nightmares so bad while renovating Cashore that she'd bought a dreamcatcher. It was like she'd switched places with Dad while we lived in this house. A self-proclaimed agnostic, and prone to superstition, Dad turned to prescription-strength sleep aid.

As for today's experience, I don't know what ticked me off more—that the ghost was fake, or that I thought chasing after said ghost would lead me to Layla.

My recollections of the morning are already blurry, drowned in this unexpected rage I've been feeling since "Vermillion" spoke to me.

After that, I remember Raina helping me out of my gown, the stiff collar loosening its grip on my neck. If not for her timely assistance, the dress would've likely ended up a torn mess at my feet.

I remember Erasmus approaching me, gesticulating in a placating manner. The woman hired to play the role of Vermillion stood next to him, and Erasmus introduced her as Francesca.

Francesca had enough wisdom to step aside after I said I needed to be alone. I stomped away.

Which led me here.

I avoid my reflection in the bathroom mirror, focusing on the movement of running water. I don't care if my feelings are justified or not. Yes, I signed up for this, but I still feel tricked and used. My thoughts swell and overflow as I scrub my face clean of makeup. I've placed my souvenir, the piece of red fabric, on the bathroom shelf. I'm sure Serge wants it back, but I don't care. I throw it in the trash.

Someone knocks on the bedroom door, but I ignore it.

I brave the mirror. My face is painfully red from my scrubbing and crying. All I see is that ghoul looking back at me, as if all color has left my complexion. I look more fragile, less real.

I walk away.

I'm sitting on the bed, massaging some tinted BB cream into my skin when someone knocks again. This time the knocking is insistent, urgent.

"Sophia?" Arthur's voice comes from the corridor, and my heart beats faster. I'm not sure I'm ready to face anyone.

I can't trust Arthur, *I know that.* But also . . . I need him. With CrimsonDreadNet giving out information in small doses, Arthur's my answer to finding more about the Path. Besides, I can't stay in my room forever, wallowing in self-pity.

I open the door. His right hand is raised, like he's about to knock again.

"You don't give up, do you?" I say.

"No, ma'am."

He meets my eyes, and we stand like that for a second, just looking at each other. There's a big bubble of tension between us, and an intensity to Arthur's stare that kind of makes me squirm with unease. But it also makes me feel a peculiar way that's not completely terrible.

I let him in.

"We need to talk," he says. Before I can respond, he adds, "I asked the chef to pack us a lunch. The weather's improved. Let's go for a picnic? Just me and you."

"Oh. *Um.* Okay?" He catches me completely off guard, and I shift from one foot to another. We do need to talk, that I agree on. "Where are we going?"

I hope he has a place in mind that's far away from here.

"The beach," he replies.

My skin ripples. While I have no bad memories associated with the beach itself, its proximity to the tidepools worries me.

"Have you checked out the rock steps yet?" Arthur asks.

His question sounds casual, but I know it's anything but. The Baron's semi-secret passageway to the beach, and the rocky path polished by the tread of the comings and goings of his mysterious guests, is anything but casual.

But I know where Arthur's going with this, and I'm ready to reclaim that Second Sign on my own terms—walking in the footsteps of both my sister and the long-forgotten secret society's acolytes.

"Not yet," I say, forcing a carefree smile. "Will there be cameras at the beach?"

When he shakes his head, I boldly take his hand and lead the way.

Arthur goes to the kitchen to pick up our lunch, and we agree to meet outside, by Cashore's sea-facing entrance.

For the first time since I got here, I'm excited to explore—

as long as we stay far away from those putrid tidepools. I give myself permission to do this one thing that feels like it's not directly connected to the film or this house, or to Layla. I'll breathe some sea air and eat sandwiches with a good-looking boy. Almost like what I'd be doing at the lake house with my friends, if my life was different.

The Path and the Signs feel like some forgotten thing, dancing at the edge of my consciousness.

The best way to remember something is to pretend like you're not concentrating on it at all, right? Perhaps, like a skittish deer, my next Sign will somehow show itself eventually? In its own time, on its own terms.

With Arthur off to the kitchen, I duck back into the bedroom to grab my phone and a light jacket. The weather outside might have indeed improved, but I don't trust the warmth, not for one second. Besides, I don't remember the last time I was by the water and didn't end up shivering.

When I leave my room, the corridor is empty. I hear voices and other noises from afar. Perhaps Erasmus will leave me alone for the rest of the afternoon.

My childhood knowledge of Cashore comes in handy, helping me avoid unwanted encounters, though I still feel watched, observed, and I don't just mean the cameras that are everywhere I look. I take the back stairs and exit the building out onto the wind-beaten circular platform, which is an extension of Cashore's foundation jutting out from the cliff.

The endless blue of the sea meets the horizon, and the horizon becomes the sea. Only the white of wave caps tells me I'm looking at the ocean, mirroring the spots of seagulls in the sky. It's easy to believe in a higher power when you're out here.

A chain-link fence runs around the outer edge of the observation platform. My parents had it installed that summer, five years ago. In fact, they fortified the building's entire foundation back then as an anti-earthquake measure. The dramatic image of Adrianna slipping from the collapsing patio to her death was as fresh on everyone's mind then as it is now on mine. It's impossible to exile the dead ballerina from my head.

My hair comes alive in the salty wind. The sun is behind the clouds, but it is unexpectedly warm. I present my face to the sky and take the sea air into my lungs.

Arthur takes his time, which gives my mind space to recalibrate. Thinking back to this morning's reenactment, the moment I thought of the Baron's disguises in connection to the Second Sign, I expected something to happen, for my Second Sign to reveal itself. What if it did, and I didn't even notice? I couldn't tell if my weird dream last night was a Sign either, not at first. But as I mull over this morning, the one thing I keep returning to is the dry ice. Why? I don't know.

"Sorry to keep you waiting," Arthur says. His nearly-silent arrival takes me by surprise. When I turn around, I find him grinning. The smile lights up his entire face. "Our lunch." He nods at the neat cooler bag over his shoulder.

I smile back. This side of him, this eagerness to please, is something I've yet to reconcile with the Arthur I saw last night in his room. He seems mercurial, changing in the way atmospheric pressure does. Right now, he's all sunshine and warmth.

"Let's go then." I start moving, and Arthur follows.

Though dry, the terraced, rocky surface is smooth to the point of slippery. I need to watch my step. The serpentine quality of our descent sends my world spinning. With each step, the stairs veer farther and farther away from Cashore, at some point taking us nearly parallel to the beach below. Underfoot, white alyssums fill in every crack and crevice of the steps, their heady floral sweetness hanging in the air. But the crisp breeze blowing from the sea keeps me focused. I expect to see V-heads hiding in the rocks, crawling toward Cashore, but there's no sign of them.

"I didn't want to talk in the house." Arthur is closer to me than I expected. I take a wrong step and start to slip. A hand wraps around my forearm, his fingers' grip hot through my clothes. "Careful," he whispers.

The soft imprint of his fingers stays on my skin long after he lets go. Damn it, that's what happens when I shun all romance and human touch in favor of plotting my way back to Cashore. Suddenly, it catches up with me in the least appropriate moments.

But I won't allow myself to look at Arthur as anything other than a source of information. I can't allow myself to see him as anything else, anything *more*.

For the rest of our walk, I focus on the stairs, trying not to think about how close I am to Arthur.

"Afraid your dad will film us and put it in his movie?" I say, trying to pay attention to what's under my feet. The wind carries my words.

"Well, yeah," Arthur says. "But besides, the Path is a personal thing."

"Erasmus doesn't know you're on the Path?"

"No. It's none of his business," Arthur says, a subtle disdain in his voice.

That's the first sign of rebellion, however small, that he's shown against his father. Maybe I can use it to my advantage.

"That was quite a performance this morning, by the way," I say. "I knew Erasmus promised me better special effects, but I wasn't expecting him to actually cast an actor to play . . . V."

I try keeping any form of accusation from my voice, but who am I kidding? I'm still bitter. My swift over-the-shoulder glance briefly captures Arthur from a flattering angle, his hair disheveled by the wind, eyes downcast.

"Would you believe me if I told you I had no idea? I hadn't met Francesca before this morning." His voice is so low I barely hear him against the wind.

"I would find it hard to believe," I admit. "But I can make an effort."

He chuckles but doesn't meet my eyes.

The rocks become more slippery and unstable the closer to the beach we get. A patchy layer of sand, empty seashells and dried-up algae cover the final steps, crunching underfoot. Wind blows my hair into my face, and the breath of the ocean dances on my skin. I peel off my jacket, tying it around my waist.

My shoe-clad feet sink into the sand.

We walk toward the water. The shadow of the cliff stretches diagonally across the shore. I exhale in relief when I step out of its darkness and into the sunlight.

Arthur picks a spot for us near a large boulder, which I remember from five years ago. It used to sit higher up the shoreline but must've slid closer to the water over the years due to erosion. The boulder casts a shade, but it's gentle, not imposing. For most people, California is a sunny place with surfers, sunshine, and the beach. But for me, Cashore's dark presence saps all that light and warmth away.

I remember one time Layla took me out for a drive at night. It was supposed to be a sisterly bonding thing, but instead, I felt tense and claustrophobic the whole time, like the building watched us from a distance as we sped down Mulholland Drive.

But not even the prospect of the creepy tidepools that mar the farther portion of the beach directly underneath the house will ruin this moment. I won't let it. I can't allow my childhood fear of the pools to crawl back and taint this unexpected moment of joy.

I peel off my tennis shoes, digging my toes into the fine-grained sand, while Arthur opens the cooler and spreads out a picnic blanket. Making sure my back is to the tidepools, unseen from here but felt on some deeper level, I sit on the blanket's edge to keep it from being blown away by the wind. Arthur takes a seat on its other end, facing me, his back to the sea.

He reaches back into the cooler and produces a napkin. "You have some white makeup, by your ear. May I?" He leans in just as I nod in consent. I brace for his touch, but much to my disappointment, all I feel is the sensation of napkin against my skin.

Later, when we sit facing each other, a sandwich in one hand and a can of some European fizzy drink in another, our eyes meet. We speak at the same time.

"What was the last Sign you—"

"My father thinks you know what happened to Layla," he says simultaneously.

Sixteen

I stare at Arthur in shock. The ocean frames his silhouette in shades of blue.

Did he really just say that?

I look away, pointedly focusing on my sandwich. Egg and mayo, an improvement from the misguided chicken salad decadence of last night. But I'm happy for anything that gives me a reason not to meet Arthur's questioning eyes.

Erasmus wouldn't be the first to accuse me, or at the very least suspect me of knowing more than I claim to know about my sister's disappearance—and I'm not even talking about me seeing the photo of Layla entering Cashore. This suspicion goes much deeper than that, and it links to my alleged connection to the titular entity of Layla's film. There are interpretations of the movie that claim I died in the end, or that I was dead the entire time, or even that Vermillion and I are one and the same.

In this interpretation, Layla is the real victim of the haunting that allegedly took place in Cashore House, which makes me the perpetrator, the ghost, the ghoul. In some viewers' eyes, I'm both the possessor and the possessed; I am the true haunted house in Layla's film.

It's been some time since I've been accused of doing something to my sister firsthand, being blamed for her disappearance. Though *technically* Arthur is relaying information to me, not accusing me of anything himself. Or is he?

As if he can see right through my pointed silence, he says, "I don't share his belief. In case you were wondering."

I arch an eyebrow but say nothing.

Unperturbed, he continues, "My dad doesn't exactly open his heart and soul to me these days . . . but I think all that Francesca-playing-V business is him hoping to get a reaction out of you."

"You *think*?"

Arthur scoffs; there's a bitter undertone to the sound.

I say, "Every single V-head and their mother think they're better equipped to investigate Layla's disappearance than the detectives assigned to her case. And guess what, Layla's still missing."

I think about that photo of Layla entering Cashore. I need to know if Arthur saw it too, but I don't want to show my cards. I wasn't taken seriously before—if I bring this up now, will I be burned again? Somehow the prospect of Arthur laughing at me feels more grievous than getting that reaction from the police.

"What do *you* think happened to my sister?" I ask.

Arthur gives me a long look, the wind moving his hair, sunshine glinting off his eyes, a cinematic moment. "She reached the end of the Path."

He looks away, focuses on the waves.

"You think Layla was on the Path?" I ask, as the world drops away from me, as I fall into an abyss. I didn't even consider a possibility that my sister would buy into the fandom lore created around her film. Leading up to her disappearance, whenever we talked, it was about anything but the movie. Layla was highly skilled in evading conversations she didn't want to have.

"Well, it's a theory," Arthur says, careful with his words. "I'm not the only one who believes it. There are fans walking the Path themselves who search for Layla's presence on Crimson-DreadNet. They think the entries she wrote to unlock her own Signs are clues to what happened to her, to where she is now, and whether she got her wish or not."

"Her wish?"

"Shouldn't you be an expert?" Arthur chuckles. "You're behaving like a newbie."

"I've only gotten access to __OnThePath this morning," I admit. "But I've been on the site for years, I've seen every single photo claiming to be of my sister, read every wild theory about what happened to her. I've never heard anything about V being some kind of genie who grants wishes."

"I think it started with some guy years ago, claiming V met him at the end of the Path and offered him a deal. He actually got kind of famous after that—his IT start-up went big; he's made lots of money."

"So, V is the devil then? She wants your soul in exchange for fame and riches?" Perhaps it makes sense that *Vermillion* lore has evolved into this deal-making stuff. After all, Cashore's original owner, the Baron, had also allegedly made a deal with the devil, which backfired. I've even heard of V-heads attributing Layla's fame to a demonic pact too. There's twisted logic to all of it.

"That's one way of looking at it," Arthur says.

"But how do people decide they even want to walk the Path? I definitely didn't choose it."

"This is going to sound esoteric, but the way I understand it the Path chooses you. It begins when it chooses to begin, and it only extends an invitation to those it deems worthy."

When I stare at him, he adds, "I'm not the one making the rules, Sophia. But you know what I think? Those desperate V-heads who fake sightings of your sister online would never get the chance."

I sit on that. So, the Path is only for *real* V-heads. But again, who decides on their worthiness?

"Okay, so if Layla was on the Path, why instead of fame and glory did she disappear? Was that her wish? I really don't get it.

And where do I come in—how is whatever happened to Layla my fault?"

"I told you," Arthur adds, gently. "I don't share my father's views. And I don't tell him anything either. Anything important, anyway." He gives me a pointed look. I shiver in response. "And maybe Layla's deal turned out bad—demons can trick you, right? Just take a closer look at the __OnThePath. There seem to be fewer and fewer comments as the Path progresses. Very few make it to the end and stick around long enough to leave a post about it."

"Maybe it just takes some people longer to reach the end," I say, ignoring the cold lick of dread along the back of my neck. "Maybe they'll catch up."

"Maybe. To answer your earlier question," he continues, switching gears. "I'm on my Fourth Sign, waiting for the Fifth."

Seventeen

Arthur is way ahead of me.

I make a shapeless ball out of my sandwich wrapper and place it inside the cooler. My knowledge of the Path and the Signs is so limited. I bite my lips in frustration. In all my research, how come I've never considered that Layla herself might've been on the Path? But does that mean she *believed* in what it entailed, believed in the supernatural? My sister went to great lengths to convince me that everything strange and scary happening in this house was a setup, with DIY props and effects. But she was into the occult too, I just always assumed it was more of a symbolic thing, that she was drawn to the appearance of it, not because she actually believed it. Hearing Arthur share his thinking with me makes me reconsider everything.

I need to know more.

"If the Path is only available to those believed worthy, then how do we know we have indeed received a Sign? Are there, like, specific things to look for? I received a riddle when I unlocked __OnThePath, but it wasn't much help. Do you get hints and riddles for every Sign?"

"Each Sign I've received so far was linked to a specific scene in the movie," Arthur says. The words come slowly, like he's weighing each one, unsure how much he can spare.

"Oh, like the Second Sign had to do with the Baron's Preparation Room?" I say. "The riddle mentioned 'disguises,' but it also said something about the past returning. Which scenes do the other Signs correspond to?"

He said he's waiting on his Fifth Sign. But do the Signs follow the sequence of scenes in the movie? The memory of walking in on Arthur watching *Vermillion* just this morning is fresh on my mind. Was it a coincidence that I caught him at the exact moment the Dance of the Unquiet Spirits unfolded, or was he just watching that scene over and over again, in the hope that his next, penultimate Sign would reveal itself?

Arthur doesn't say anything until I meet his eyes. "Haven't you learned the rules yet?" When I shake my head, he adds, "We can only discuss the Signs we've both received to date."

"Oh." My fingers dig into the sand, burrowing below the crumbling, dry layer until I hit the grave-cold, wet one. The chilling sensation against my fingertips is not a pleasant one, but it gives me unexpected clarity. "It's just that I feel stuck," I admit.

"Before coming here and joining your father's project, I didn't believe in the Path or the Signs, not as a supernatural thing. But I had a dream last night and it felt so real, and I don't know what to believe anymore. A part of me really thought I'd get my Second Sign this morning, but then the fake Ver—*V* made an appearance, and now I feel even less certain of everything." I catch myself before I can utter the banned word, as if saying the name Vermillion will create a tear in reality, letting something bad pass through.

Arthur is nodding like he really gets my frustration. And maybe he does, maybe he's also "stuck."

"I'm . . . I'm going to break the rules," he says. The slight rise in his voice at the end implies a question, like he's asking me, or the universe, for permission, a blessing, or for forgiveness.

If my eyes were closed, with the noisy wind, I could've pretended Arthur hadn't spoken. But he did. And now, his words begin to expand, they surround me like those hazy images from *Vermillion*'s negative space. There and not there. But ultimately, most definitely, *there*.

I'm scared to spook Arthur back into silence, so I say nothing. I wait.

The tactic pays off.

"You probably *have* received your Second Sign already," he says. I lean slightly toward him, a movement not entirely my own. Not even the wind whistling in my ears can suppress his words now. "The hardest task is not to receive the Sign, but to recognize it for what it is."

His speech is fast, like he's a man pursued by a wild beast, like there's a timer on what he is saying, a bomb ticking away. "When I got my Second Sign, at first it looked like a random thing. Insignificant, you know? But when I saw it for what it was, things clicked into place. It was terrifying but also incredible."

The quality of light dramatically shifts, clouds swallowing the day. Whether it's Arthur's nervousness or just my own sudden change in perception, the boulder's shade seems unnaturally darker, and Arthur's face paler.

I avoid looking down, irrationally scared to catch a glimpse of myself, expecting my skin to look pale and rotten too. The wind must've changed direction because it carries the familiar stench of mulch and decay. The odor has its own gravity, thickening its hold on me; icy fingers cup my chin, making my head turn to acknowledge its source. I resist. I know where the smell comes from: the shallow tidepools that taint the beach's perfection a short distance away.

It takes all my mental power to resist the pull of this force. I focus on Arthur, as if he's my anchor in the world of the living. I refuse to miss a single word of his unexpected confession. But he seems lost in his own head.

"What happened? Can you tell me?" I nudge. I don't understand why Arthur is willing to break the rules surrounding the

Path, but I don't stop him.

"Might as well. I've told you this much already. If I'm found dead in my bed tomorrow morning, you know what got me, and why." He chuckles, but it's a dark sound.

"You shouldn't say things like that." I channel Dad, the superstitious counterweight to my atheist mom. "Don't mock death, don't tease the spirits, regardless of whether you believe in them or not." Dad's not religious, though his parents kind of are, but he's the kind of person who'd throw spilled salt over his shoulder and avoid stepping over a crack. I wonder what made him this way. His paternal grandparents came here as kids from different parts of Poland, so maybe their families brought these traditions and superstitions with them.

"Oh, I *do* believe," Arthur says, without missing a beat. "But I was just kidding." He gestures in a pacifying manner, offering me a smile. A lock of wavy dark hair falls into his eyes. A misguided impulse makes me want to reach out and clear it away, but Arthur beats me to it.

"Anyway," he says, all business. "A Sign can be something random that sticks out, but it's always deeply personal. Like, in my case, about a year ago an ex-girlfriend called me up out of the blue. She wanted . . . it's not important what she wanted. What matters is that her call triggered my Second Sign, something from my past coming back. Hearing her voice made me remember how we were in *The Crucible* together in high school,

I was maybe fourteen then. She played Elizabeth. I remembered us on stage together, we were rehearsing, and as I watched her move, I kept seeing a figure hiding behind her, a red silhouette in sync with her movements. Like double vision."

I grow still, barely noticing the wind and the breath of the sea on my skin. My imagination offers a morbid visual of a shadowy red person clinging to someone's shoulders from behind. There's something terribly familiar about the image. In my mind, it's Layla who's on stage playing Elizabeth, a girl accused of witch-craft, and Vermillion herself is holding on to her shoulders and her neck, fused with my sister until they are one.

That raw imagery aside, there's a lot to unpack in Arthur's story, though against my better judgment, I really want to zero in on this ex-girlfriend business. But I don't. I must focus on the Signs, the Path.

"Double vision. Got it," I say, faux-perkily. "So you didn't remember seeing that . . . that *thing* until you had this talk with your girlfriend a year later?"

"*Ex*-girlfriend," he corrects. "But yes. After that phone call with Carolyn, I remembered that I was feeling sick during that particular rehearsal. I was coming down with something nasty, I just didn't know it at the time. It wasn't until much later, until after I'd shed the virus, that I revisited that weird memory of watching Carolyn being shadowed by this thing on stage. At the time, I'd written it off as a hallucination, a play of light. But after

Carolyn's call, I knew it wasn't a distortion of light or a fevered vision. It was V."

"V was on stage with you during a high school play rehearsal, hiding behind your ex-girlfriend?" I don't even bother to conceal my skepticism, but I do feel like trash for not accepting his words at face value.

When Arthur meets my eyes again, he makes a point of holding my gaze for a moment before looking away. For a long while he concentrates on the task of smoothing a patch of sand next to him.

"Don't you think I know how this sounds?" he says. "But that's how the Path is. When you know something is a Sign, you just know it."

"Okay." I play along. "So, it's like a new memory or . . . more like an old memory seen in a different way?"

"Exactly!" He abandons his sand smoothing and gives me a look like I've just won the lottery. "What?"

I give him a playful, crooked look. The words are out of my mouth before I can think better of it. "You did *The Crucible* when you were fourteen. That's kind of a full-on thing to do, isn't it? I mean, we did some Don Zolidis, and also the *Addams Family* that other time."

"Oh yeah." He laughs. "We had a creative director with a specific vision of the world. She deviated from the script quite a bit, too. We even had this fake bonfire made up of red scarfs, and a fog machine . . ."

"Impressive. Layla used dry ice in *V*. That's how she created all that fog."

The fog in Layla's film, abundant, swirling, alive, acquired its own legendary status. It's no surprise that so many people believe *Vermillion* captured a real haunting on camera, evidence found among the unsettling snippets of "scenes" involving me and the film's titular ghost, locked in a weird dance, veiled in fog. Back then, that fog followed me everywhere I went, inside the house and out.

"Dry ice? You're sure about that?" Arthur asks. I can't decipher his tone.

"Of course I'm sure," I insist. Even if I feel like I can no longer be sure about anything anymore.

"I get it, you know," he says, looking between me and the patch of sand he'd smoothed earlier, which he'd absently covered with the letter V while talking. He adds more Vs as we talk, and they're packed tightly, crowding each other, overlapping, like a bird murmuration that's lost its direction. "The difference between you and me is that I accept the Path for what it is while you continue to deny its 'realness' or, worse, try to explain it with logic. That's what's blocking you from seeing your second Sign."

Back when I was twelve, I used to take things for granted all the time. Growing up, we really do lose some of that spark. I've definitely lost some of mine. And I'm barely eighteen. How can I already be so jaded?

"Perhaps that's because I find it super hard to believe that all these Signs are really going to lead me to V herself," I say.

He's nodding, like he gets it. "Well, the 'Path' metaphor is a bit misleading. When I say 'Path,' what image do you get in your mind?"

I stare at him for a moment. Then decide that I'll keep playing along. "I'm thinking of a way of getting from point A to point B. Could be a straight line or a long and winding road. But either way it's about *moving*, about getting somewhere . . . You're smiling mysteriously, so why don't you just tell me where I'm wrong."

"You're not wrong, Sophia," he says gently. My skin ripples with goosebumps like tiny pebbles in sand, and I experience a brief sensation of light-headed vertigo, like I'm standing on the edge of a cliff. This all-body tingle is not unpleasant at all. I could stand on that edge of a cliff forever, relishing this sensation.

I focus on the sound of Arthur's voice. "Whoever came up with the metaphor of the Path may have oversimplified things," he says. "I think the Path is not so much about progressing forward as it is about moving *backward*. Each Sign, all but the last one, while linked to specific scenes from your sister's movie, is also connected to our individual memories, and all memories live in the past."

"So, the Signs are like triggers that help us rewrite a particular memory," I think out loud, not expecting an answer. Perhaps

Arthur is on to something. Thinking of the Path this way, like it's a device that helps us move forward by sending us backward, and that is kind of paradigm-shifting to me. Yet, it's also so obvious it almost hurts that I didn't think of it myself.

But then, as suddenly as I gain this understanding, my old, familiar doubts creep in. It can't be helped. "But do you really *believe* in it? That there's an actual supernatural *entity* waiting for you at the end of this metaphorical path?" I ask him.

"Yes, I really do believe that, Sophia," he says softly. "Being on the Path is about believing in all of it, not just bits and pieces that are convenient or that make immediate sense. I think the moment you allow yourself to *believe* will bring you closer to what you seek. Like everyone else on the Path, you're moving toward conclusion."

"And what do *you* want to gain from it? What are you going to wish for?" I ask, eager to shift the focus away from me.

"I really can't say." He looks infinitely sad when he says that.

Can't or *won't?*

"Is it like a birthday wish? If you speak it out loud, it won't come true?"

"Something like that . . ." He exhales, then looks at me in a way I can't decipher. For a moment, the world around us quiets, the sea stops mid-movement, the breeze pauses its incessant whistling, growing nearly silent for once. Even the foul, decaying smell of the shallow tidepools retreats, giving me just enough clarity of mind to understanding something. And when I do, it's like a little bit of fog is lifted from my eyes. Not all of the fog, mind you, but just enough for me to see the shapes of objects that were previously occluded.

My Second Sign emerges from the past.

Eighteen

Things—faraway, strange, unnamable things—begin shifting. But in the end, they fall into place.

"Dry ice," I say, and the meaning of the words resurfaces, white and blind and shapeless. "Dry ice," I whisper, but now the words appear to waver, as if saying them over and over again renders them temporarily meaningless. As if the words come out of my mouth as fog, thick and milky white and moving in a sentient way.

I meet Arthur's eyes again. "Why did you ask me if I was *sure* Layla used dry ice during filming?"

Voicing the question transports me back to the Baron's Preparation Room, his mirror-clad psychomanteum. This morning, but also five years ago, I distinctively remember the white, wispy fog carpeting the floor, clinging to the walls, coming down from the ceiling. I vividly remember how, as a child, I stood on tiptoe, to limit how much of my bare feet touched the fog-covered floor. "It's just dry ice," Layla told me then, and her words stuck, they set root, burrowing deep into my marrow, until they became unshakable reality.

Arthur watches me, like he can somehow see inside my head, read my thoughts, my memories, my most intimate fears now bobbing on the surface of my mind like unsinkable buoys.

"Think about it," Arthur says. "Where would a seventeen-year-old get her hands on unusually large quantities of carbon dioxide? Did she steal it from school? Buy it illegally from a farm? What does your logical mind tell you?"

I stare at him blankly, before refocusing on the patch of sand to his side, where a crowd of Vs multiply into infinity. My eyes water.

Despite my obsession with her, Layla and I weren't particularly close before Cashore. The age difference was a part of it, but it also didn't help that I was the epitome of a pesky little sister. The brat of the family, I seemingly existed to ruin my big sister's me-time, invade her privacy.

Our time at Cashore House changed all that.

We became nearly inseparable. Left to our own devices in a big, old, mysterious house with nothing much to do brought us closer. Reinforcing the situation was our parents' decision to switch our enrollment to online schooling, a move that confined us to the house even more. I hated the idea of studying online. Layla loved it. She didn't seem to care about the high school milestones she was missing out on, even graduation. She didn't miss her pre-Livadia life, or her old friends from school; her times sneaking out to party and hang out seemed to be over. She didn't want to leave the house anymore. Of course, by then my sister was already neck-deep into her creative project, busy unearthing Cashore's old ghosts and creating one of her own in the process.

Which brings me back to Arthur's question.

Where would a seventeen-year-old kid buy lots and lots of carbon dioxide?

Where indeed. Her credit card was linked to that of our parents, so they would've noticed if she was buying up chemicals in large quantities and having it delivered to the house. I don't remember any big deliveries anyway, nothing that wasn't construction material Mom and Dad needed for their work.

The only two places in Livadia that Layla frequented, often with me in tow, were the local historical society, and the long-closed gadget-slash-memorabilia shop. If I were to make an educated guess, neither place could supply her with carbon dioxide, definitely not in the quantities she needed to fill most of *Vermillion*'s scenes with mysterious smoke.

The question of where the chemical could've possibly come from is making me reanalyze an entire year of my life. I'm rethinking things I took for granted. Because Arthur is right. There's no way my sister could've acquired large amounts of carbon dioxide, let alone hide it around Cashore House, right under our parents' noses while the renovations took place.

And if Layla lied about dry ice being the source of all that fog, then what else was she hiding from me?

I see the "dry ice" conundrum for what it is.

My Second Sign revealed. I'm one step closer to finding Layla.

"You all right?" Arthur asks me. "Should we start walking back?"

His words vibrate faintly, reaching me as if through a wall of cotton. I'm cold. Shivering. The boulder's shadow has grown too large and dark for comfort. This strange, desolate beach hasn't been visited by a single soul the entire time we've been here. A coincidence? Or do Livadia residents keep away from Cashore and its surroundings because they can feel what I know deep in my bones—that something's terribly wrong here.

I nod in response to Arthur's question. But as much as I want to leave, I also don't particularly look forward to being back in the house. Because, aside from having to deal with Erasmus and his agenda, I don't like where this train of thought is leading me. But I must deal with it. And I must move past it. I'm starting to believe that the Path is something more than can be defined by logic, which can be objectively understood. It's time for me to reconsider my experiences in the house, to see what my sister created, what she made me believe in a new light.

Erasmus can do what he wants, I'm sticking with my plan. Not his.

Get the rest of the Signs, complete the Path, and find Layla.

We pack up our picnic and start the climb back to Cashore in silence. The wind has picked up in the past half hour, and while I could really use my jacket right now, the fear of losing my footing keeps it tied around my waist.

I begin counting steps. It's an old habit. Just like five years ago, now I find the monotony of it soothing. The assailing wind makes me stumble, and I have to start from scratch. But it's okay, the point is the process, not determining the exact number of steps.

The familiar edge-of-the-cliff vertigo comes and goes, painting my windswept world with the bold brushstrokes of silver. I wonder how it felt to traverse this rocky passage at night, with the Baron and Adrianna leading their guests to the shore to witness sunrise. Did the procession carry flaming lanterns, or did they use unreliable flashlights like the one I was given this morning?

Unlike on the beach, I sense Arthur's nearness now as we climb the steps, a warm presence against the chilly wind. We've shifted positions to walk side by side. Every time our shoulders brush, I feel more anchored in this reality, more alive.

"You've got it, haven't you? Your Second Sign?" Arthur asks.

"I thought I wasn't supposed to tell you?" I say, and he looks away, smiling. "But yes," I admit after a couple of heartbeats. "Even if I still don't fully understand it, I have that feeling of rightness you've mentioned."

The moment I say it out loud I believe it completely, without any doubt. I experienced my Second Sign this morning, and yet I'm still me, same as before, but also different.

Does it mean I'm another step closer to believing that *Vermillion* is something more than a movie, and that my sister's fate is somehow tied to its grim storyline, its unsettling ending? Fear blossoms in the pit of my stomach. I'm not ready.

It wasn't real. There isn't a ghost haunting Cashore. Only memories. I cling to these statements like they're a life raft and if I let go, the churning sea will drag me under.

"You should start thinking about how it ends," Arthur says. Before I fully grasp his meaning, I register the prophetic nature of his words. "I mean, the end of the Path," he clarifies. "You need to start thinking about what you want out of it. The thing you're going to ask for in the end."

Ask Vermillion herself, he means.

I nod, acknowledging his words, but say nothing. It's easy to justify the silence by my dutiful adherence to the rules surrounding the Path. After all, with all his chattiness earlier, Arthur wouldn't tell me about his own wish—what is it he plans to ask Vermillion when she greets him at the end of the Path? But then, I suspect he's perceptive enough to already know what I want. Isn't it obvious, written all over my face in the biggest letters?

I want my sister back.

Nineteen

We return to Cashore to find it abuzz with activity.

It turns out no one in the house but the chef who packed our sandwiches knew about our little beach date. If it wasn't for the chef speaking up at the right moment, I'd have a real problem on my hands: Erasmus was about to launch a search party. Evidently, our phones were out of range when we were down by the sea.

Which means that the first moment I can, I slip away to my room to check my phone. Mixed in with all the missed calls from Erasmus and Petra-the-producer, there's also one from my mom, along with a text from one of my friends at the lake house—my alibi.

In the cold of my room, I grow hot with unease.

I read my friend's message first, low-key shuddering as I realize how close I've come to being discovered. It turns out, Mom called the lake house gang after she couldn't reach me. Of course, she chose to get in touch with me exactly when I was on the beach. Perhaps parents do possess a special sense that tingles when their kids are up to no good.

But my friends at the lake house did well. Whatever they said to my mom must've calmed her down. I don't hear police sirens blaring, and authorities aren't rushing in to return me to my parents. Some of my tension lifts.

Still, I feel the fragility of this lie I've constructed to justify my absence from home. One push and this precarious house of cards will fall. It's been a small miracle that Erasmus has kept his promise not to talk about the production to the media. A *Deadline Hollywood* article about *Vermillion: The Return* starring Sophia Galich is the absolute last thing I need right now.

None of this would be an issue if I was already eighteen, but sadly I am not, my birthday is still a few months away. I just hope that once the truth comes out, Mom and Dad will forgive me, that they'll agree the end justified the means. Of course, this will only work if I bring Layla back.

I finish talking with Mom, and by *talking,* I mean lying through my teeth, and open my laptop. I don't know how much time I have before someone comes to fetch me; I need to move fast. I log in to CrimsonDreadNet and navigate to **__OnThePath**.

After I enter my Second Sign revelation and hit enter, the next level unlocks.

Third Sign:
Twisted inside out
Hanging upside down
My nature is revealed

This riddle feels even more convoluted than the previous one, at first. If my Second Sign was connected to the Preparation Room scene, which scene would the Third Sign correspond to? I can only think of one option, only one scene in *Vermillion* involves hanging upside down—the one in which the titular entity makes her first appearance. Before that gravity-defying scene, Vermillion is a true ghost, unseen, unheard, only a suggestion of dread, a sinister atmosphere woven from the shadows of the house, a herald of things to come.

The more I dwell on my memories of filming this scene, the more I shudder. Memory can turn us into little kids again, fearful of shadows and dark corners. I hope my Third Sign is worth it since it likely means going through that particular encounter again. Even though I know whatever is going to happen is a setup, I still coil in discomfort.

At the same time, there's really nothing that Erasmus can throw at me that can truly scare me. My blood-curdling experiences with Layla's extra-realistic ghost dummy set up certain expectations. Erasmus's version of Vermillion played by Francesca, while undeniably freaky, was nothing like my childhood encounters, when terror turned my vision blurry, adrenaline twisting my memory. Past me would never chase after the ghost from Layla's film, would never try to touch her. Maybe I'm just braver now, or maybe without Layla by my side, without the tug of our sisterly connection, I'm not the same, none of it is. Erasmus is a stranger, someone I work with. Layla is someone I love, and love transforms perception, though not always for the better.

Someone knocks on my door. I hope it's Arthur, but it's Raina standing in the corridor.

"It's time for your makeup," she says, barely meeting my eyes. "Erasmus wants to shoot the next scene in the late afternoon light."

I'm heavy with exhaustion, still drained from starring in the reconstruction of the Preparation Room scene. I'd much rather be left alone to regroup and do more research, but Erasmus has other plans.

When I ask Raina what Erasmus has in mind this time, she smiles mysteriously.

As I follow Raina to the makeshift makeup station, I catch a glimpse of Arthur at the far end of the corridor. Partially hidden in the shadows, he's talking with his father. As if they can feel my stare from the distance, in eerie synchronicity, their heads turn my way. From where I am, Arthur's dreamy, gray eyes appear darker, nearly black. I look away quickly.

On the beach, Arthur told me he doesn't share anything

with Erasmus. Was I too quick to trust him?

Raina sits me down in front of a rectangular mirror leaned against the wall. The mirror's art deco design is one of several anachronisms throughout the house. Perhaps these new objects are courtesy of the current owner. I keep forgetting that someone actually owns this place—the same someone who had contracted my parents five years ago. I wonder who'd want a house like Cashore. While architecturally stunning, its history is terribly morbid. Despite its glittery interiors, this is a perfect setting for a horror movie, not a place to raise a family or to simply live in. No wonder Cashore today doesn't look lived in. Perhaps the owner, whoever she really is, simply likes to own this building, not actually make a home in it.

Back to my own predicament, I take the presence of the mirror as a positive sign. At least I'm allowed to see what Raina is doing. And that's despite my general cautiousness around reflective surfaces. To this day, whenever I see my own reflection, I half expect to catch something else in there, something that doesn't belong. Seeing *Vermillion*'s negative spaces filled with faces pressing out of the wallpaper, furniture moving in the background, has left its mark on me.

Watching Raina work with "normal" makeup, accentuating my features and enhancing my natural complexion, enhances my calm. No undead clown-slash-bride of Dracula look for me this time, thank you very much.

But slowly, my suspicions crawl back. I still have no idea what to expect from the upcoming filming session. I thought over the course of this documentary I would be expected to talk about the past and about Layla. I expected lengthy interviews and uncomfortable questions. And maybe that's to come, but so far, it's as if Erasmus is waiting for something to happen, and the longer it takes, the more stressed he becomes. Do the members of his crew know what he hopes to achieve, or are they as much in the dark as I am?

Raina's nervousness feels contagious. Arthur is definitely not telling me everything he knows. I have my secrets too, and I have good reasons for keeping them. But I can't say the same for the rest of these people I've temporarily thrown my lot in with.

I should be focusing on my Third Sign, but all I can do is stress about the staged horrors Erasmus is surely about to unleash upon me. My body reacts in kind, my injured ankle from long ago flaring up with dull pain; the scars around my left wrist appear whiter in Cashore's dulled light. And then there's a new sensation, deep in my chest, like my rib cage is shrinking around my heart. I have a sudden memory-jolt of falling through darkness and landing badly on my back. There was a flash of pain, followed by the violent sensation of being torn out of my body, and then . . . nothing.

"Hey, Sophia? Check it out. All ready!" Proud-looking Raina pulls me out of this unsettling barrage of memories I can't place.

I stare at my face in the mirror.

Raina's efforts have made me prettier but also more dramatic without being obvious about it. My eyes seem bigger and . . . sadder. My lips appear to not know what a smile is. I look like a girl who knows her own fate.

Before I can shake off this maudlin mood, Serge joins us. He brings my evening attire with him. I'm instructed to change into a peculiar period piece that consists of a red dress falling just below my knees, black strappy pumps, and a hairband with a bejeweled feather fastened to the side.

I take one look at this ensemble and frown.

Raina twists my shoulder length hair to create the illusion of a shorter cut, the tight, feathered hairband completing the look.

When I stand up and see myself in the mirror fully, I grow cold. This old fashioned style is a clever imitation of the bedraggled attire Vermillion wore when she crawled out of the hole in the ceiling five years ago as I watched on, in terror, from outside.

Twenty

"**A**-a-and action!"

The clapperboard's chopping downward swing reverberates long after I leave the reception room and assume my position outside, on the balcony. As with the morning filming experience, Erasmus gave me limited instructions, telling me not to overthink it.

Though I did overhear him talking to Miriam about capturing my face when "she appears." She must refer to Francesca, I'm assuming. I roll my eyes. Surely, Erasmus doesn't think I can be tricked twice in one day?

And while a part of me is annoyed, another part grows more and more filled with simmering dread. The wind battering the balcony brings a chill, but I'm burning on the inside. I can't simply will the Third Sign to show itself; I don't even know for sure if it is linked to this scene. But I have a feeling it is, and if I'm right, it's like Erasmus is following the exact order of the Signs on purpose—could he be drawing on his own experience of the Path?

I search for his face in the room I've left behind, but from out on the balcony, the view is slightly distorted by the window's mullioned glass. Now, I see much better, clearer, than compared to five years ago when pouring rain muddled the view. I'm not sure if that's a good thing, though.

Today, Erasmus and his crew have gone to great lengths to keep the chandelier's gaping hole in the ceiling blocked from my view. As I take in the room from my spot on the balcony, Miriam climbs halfway up the safety ladder, concealing the patch of ceiling behind her. An old suspicion returns, sending my thoughts back to the dinner last night. Arthur swore Erasmus hadn't planned for the chandelier to end up on the floor, but what if he doesn't know the truth himself? While Arthur claims he doesn't share anything important with his father, the reverse might also be true: Erasmus is keeping Arthur in the dark.

I'm shivering now, and I can't tell if it's the wind blowing from the gray sea, or if it's my levels of anxiety rising.

Probably a little of both.

I stick close to the wall as I pace the length of the narrow balcony, struggling to keep my balance in these elaborate, high-heeled pumps. I don't trust myself to venture too close to the railing—the drop beyond it looks sudden, absolute. The feeling of vertigo never fully leaves me.

If Erasmus has any further instructions for me in addition to "please go outside and wait," he'd have to scream them at me at the top of his lungs. I can't even hear the clicking of my own heels against the stone. It's like I've shed my corporeal body and entered a new realm of existence, where I float above the room.

A piece of dust gets stuck in my eye, and I force a handful of blinks.

As my vision clears, I notice something's changed inside the salon.

There's no Erasmus, no crew. The step ladder is gone too, along with Miriam. Though strangely, I can still feel her presence, her steely eye following me everywhere I go.

I put my hands against the window, bringing my face close. My exhale's warmth coats the glass briefly before vanishing.

When a hand emerges from the hole in the ceiling, my breath hitches.

The faint half moon scars circling my left wrist flare up in pain. It's like I'm in a horrible, prophetic dream. I know what's coming but I can't stop it. I can't stop it.

Dislodging dust and cobwebs and god knows what else, Vermillion crawls out of the ceiling, headfirst. Her black hair, filthy and tangled, is first to emerge from the hole.

Temporarily paralyzed, in complete and utter fright, the heels of my pumps fuse with the balcony's stone surface. I can't see the details from out here, but deep down I know that Vermillion is wearing a hairband with a feather, exactly like the one Raina's placed around my head. And I know that Vermillion's red dress is a copy of my own. The only differences between us are that she's barefoot, and I'm not. She's dead, and I'm not.

I know I'm being tricked and yet . . . maybe it's my newly found, tentative faith in the Path, in the Signs, or perhaps Raina went above and beyond in her task of making Francesca look more . . . dead, but the illusion is nearly perfect. So perfect that a part of me believes it. My panic rises, along with the primal need to give in to the legs-jellifying fear. It is Francesca behind the glass, and it is . . . not.

Whatever that thing is, I need to get the hell away from it. From *her*.

I scramble for the doorknob and turn while pulling at it at the same time. The door rattles but doesn't budge.

Inside the room, the red ghost moves with slow deliberation, self-assured like a python ready to swallow its prey. Me.

But there's still time. I have to believe that. I still have time to reenter the salon and run before Vermillion fully emerges from the ceiling. But much to my dry mouthed shock, I find the door is locked. No matter how hard I push and pull.

I'm alone, on a windswept balcony, with only a glass window between me and the monster that's haunted my dreams for five years.

Twenty-One

Filming with Layla at Cashore was like walking in a dream, my feet light and barely touching the ground. It would have been easy to write off the entire experience as such, if only the evidence of it didn't exist in the form of an actual movie. I have avoided watching *Vermillion* for years, only catching bits and snippets of it, but I've made myself sit through the entire film before returning to Cashore. Working off a hypothesis that a fan may have been involved in Layla's disappearance, I needed to experience *Vermillion* the way a fan would. The task turned out to be harder than imagined. It was like someone made a home movie reel of my worst nightmares, having reached inside my head, pulled out my biggest fears, and made a spectacle of them. Against the backdrop of sinister atmosphere woven from the shadows of the house, heralding things to come, some scenes appeared more real, sharp, and precise, while others possessed the same dreamlike quality I remembered from my time here. It's my memories of Vermillion, of my interactions with her, that are clouded in this gauzy fog that thickens whenever I try and focus on it.

As I stand now, immobile and windswept on a balcony, watching Vermillion emerge from the ceiling headfirst as if gravity inside the house has flipped upside down, I know this is not a dream.

This time she is real.

As I watch Francesca unfold from the ceiling, I struggle to reconcile the memories of Vermillion from my childhood with the reality of an actor *pretending* to be the ghost who terrified me then. My brain's meshing the two experiences together, aligning my past with my present, twisting my reality inside out.

Battered by the wind, I can't hear my own rapid breathing. I wonder if the microphone that Ivor hid in the dress's collar captures my hitched inhales and whimpers.

I locate the mic and cover it with my hand before whispering the words only the wind can hear. "I'm cold. I'm on a balcony. I'm acting in a movie. There's an actress, her name is Francesca . . . Shit!"

I whimper when the fake Vermillion muscles her torso out of the ceiling, then flips in midair, her arms holding on to the edge of the hole.

She lets go, and her legs meet the ground. My eyes water from the wind; I can't see any straps on her, no harness. The illusion is perfect. It's impossible to recognize Francesca in this getup, a hellish reflection of my own.

I try the door handle again. Still locked, or jammed.

Through the glass, I see Vermillion test her spot on the floor, cautiously so, as if she doesn't fully trust it won't break beneath her.

She shifts her head from side to side, angling it like a bird, then faces me, dead ahead. Impatient, eager. Her dry lips move.

She begins her slow trek toward me. Alternates between shuffling her feet and jerking them in a way a resurrected corpse would, its stiff, rotting body not working as it should. I can't smell her, but I gag on the memory of decay all the same.

"This isn't real. This isn't real. This isn't . . ." I whisper, bound by the rhythm of my hammering heart. I can't think straight with all the adrenaline coursing through me.

The edges of my reality darken, and memories rush in.

The Vermillion of my past could walk through walls. She could float. She'd vanish in one place of the house only to pop up in another. To her, nothing was sacred or unbreachable. She respected no boundaries or barriers inside Cashore and remained indifferent to my pleas and tears. She was Cashore itself, her bleeding, flayed soul fused with the bricks, baked into the crumbling foundation.

Only about nine feet separate me from the creature in the salon, but she takes her time to cover it. With each step she takes, I grow colder. My right hand's fingers encircle my left wrist, as if that can stop this unholy buzzing under my skin. The old scars are more raised, more painful to the touch, as if whatever pierced my skin five years ago has poisoned inside me, and now it's reacting to Vermillion's approach, no longer able to distinguish between now and then, real and not real.

It's not real. It's not real. It's not real.

No one but Layla and I know how the original scene, the Upside Down or the Awakening as it's also known, actually ended. The footage was heavily edited by Layla before anyone could lay eyes on it. It means the memories of what really happened that day are my own, but they are incomplete, foggy in parts. With Francesca-as-Vermillion moving toward me now, it's all coming back.

I'm twelve years old. I'm out on the balcony, this very balcony, watching Vermillion through the glass. She emerges from the ceiling and cascades down to the floor, a jerkiness to her movement—she is inanimate, an empty shell. Layla is her invisible puppeteer, pulling the strings. Vermillion unfolds upward, her head jerks up, pale chin jutting out from beyond the mass of her hair. And then, and then . . . she floats toward me. I can't see her feet, which makes for a perfect illusion of ghostly flight.

As I am on the balcony now, the nightmare is repeated. Only this time, my sister isn't here to soothe me with her explanations and promises. As a child, I just wanted to be close to her, to be a part of her world, to be an equal participant. Now, I just want out of here, to run, to hide. Francesca's labored approach fosters a deeply uncomfortable, constricted feeling in my chest.

Plastered against the glass, I watch the animated mannequin approach, expecting Layla to appear any moment and end this. Surely, she's gotten enough footage by now. But Layla is not rushing to get to me. She's far away, cowering in the corner with her camera, a shadow of a girl, looking as terrified as I feel. I'm on my own. Vermillion is right there, reaching for me. One moment she is banging her bloody fists against the glass and the next she is walking right through it. She's next to me, towering over me, the balcony is too small for the two of us.

My breathing is frantic as this memory, one of those that used to be a gap, emerges from the mental fog, and takes its place in the puzzle of my mind. There are others empty spots that remain, but this recovered memory is important. I know it from the way it feels—heavy pressure and the thudding of blood.

Vermillion is right next to me, and she reaches for me, she grabs my wrist as I scream. Her fingers, nails razor-sharp, dig deep into my skin, leaving me forever marked. The pain spreads from my wrist, the pain fuels me. I transform into a feral animal, hissing and biting and screaming, as I fight off this creature—not a dummy or a mannequin but a being with a mind of its own—and run, without looking where I am going.

It wasn't until later that I learned I was missing for over an hour before Layla found me in my bedroom. It was the third time she'd checked there. Neither of us could account for the seventy minutes or so of our lives that preceded it. At the sight of my bleeding skin, Layla paled. But the words out of her mouth didn't match her horrified expression. She dismissed my story of the dummy coming to life. She said it was just my imagination. My own fingernails that dug into my skin.

But while I still can't account for the time I was allegedly missing, I know I didn't harm myself.

And I have no logical explanation for how the dummy came to life five years ago, how it walked through the glass and ended up right next to me. I remember all this now in detail, down to the way Vermillion smelled, of ages-old dust and dried blood, and how her pale hand possessed a terrifying strength when it wrapped around mine.

This new understanding eats away at my old belief, corroding it.

Was I wrong to listen to Layla's explanations and assurances that everything that was happening to me, around me, was staged and completely harmless? I have scars to prove otherwise. And I have this new memory—from my own perspective and not as a viewer of Layla's film.

And now, Vermillion is nearly at the window again. The distance between us gives me a better view of her features and her expression.

I can't look away.

I watch her arms move. I wince when she slams her fists against the glass, and the shock of it sends me backward. I hit the balcony's railing and it's cold and hard against my back.

My hands find the railing, my stiff fingers wrap around it. The creature of my nightmares is about to pass through the glass, to get to me, to finish what she started five years ago.

But the ghoul behind the glass remains where she is. Her eyes don't leave mine. We're at a stalemate. And then I know in my bones that this isn't at all like five years ago. Francesca can't walk through walls. She can't hurt me.

The original version of this encounter superimposes itself upon my brand-new experience of witnessing Francesca do the same moves Vermillion did five years ago. In my head I can see one red figure moving behind the other, two pairs of limbs moving in near unison. The two Vermillions appear near identical, but one is flesh-and-bone and the other is . . .

This current version of Vermillion slams her hands against the glass. The window shakes but doesn't give. I let go of the balcony railing. I approach the glass and press my hands against it. I stare at the woman on the other side.

I can see that she is indeed human. The natural lines of Francesca's skin crease against her makeup. Lean, wiry muscles move under skin. She's athletic, a former acrobat maybe, that's why Erasmus must've chosen her. Her movements, jerky and sharp, now seem honed and precise, practiced. It reminds me of Rie Inō, a Kabuki student who played Sadako, the terrifying ghost in *Ringu*. To get the footage of Sadako crawling out of the well,

Rie Inō was filmed walking backward, moving her limbs in the signature jerky Kabuki motions which are traditionally used to portray powerful emotions. When the footage was run in reverse, the effect was unnatural, blood-chilling.

My past and present blend into one narrative. The red ghoul from the past moves with the fluidity of a real person while Francesca's face distorts into a familiar snarl, with black eyes and rotten teeth.

The Third Sign lights up roadside neon. It crackles and flickers.

It wasn't a dummy five years ago.

And it wasn't an actor.

It was something else entirely.

Something able to walk through walls and leak into my dreams but still tangible enough to leave me with real scars.

And then, as if Cashore itself can hear the frantic, panicked clicking of my mental gears, the house groans and shivers against the wind and my vision swims.

I don't hear the lock clicking open, but I do notice when the handle moves. The threshold is immediately claimed by the scary-looking Francesca.

I know she is just a human, just like me, but still my knees want to give out. I need to get the hell away from her. I need to process what I've just learned.

I rush Francesca, ram into her shoulder, forcing her to turn sideways and let me pass, but before I'm free, her freezing fingers wrap around my left wrist, and I shriek in pain.

"Cut! Cut!"

People rush into the room, Erasmus among them, but I see them distorted, as if through a veil.

The air moves around me in a strange pattern.

Even after Francesca lets go of my wrist, the searing pain lingers, like liquid fire under my skin. I'm too afraid to look, but I know my old scars have opened up. I'm bleeding.

The floor swallows me up.

Twenty-Two

As a kid, I hadn't seen Vermillion outside of the movie context. Layla said it would be better that way. To see the monster of her making in a safe environment separate from filming was to destroy any cinematic sway Vermillion had over me. And while Layla claimed the entity was a mannequin, she never told me where she got it—same with the dry ice. Naturally, at the time, my imagination ran wild. I imagined my sister breaking into a department store at night and stealing a plastic body from a display window. I imagined Layla visiting a secondhand shop to purchase a red gown, buying human hair from a salon, bringing dirt in from a mulchy garden to rub into the dummy's feet.

At some point, when the actions of this "mannequin" became too complicated, I thought Vermillion was played by a friend of Layla's, or someone she had hired. But like Francesca, that actor must've been skilled.

And able to pass through walls.

But now I know Layla's dummy was no dummy at all. It moved of its own accord. It had a purpose.

I wonder if Vermillion, that *thing*, whatever the hell it was, is still in the house.

If my recovered memory is as much a warning as a Sign?

The Signs I've already received rush before me. The Invitation, with Layla staying just outside my view as she implores me to "give it back." Then, the past returning, bringing with it my Second Sign. And now, something Upside Down.

At this rate, I'll be at the end of the Path by tomorrow. But instead of steely determination, I feel heart-pumping terror. I'm not ready. My entire life I've been cowering by this door, the symbol of Layla's legacy, only brave enough to open it a crack. Now, this door is flying open in my face.

Arthur was right. Experiencing the Signs is not the same as hearing or reading about them. My perspective has shifted completely. My stern belief that there must be a logical explanation for everything has been fundamentally shaken over the course of a single day, a single afternoon. This is how people start believing in ghosts, gods, spirits, anything outside the rational realm—by seeing these things face to face, by feeling their breath upon their own skin.

But if I allow myself to believe that *everything* that happened to me in this house five years ago was real—that there was a ghost named Vermillion and it haunted me day and night, and my sister captured it all on camera—did Layla know what was happening? Why wasn't she scared then?

Layla's terrified face flashes before my eyes. That's my answer. She *was* scared. Terrified. And yet she was wielding her camcorder fearlessly, talking me down after each of my panicked encounters, telling me it was safe, that it was all pretend.

But was she protecting me, or exploiting me?

Love for my sister is at war with anger, but love is winning. It always does. Love is what drove me here. Love and the need for truth—something I believe would release me from the demons of my past.

But I have so many questions. Was Layla really on the Path? Has she reached its end? What did she ask for? What did she get?

"Sophia? Are you all right? I'm a doctor. My name is Evie Patel."

I look up to find a woman hovering over me. I must've seen her in passing before, but back then she was just one of the faces in the crowd calling Cashore a temporary home. The doctor's black tresses are pulled up into a tight bun and her brown eyes are in equal measure kind and concerned. I zero in on her voice, letting it pull me out of my petrified state.

As the room stops spinning, I see more of Erasmus's crew. They're sticking to the salon's periphery, pretending to go on with their business, giving me and Dr. Patel a wide berth.

Francesca lingers just behind the doctor. Through the layers of her deathly makeup, I read her expression as apologetic. She's still wearing her Vermillion getup, the crawled-from-the-grave version of my own outfit, and I look away, hoping she'll just leave me alone.

"I'm all right," I tell Dr. Patel, training my mouth into a smile. Evidently, I convince no one.

"That was quite a fall," she says, frowning. "I heard your knees cracking from the next room. Do you mind if I have a closer look?" She studies me with such concern that I feel the beginning of an uncomfortable shiver starting in the back of my neck.

"Fine," I mumble because the alternative might mean the end of my ruse. Any hospital will see through my charade and inform my parents immediately.

While Dr. Patel inspects my beat-up knees and bleeding wrist, I seek out Erasmus. But suddenly, he is nowhere to be found. Arthur is also conveniently missing.

I watch the doctor produce rubbing alcohol and gauze from the open case by her side. As she takes care of my wrist, her expression darkens. "What happened?" she asks as my opened-up scars disappear under layers of bandages.

"I . . . must have scratched myself when I fell," I say, but I don't sound convincing even to my own ears. I realize I sound just like Layla did when she was telling me my original wound was self-inflicted.

I cry out when Dr. Patel probes into the pale skin of my right ankle. The injury is old but still hurts-with-a-capital-H when twisted a certain way.

She looks at me, her eyebrows drawn high in an unspoken question. I wonder how much Erasmus has told her. But her face doesn't give anything away. I relent. "It's an old injury. I broke it years ago. It never healed properly. It doesn't usually bother me."

I'm so used to giving the abbreviated history of my injury that the words come out sounding practiced and untrue. But Dr. Patel doesn't need to know the gory details. Like that on the day I received my injury, the day I danced like one possessed and ended up falling through the wooden rafters and hurting myself terribly, was the first time I blacked out during filming.

Some V-heads might know this from the few rare interviews Layla gave while reluctantly promoting the movie, but it's not common knowledge that the Dance of the Unquiet Spirits was actually the very first thing Layla captured on camera, before *Vermillion* was even a solid concept in her head. The scene in question wasn't planned. Something made me do it, put on my ballet shoes and begin my possessed dance. And after I'd fallen through the rafters, Layla couldn't immediately find me. When I came to, my legs folded painfully beneath me, she was right next to me, her face faint, completely washed of color. When I asked her what was wrong, she said "everything is perfect now." Her voice shook.

But Dr. Patel doesn't need to know any of that.

She finishes her examination, then offers her hand to help me stand up. I'm shaky at first, but my motivation to get the hell out of there improves my balance faster than is probably safe.

I thank Dr. Patel, unlatch my lapel mic, and leave the salon on unsteady feet.

Daylight leaks away from the sky. Then twilight comes, wearing a dark purple mantle. The incessant wind morphs into a storm, and Arthur arrives to check on me in my bedroom.

"Are you coming to dinner?" he asks. His face is familiar, yet mysterious. There's concern in his eyes and something else—a question he wants to ask, but he holds it back.

"I was just getting ready," I say, as I invite him in.

There's a certain caution to his movement. His shoulders are tense, his mouth reduced to a tight line. The way he looks at me gives me a pause. He stares at my bandaged wrist but doesn't say anything.

"I didn't see you earlier. When I was filming the balcony scene." I don't exactly mean to sound accusatory, but it comes out that way. I look away and pick up my hairbrush. When I see Arthur's face again, he looks decidedly guilty.

"Look, it's fine," I say. "I don't expect you to be by my side or even *on* my side all the time. Your father has his own agenda here, and I know you do too."

"It's not like that . . ." he begins to say. The alarm in his tone makes me look away from the mirror. I set the brush aside and turn to face him. His hair sticks out, and the left side of his face carries a faint indentation, like the one formed from pressing against a fold in the sheets in your sleep. But Arthur doesn't look well-rested. Quite the opposite. I take a careful sniff, almost expecting to smell alcohol on him, but all I get is a faint whiff of mint. He looks younger than his age, more vulnerable and relatable. Concern for him takes root in my heart.

"What happened?" I ask. "Should I go get Dr. Patel?"

"No." He dismisses the suggestion with a jerky wave. "It's nothing a doctor can help me with. I . . . I forgot."

My breath hitches, but I don't understand why his words spook me so.

"What did you forget?" I ask carefully. He just frowns, as if in concentration, his eyes darting. I follow his eyes' movement to the corner, where the wardrobe doesn't quite meet the wall. The blind spot. I watch Arthur grow a degree paler, if that's even possible.

"Arthur? Focus. Why don't you start from the beginning? You were saying you forgot something?"

He nods, meeting my eyes. "Earlier, I went to my room to try and have a nap. I didn't want to watch you film the balcony scene with Francesca. I think what Dad's doing is weird and it goes against the very nature of your sister's art. *V* was spontaneous, it was authentic, you weren't told when to be scared . . . What's happening here is staged. It's wrong. But my father is beyond the point where he can be reasoned with . . ." He stops, taking a long breath.

I wait.

I sit on the bed and beckon him to join me, which he does. We're closer now than when we were on the beach, but instead of warmth, it's nervousness that radiates off him.

"You went upstairs for a nap . . ." I nudge.

"And when I woke up, I forgot my Fourth Sign. It's gone. Completely erased from my mind."

His admission thunders through me as he reaches for my hands, a sudden movement. I let his touch seep into me, exiling the ghostly sensation Francesca's fingers left on my scarred wrist. I wrap my fingers around Arthur's and squeeze. The connection is more intimate than I expected. A shudder goes through me, warming my insides. My heart beats fast.

"How could you forget a Sign?" I ask.

"It's punishment," he whispers, fingers curling around mine. I break into a deep blush. But I don't think Arthur can see it. He's lost in his own thoughts. "For sharing my Path progress with you," he says. "She made that clear when she reached inside my mind and pulled out those threads of memory. She took it away, Sophia. She, she pushed me back a step."

I'm still digesting what he's telling me, and the more it sinks in, the colder my hands get. I can't even feel the warmth of Arthur's fingers against mine anymore. I strengthen my hold, afraid that if I let go, he'll fade away along with the afternoon light.

"Maybe it was just a bad dream?" I ask, though I don't really believe that. In Cashore, nothing is "just a dream"—I understand that now.

Arthur shakes his head. "It wasn't a dream. It was a visitation. She's done it before, to others—I've read about it. That's why it's very rare when people talk about their experiences, about the Path, because when you do, when you share things with those behind you, you break the rules, and there are consequences. I didn't believe it could actually happen, but she did it to me. She made me forget. I've even been kicked out from the Fourth Sign thread of CrimsonDreadNet—how could the mods even know to do that?"

A chill runs through me. Arthur lets go of my fingers, digs his hands into his hair. I reach for his hands again and gently loosen his fingers, bringing our locked hands back to rest between us on the bed. I find his eyes again. This is the most vulnerable I've seen him, and it scares me. I refuse to believe this is all an act he's putting on to trick me. Something frozen inside me melts a little.

"Arthur, listen," I say. "Look on the bright side. You've been pushed back a Sign, but I've gotten my third one today. We can look for the Fourth Sign together."

Twenty-Three

We leave my room to procure dinner from the kitchen. We don't need to articulate it, but neither of us feels like socializing, so we go back to my room and have dinner together, just the two of us, sitting on my bed, huddled under the blankets, fully clothed. If Arthur notices how freakishly cold my room is compared to the rest of Cashore, he doesn't say so. He's calmed down a little since his earlier outburst, but there's still a darkness in his eyes.

He shoots glances into the corner where the wardrobe makes a corridor against the wall. Arthur's nervousness is contagious, and soon I join him, looking for something in that darkness, too. We consume our chicken anticucho skewers and sweet potato fries to the relentless soundtrack of the ocean gale slamming repeatedly against the house. Cashore groans and moans, but its integrity holds.

"Something happened while you were filming the balcony scene," Arthur says as a statement, not a question. "You seem different."

"Something did happen," I admit. I wonder how much to tell him, how to steer this conversation without endangering my progress on the Path. I don't want to have my latest Sign erased from my head. But I want to share something meaningful with Arthur, this desire overriding my cautiousness. "Let's just say, I had a shift of perspective."

"That's when you've received your Second Sign—during the filming," he says. He shifts on his side of the bed, and gravity beckons me to slide closer to him. "I wonder if my father did too, or if he's further on than he lets on."

"I bet this whole house is on the Path. Ivor, Raina . . ." I say, the calm in my voice not reflective of the turmoil inside.

"No, not them. Just him," Arthur says.

I wait for him to share more. He looks like he wants to, fingers gently tapping against the bed. Our dinner is finished, and Arthur could've left by now. And yet, here he is, perfectly behaved, yet stiff with tension. I wonder what it might look like to the crew, to Erasmus, this thing I have with Arthur, where he spends time in my room, in my bed. But also, do I care? We're not doing anything, just talking. If someone watched the surveillance footage and got scandalized, I'm sure we'd have heard from them by now.

"I didn't know until today, not for sure," Arthur says. "But I . . .

was looking for something in his room and came across his notes."

"You went snooping?" I shake my head in mock judgment. I can't say it didn't occur to me to invade Erasmus's private space and look for anything incriminating, but what if I got caught? Would he kick me out from his movie set? Besides, I didn't really have a good reason before. The director may be suspicious, but so is everyone else currently trapped with me in this house.

"I needed to know what we're *really* doing here," Arthur says.

"Are you saying we're not really reenacting scenes from a cult teen horror movie to reinvigorate your father's career?"

"He does want to be relevant again, that's true," Arthur says. "And nothing will make him more relevant than attaching his name to something evergreen, like *V*. But . . . when was the last time you logged in to CrimsonDreadNet?"

"Earlier today. Why?" It feels like days ago, weeks even. I'd check the site more frequently if there was a way to access it on my phone, but of course there is no app, and CrimsonDreadNet only likes desktop browsers. Whoever built it didn't care about user friendliness or mobile integration.

"Bring it up. I want to show you something," Arthur says.

My first impulse is to decline. My experiences with the site have always been personal, intimate even. CrimsonDreadNet is not a place you casually check out with your girlfriend, or with a good-looking boy next to you in bed. But Arthur's serious voice makes me reconsider. He might have an agenda of his own—I *know* he does—but every time we talk, it's becoming harder and harder to believe that this agenda is to harm me. He's here with me now, willing to share something important, inviting me into his world.

I grab my laptop and enter my login details, while Arthur politely looks away. As I type the name of the site into the search engine, I expect that today of all days it'll choose to stay out of my reach. But the site emerges from the digital depths.

I suppress a sigh. Clearly, something wants me to have this moment with Arthur. He's about to know me by my user-name, and that means he'll be able to read my contributions to **__OnThePath** so far.

Something inside me squirms—this whole website may be dedicated to my sister, but it's got plenty on me as well. If only I could just come in with a digital eraser and delete everything that has my name or picture . . .

"I can use my login, if you prefer," Arthur offers as I hesitate, fingers hovering over the keyboard.

Without a word, I hand the laptop over to him.

Arthur is *@SleeplessReveler*.

I can't help but snort in amusement. "Very appropriate."

"*@AlwaysTiredInsomniac* was taken," he deadpans, while navigating to the one CrimsonDreadNet thread I rarely visit: **__LookingForLayla**.

Despite what its title suggests, this thread does not imply

fans are sharing the results of their own active investigations. The thread is dedicated to the official search for my sister, as conducted by the police. It started when some well-connected V-head leaked several official documents online in the months following Layla's disappearance, including the 911 recording that first alerted the authorities to something wrong. The call's transcript was the only moderately useful thing though. The rest of the thread is just recounting police's official theories, posting screenshots of news articles chronicling Layla's vanishing, making diagrams of suspects (I'm always included as one), and so on. No one on this thread, or any thread on CrimsonDreadNet, has ever mentioned that photo I saw for a split second on **__LaylaGalichIsAlive**. I admit, there are times I doubt the photo was real, that it was a hallucination caused by anxiety and grief, a momentary lapse of synapses.

But I have to trust myself, trust my own mind.

"Have a look at this," Arthur says as he hands my laptop back to me.

My heart does a painful flip in my chest when I see the screen. It's a photo, one I've seen before. Framed in the gloomy light of an overcast day, Cashore's front porch is smothered in flowers and videotape rolls—the latter is purely symbolic, since Layla's camcorder was digital. This is from the week of her disappearance, when her fans swarmed Cashore to show their devotion to my sister. Some even broke in and took a quick stroll through the building's empty rooms, posting blurry photos to the forum afterward. Cashore always seems to occupy this liminal space between empty and inhabited. It's never completely abandoned, but no one lives here either—no one alive that is, not for long anyway.

The building's security system must've alerted the cops, which brings me to the photo at hand. There's a hint of a police cruiser on one side, while a group of people, V-heads, are gathered to the right the porch. Everything is just a tad blurry; the crowd appears faceless, washed out.

"I've seen this before," I say, barely containing my disappointment.

"Sure, but have you *really* looked at it?" Arthur points at the group of V-heads.

Zooming in on the mini crowd decreases the quality of the photo by a degree, but I study the fuzzy faces anyway. I sense Arthur's tension next to me, his body radiating heat.

I gasp. It's Erasmus, blending in with the crowd. His beard, his height, his build. I look away from the photo and meet Arthur's eyes. He looks as unsettled as I feel. "You didn't know your dad paid a visit here the week Layla went missing?"

He shakes his head. "He's never even mentioned anything about his V project until the week after Layla disappeared. And it usually takes him years to develop his movie ideas. I suspect he's been planning this for a while, he just kept it to himself. But there's more—I told you I went through his stuff . . ."

"Were you looking for something in particular?"

"Not really, not at first. But then I found this." He brings up a picture on his phone. Arthur went full spy-mode and photographed what appears to be photos of book pages. Copies of copies.

Instructions for rituals, how to draw an invocation circle, a list of obscure ingredients. Paragraphs of texts, something about using repeated patterns to enable manifestation magic.

"Manifestation magic?" I read out loud, dark thoughts racing through my head. Repeated patterns lead to manifestation, I read. Are reenactments repeated patterns? Am I being used, but to what end? "What is Erasmus hoping to manifest?" I ask, despising the shiver in my voice.

Arthur doesn't respond and he avoids looking at me.

"You've already told me as much," I prompt.

The old me, the one who didn't have her perspective shifted dramatically just hours ago, would ridicule the idea that Erasmus's movie is a charade to enact some arcane manifestation ritual. But the new me? The new me fights the urge to pack up my bags right now and run into the night. I may have gotten myself into something a lot more sinister and dangerous than I thought. Layla's disappearance may have truly had a supernatural culprit. But what is Erasmus's role in all this?

"I can only guess," Arthur says. "I mentioned before, my father and I, we don't talk. I mean, we talk but not about things that matter, not since— I think these photos I found are from the *Book of Ka'schor.*"

"I keep hearing about this book," I say. The way he pro-nounces its name, emphasizing the harsh consonants, sends a wave of discomfort through me.

"It's a book of spells. Supposedly this famous medium, Lady Parschalli, gifted it to the Baron and he became obsessed, but I don't know," he trails off. "Many people take it at face value, like its spells work; my father might be one of them. What are you going to do?" he asks when I remain silent. "You're going to leave?"

Something, an imagined hint of a movement, draws my attention again to that blind spot in the corner, the tight corridor formed between the wardrobe and the wall. Unblinking, I stare at it until tears form in my eyes.

"Your dad might have his weird secrets," I say. "And he might think he's using me, but I'm also using him. I need to stay here. I-I want . . ." I'm about to say it: *I want my sister back*. But I chicken out in the last moment.

"I'm staying," I say firmly.

When Arthur stands up to leave, I try not to read too much into his hesitation. He seems more or less recovered from the shock of forgetting his latest sign. Perhaps sharing with me helped him shed some of the burden he was caring.

His eyes linger on my face. As he walks out the door, a yearn-ing unfolds in my chest. I imagine there's a red, glimmering string that connects me to him, like we're forever linked.

Twenty-Four

I try compartmentalizing. Try shoving the disturbing information about Erasmus into a drawer in my head dedicated to things I'll have to deal with later, but it's a difficult task. I can't stop thinking about Erasmus: picturing him stalking Layla, coming to Cashore in the wake of her disappearance. I'd read somewhere that criminals like to return to the scene of their crime . . . Has Erasmus done something to my sister?

The longer I stay in this house, the more dangerous it might become, but . . . the longer I stick around, the more likely Erasmus will slip up, make a mistake, or reveal something he shouldn't, and I'll be there to witness it. I need a solid piece of evidence that will implicate him.

But guilty or not, what does Erasmus hope to manifest? Is he attempting to recreate *Vermillion*'s wild, underground fame by capturing real ghosts on film?

I fight a shiver and wrap myself tighter in a blanket. I'm on the Path. Whatever Erasmus ends up manifesting might play in my favor, might help me progress faster. I know exactly what I'll ask if Vermillion makes an appearance. But what price am I willing to pay to have my wish come true?

I barely sleep that night, and when the dawn comes, I greet it with bleary eyes and a heavy heart. After my Third Sign, I now believe that what happened in this house five years ago wasn't just props and morbid creativity. My memories of filming *Vermillion* are being rewritten. And while I fear the next Sign, dread the next bend of the Path, I also yearn for it. Like it's a black, pulsing star, and I'm the light it hungers for. I want to walk the Path to the end, but I don't want to end up like Layla, to vanish without a trace. I hope that our Paths will cross, that as I chase the scary ghost of my childhood, it'll lead me to my sister.

Ever the pragmatist, I prep for the Fourth Sign. I bring up CrimsonDreadNet again.

When I type in my credentials and share my Third Sign experience, my next clue appears.

Reflection tells the truth
But there is a price to pay

Oh.

Reflection can refer to any one of the scenes in the movie involving mirrors. There was the one in which a taloned hand reached for me, as if from beyond the glass. And then there was that other scene when my face rippled in the mirror and rearranged itself into a ghoulish sneer. But I suspect that the Fourth Sign has to do with the tidal pools festering in the shadow of Cashore, where we filmed *Vermillion*'s most misunderstood scene.

As a kid, I felt simultaneously drawn and repelled by the rocky shallows. But just like the smell of Cashore's west wing, the briny rot of the pools seemed to exist solely in my mind, beckoning me and luring me in. What Layla filmed at those pools that one night is the reason I'm wary of filled bathtubs to this day.

But despite my determination and my readiness, the next two days offer an unwelcome change of pace. Everything slows down, even the air inside the house feels stagnant and foggy, despite powerful ventilation that keeps the rooms icy.

Instead of tackling *Vermillion*'s biggest scenes, Erasmus focuses on minor, shorter ones—snippets, not full-length re-enactments. Francesca in her red ghoul getup is no longer a shock, and the director knows it. His hired ghost grows more and more scarce, a number of scenes restructured without her.

My Fourth Sign refuses to reveal itself. As time slips through my fingers, I feel like I'm disappearing into the walls of the house, one particle at a time, like my feet are drowning in the lush carpets.

It's as if Erasmus can sense my frustration, because suddenly he wants to talk to me all the time, to give me his directorial "notes."

We're outside, filming atmospheric shots on the beach when Erasmus approaches, his expectant smile immediately making my innards coil.

"I want to create imagery of you walking toward the tide pools. I'll overlay it with Layla's footage from the beach, inserting you into the original visuals. What do you think?"

"Sounds good to me," I say, though what I really want is to ask him why he suddenly cares about what I think. But then I think of an even better question. "You know, I've been meaning to ask why out of all the options in the world, you chose my sister's movie as your inspiration here. Why *V*?"

He gives it a moment, his eyes scanning the shore. We're as far away from the tide pools as the strip of the beach allows, and I'm already in makeup and wearing a cerulean gown that glitters in the sun. In the distance, below Cashore's neck-breaking cliff, Erasmus's crew busies about, carrying equipment and whatnot.

"I don't like talking about what inspires my art," the director offers at last.

"I get that. Layla is like that too."

That earns me a look. "You speak of her like she's alive."

I glare at him, which is not a difficult task against the sun in my eyes. "Why wouldn't I?"

I hide my anticipation behind an innocent expression.

"I know how we all crave resolution, closure," he says. "But it can also be tempting to hide behind uncertainty."

"What do you think happened to Layla?" I go for it. At the very least, I can study his face, see if there's any change as Erasmus formulates his response.

But the director's features remain smooth, unrattled. "I don't like to speculate," he says. "But I must say I admire your bravery. Being here, doing this, must not be easy for you. I understand it though. I'd do the same thing, if I thought it'd bring me closer to the one I've lost."

The director clams up after that, evading my prompts and questions. There's sadness clinging to him like a cloak, and though I suspect him of darkness, I wonder once again about his true motives for being here, for doing the things he does.

We begin filming, and I focus on the task at hand as I walk the length of the beach toward the tide pools and cameras. I look straight ahead, resisting the temptation to study whatever flickers in my peripheral. In Layla's film, the scariest things took place in the backdrop. Even now, with the sun shining down on me and pushing away all shadows from the beach, I expect to see Vermillion walking side by side with me, her red dress semi-transparent, her rotten feet leaving no marks in the sand.

I spend my breaks with Arthur, poring over CrimsonDreadNet for clues and hints. We fall into an easy habit of sitting side by side on my bed, backs to the wall, laptop on my lap, our heads leaning together toward the screen. If this was a "normal" situation, we'd be watching YouTube videos or streaming a show. Instead, we descend deeper and deeper into the rabbit hole vortex formed around a cult horror movie.

It's during one of those rare moments of calm between shooting random scenes when I confess to Arthur.

"I once saw a photo of Layla entering the house the night she disappeared," I say.

Is it Arthur's physical closeness, his warmth, that triggered the sharing? I'm immediately horrified at having said the words, but it's too late now.

Before Arthur can speak, I rush to add, "The photo was gone before I could go to the police."

"I believe you." That's all he says.

I glance at him sideways. His expression hasn't changed, but I sense a wave of tension rising from his body. "CrimsonDread is like that," he adds after a moment. "I think the site is possessed. It reveals certain things to certain people at just the right time but then holds back with others . . . is that why you're really here? Because of that photo?"

I nod. "Do you think I'm silly? Going on this wild goose chase, thinking I know better than the detectives? Hoping that if I receive all the Signs, I can have my sister manifest out of thin air?"

"I don't think you're silly at all, Sophia," he says. He looks at me, his gaze a magnet, pulling me closer. "I'd do the same thing. I'd follow *any* clue."

"What if your father is the one who took that photo?" I say, the words hoarse against my throat. "What if he's done something to Layla?"

Arthur shifts away, comes to face me on the bed. The weight of his eyes compels me to look at him.

"My father may be obsessed," he says. "But he's not a . . ."

What's he about to say? Killer? Murderer?

"He'd never hurt anyone," he concludes. "I don't know for sure. We barely talk, but I think his reasons for being here are the same as my own."

He doesn't offer more. Perhaps he doesn't want to be pushed back a Sign again. I hope that's what it is. I don't know what to make of his impassionate words in defense of his father, but I want to believe him. I really do.

Later, as I lie in bed, listening to the sounds of the house, doors swinging shut, showers running, I try distracting myself from my dark thoughts by imagining what life will be like when this is over. I'll go away to college, or maybe find a job first and save up some money. Layla will be back in my life and doing her thing. She might make another movie, perhaps an autobiographical one about what happened to her, or she might write a book about her ordeal. That'll put me back in the spotlight, for sure, but I don't care. I'm willing to sacrifice a bit of calm if it means her safe return.

My thoughts jump around, turning to Arthur next. I mull over the look he gave me before walking out of the room. Earlier, he shared vital information with me and paid a price for it. And it's clear he's willing to jeopardize his relationship with his father if it means answering my questions and sharing his findings. Something is happening between us. I've never felt this sense of unity and purpose with anyone outside my family. Ever.

Thanks to the house's omnipresent surveillance, there now exist several videos of Arthur entering and leaving my bedroom. I'm aware of what it looks like, but a part of me warms at the idea of it being real. Though I know it's not.

I can't do *this*. Can't be with anyone right now. Not until I find what I'm looking for. My sister comes first, no matter what.

And yet, I'm not strong enough to stop fantasizing about what it would it feel like . . . What would his mouth taste like? How would it feel to sense his breath on my skin? I close my eyes and imagine Arthur back here with me, leaning in for a kiss.

Though it's not even the physical attraction that draws me in; it's the way he is.

I've tried dating in the past, and I don't mean my experiences with V-heads trying to get into my life. I went out on real dates, sat next to a boy in a dark movie theater, our hands touching. I kissed and wanted more. It was a brief period of my life when I was trying to let Layla go, to put *Vermillion* behind me. It didn't last. Before I knew it, Layla was back on my mind, and then I began plotting my return to Cashore. Romance always lost its appeal too soon, and every moment I spent on a date or just hanging out with friends felt like time being wasted. The poison Vermillion's nails deposited under my skin was building, bubbling up to the surface. I was starting to burn with this need to find Layla. Everyone who didn't mesh with that plan was pushed away.

But now, with Arthur, those yearnings return. Despite the unsettling circumstances of us meeting, he makes me *feel* things again, things I thought I forgot how to feel. And one thing that's different now is that I don't see Arthur as a distraction. Quite the opposite. I have a strong feeling I'll need him more and more as I progress toward the end of my Path.

Maybe I'm just ruined for regular romance; the only way for me to feel anything at all is when I'm trapped in a haunted house, searching for elusive signs while walking a metaphysical path.

What happened to me here and the way that experience shaped my life has set me apart from my peers. It isolated me. The only friends I've managed to make are the kind of people that are nice to misfits—they have adopted me into their group because no one else would. They forgive me my aloofness, my occasional coldness, and they lie to my parents for me—even if I don't think they believed me when I told them I was spending this time with an older boy. I've built a complicated house of lies. I had to. I don't know whether I can completely trust my friends to tell them the truth about where I really am and what I'm doing without them leaking it, even if by accident.

Being in Cashore with Erasmus and his crew is my current reality. Today alone feels like it lasted a century. I've even stopped paying attention to the motion activated cameras. My home life, parents, school, friends, in fact, the past few years of my life barely seem real to me anymore.

I pull out my phone and open my chat history with Layla. Her horrifying profile picture of a snarling Vermillion stares back at me. I don't flinch. Layla—or whoever has her phone—hasn't been online since I got that weird, truncated message that sent me down this vortex of the Path, Signs, memories, and suspicions.

I need a sign that my sister is alive, not the kind associated with *Vermillion*, but a sign from the universe that I'm not wasting my time. I need to know all of this is going somewhere. But the universe offers nothing.

I set the phone aside and reach for my laptop again. Crimson-DreadNet beckons.

As I stare at the page before me, I realize I don't want to read about the Path and the Signs right now. I need to *see* my sister. I head for the thread that started all of this: **__LaylaGalichIsAlive**.

It's been updated twice since my last check-in.

My fingers immediately dampen with nervous sweat. I take deep breaths, waiting for my heart to calm down before proceeding.

I click on the first of the two recent posts to find a poorly retouched photo of . . . me. It must've been taken a few months ago by the looks of it, near my parents' house in Bakersfield. The user who posted is *@IAmVermillionDemon*, and their profile pic is an external shot of Cashore, rendered in black and white and outlined in red. How classy.

I look away from the photo of "Layla" in disgust.

That's exactly why I hate this deranged obsession people have with her.

When people claim they see my sister, one likely scenario, the benign one, is that they saw me and mistook me for her. Or they deliberately took a pic of me and made it look like a **__LaylaGalichIsAlive** sighting.

I click on "report this" and type my annoyance into the box that pops up. I wish *@IAmVermillionDemon* burns in hell for this fakery, intentional or not. If they're on the Path, I hope all the Signs they've received are erased from their head, sending them back to the beginning.

I consider stopping here and now, but who am I kidding. Once I've given in to the siren call of **__LaylaGalichIsAlive**, I'm not going anywhere until I've seen all the new posts. I can't stop my fingers from clicking, powerless against this spell my sister has cast upon me. Upon all of us.

When the second new post of **__LaylaGalichIsAlive** claims my screen, the air leaves my lungs.

My eyes are immediately drawn to Layla's face, her familiar sharp features captured sideways. Though this photo of my sister isn't new, it is indeed the most recent sighting of her. The only difference is that this photo appears to be taken from a different angle, from a perspective I haven't seen before.

Not counting the elusive nighttime photo of Layla entering Cashore House, the last public sighting of my sister happened a few days before her disappearance. In this picture, Layla is dressed for early spring, a notched-collar trench coat over an inky black turtleneck. The rest of my sister is partially concealed by a small but entitled crowd. Even now I can't help but wince just thinking about how trapped she must've felt, strangers pressing in too tightly, cocooning her. Damn V-heads. What's seen of Layla's face, partially obstructed by a wide-brimmed fedora, is twisted with fury. I'd be furious too if I was being mobbed like that.

I know that iconic photo by heart. Or I thought I did. Until today, I naively thought there was only *one* photo taken that day. Clearly, I was wrong.

There are two key differences between the old photo and this new one.

One, Layla is holding a book, her hands clutching the tome possessively against her chest. Her fingers grip it just so, but I can still see the title: *The Book of Ka'schor.*

Two, the new perspective reveals new faces that were previously concealed.

And one of those faces is mine.

Twenty-Five

My memory draws a blank. I don't remember being there. I wasn't!

And yet. Clearly, I was there. *There* next to Layla, only days before she vanished off the face of the earth. We're together, going somewhere, with that damn book cradled in her hands. Caught mid-stride, our shoulders nearly touching, my expression a perfect copy of Layla's subtly furious one. I could always tell when she was pissed off, even if she had a perfect poker face. Ever since our year together at Cashore, I became perfectly attuned to my sister's mercurial moods. Sometimes I imagined I could read Layla's mind simply by looking at her. And I swear, while to an uninformed observer she might appear serene, when this photo was taken, she was *livid*.

I squint at the laptop screen, as if the photo will reveal its secrets if only I shift my gaze. But no matter how long or how intensely I stare at it, the picture stays the same.

The me-in-the-photo looks . . . determined. My body language indicates I'm exactly where I belong, walking with a purpose. But seeing me like that doesn't suddenly help me remember. This girl that looks so much like me, might as well be my double, my doppelgänger from a parallel universe. Maybe the photo is augmented? Though if it is, its author is a genius. Both Layla and I look *so real*.

The longer I stare at the image, the more it does something to my perception. I can almost *feel* my brain strain as it attempts to reconcile this new information with memories it's archived away. My mind bursts at the seams.

If I can't remember this, what else can't I remember?

My vision darkens, but not before I register the poster's username.

@DoesSophiaDieInTheEnd

I scowl. Whoever this is, they've joined the forum only yesterday. There's no bio, no profile image, no location. Nothing. This picture is their first and only post. At least I know it's not Arthur, but anyone else in this house is a suspect.

I don't read the comments.

I slam my laptop shut.

My brain grapples with my rudely altered past, and the revelation that I was with Layla that day, the last day she was seen in public. As if my unreliable memories of being a child star in her movie are not enough, this doubt about reality creeps into the world outside of Cashore too, an ink blot spreading and spreading, like blood in water.

What am I supposed to do? What if the police see the photo? Clearly, they haven't—yet. If they did, I'm sure I'd have heard from them by now. But that doesn't make me feel better. CrimsonDreadNet is passcode protected and evasive; it doesn't allow screenshots. But what's to stop someone from coming to the cops with their testimony of seeing this evidence of me being somewhere I had no memory of being?

Would the detectives latch on to this little thread and pull at it, and pull and pull and pull until they unravel something that I have a feeling needs to stay hidden? And what if I *am* to blame? Arthur said his father believes I know what happened to Layla, and he's not alone in thinking that.

I *know* this photo looks bad for me, incriminating even, but I truly don't remember anything. What were we doing that day? Where were we going? Is the photo a Sign? My gut tells me no. But it means something. It must.

And so does the *Book of Ka'schor*.

Erasmus mentioned that Cashore's owner has the Baron's annotated copy. Seeing snaps of random pages Arthur found in his father's room makes me certain Erasmus doesn't have a copy of his own. I suspect this book is not something that can be easily found and bought. To my knowledge, Layla's never owned a copy either, and yet the book somehow found its way into her hands, and then my sister vanished. My memory churns. I get flashes and glimpses. Of Layla, gripping the damn book with too much force. But in my mind, she looks younger and she's here, at Cashore. Did she find the book in this house five years ago and keep it for herself?

When I open my laptop again, I find surprisingly little information about this book, its origins indeterminate. Copies appear to be floating around, but whenever I click on links to secondhand bookshops or private sellers on eBay, those listings have been archived. There's no year of publication, no author or publisher, and no table of contents. It's like the book is a ghost, all evidence of its existence gone or in the process of vanishing.

That is, until I return to CrimsonDreadNet.

There is exactly one thread dedicated to *Book of Ka'schor*, laconically named __**TheBook**. The discussion hasn't been active for a while. Still, what I read confirms the little I already know: The Baron used the book as a manual in his occultist endeavors, which once took place under Cashore's roof. Handwritten marginalia riddled his personal copy. The thread informs that famous trance mediums and spiritualists of the time, including Lady Beverly Parschalli, frequented the Baron's soirées. During these séances, the windows and all reflective surfaces inside the house would have been smothered in black silk, leaving the guests at the mercy of flickering candlelight as the summoned spirits murmured their secrets.

Reading the thread brings back memories. In crafting *Ver-million*'s complicated lore, Layla drew on what she knew about the Baron's occult predilections. But in my sister's interpretation, Vermillion-the-entity was a demon the Baron and Adrianna had accidentally summoned and couldn't contain. Did Layla make that up, or had it actually come up during her research? I wish I'd paid more attention then, but Layla was like an unstoppable hurricane in her creative process. It was hard to keep up.

Though if Erasmus is indeed engaging in magical rites by having me reenact scenes from *Vermillion*, wouldn't I catch him muttering words of summoning at some point?

As I go over my memories of reenactments to date, I remember the handle of the user who posted the incriminating photo.

@DoesSophiaDieInTheEnd.

In my already unraveling mind, the moniker creates a new wave of disturbance. The question in the name refers to *Vermillion*'s bizarre ending, which has long drawn ire and admiration from viewers in equal measure. Even if the way the film ends is not the way our stay at Cashore ended. Even if that ending is a result of my sister stitching something resembling a semi-coherent narrative out of snippets we filmed around the house. But real or manufactured for dramatic effect, *Vermillion*'s final scene has long become a critical part of the film lore.

Did you really become possessed in the end? Does Vermillion live on inside you? These are the kinds of questions I used to get in my "fan mail" before I learned how to take better care of my privacy.

I consider reaching out to *@DoesSophiaDieInTheEnd* via DM, but by the time I navigate back to the forum, their profile, and the photo, are gone.

Not this again. Not another phantom photo appearing seemingly for me alone and vanishing seconds later.

Was it even there to begin with? Did I dream all of that up?

I shut my eyes tight.

I know I need to get some sleep, but I also know there's no way I can actually fall asleep now. Maybe I'm turning into an insomniac, like Arthur. Or perhaps insomnia is a mechanism I'm developing in order not to lose myself to this house.

The night is eerie, unnaturally quiet. I hear a sound—a faint scratching comes from somewhere in the room. I sit up in the bed so fast that wind whistles past my ears.

The arctic, chilly draft in the room suddenly turns ominous, but I'm hot, uncomfortable in my own skin, close to burning. I listen for the noise again, but all remains quiet. It's a strange, unnatural kind of silence that penetrates deep into my soul. Perforated only by the glimmer of the distant lighthouse. The darkness around me stretches, grows a pair of limbs, presses against my chest. I resist. Susurrations fill my ears.

Sleep you will, gentle spirit, night itself cradling you on its feathered wing.

The words spoken by *Vermillion*'s ghostly narrator flit through my mind, as the pushy, feathery darkness continues its expansion, filling the room to the brim. The narrator was likely Layla herself. But some say it was the film's titular entity, the red demon who said the words.

And then the smell comes.

It's horrible and familiar to the bone; it's the smell of Cashore's west wing. It's here, in my bedroom.

My mind kicks into overdrive. I get out of bed and swiftly change back into my jeans and a top. I throw my shoes on. I find my jacket and quickly slide my arms into its sleeves. I'm preparing to run, I realize, only partially comprehending my own impulses.

Because deep down I know what that smell means.

Vermillion, the real one, has finally found me.

Twenty-Six

'm gagging by the time I make it out into the corridor.

The smell fills my head with fright and strange desires. If this smell could make a sound, it'd be a keening. If it had a face, it'd be that of Vermillion, snarling, screeching, furious, and not to be denied.

The smell is one of despair, of yearning for something out of this world—the brine of the unearthly tide pools, the viscous fog, blood spilled in a summoning circle. It pulses like a heart as it follows me. I break into a run, uncaring who hears me or what they think of my nocturnal panic. I can't stay in my room. Can't stay in this house. Something is terribly wrong, more wrong than usual. And I sense it coming, a revelation. My Fourth Sign?

Reflection tells the truth but there is a price to pay.

That's what the clue said.

The Fourth Sign demands a toll.

"What do you want?" I whisper into the darkness as I run.

I don't dare look back, because I swear I hear it, the faint patter of soft feet against the carpeted floor just so behind me, the hiss of friction.

I shoot a desperate glance in the direction of Arthur's room, hoping he's got his lights on, but the doorframe is dark.

Driven by heart pounding fear, I take to the stairs, clutching the railing with slippery fingers. The graveyard smell crawls into my lungs, and I can already feel it do its dark work. It permeates my skin and bone.

Without thinking, dogged by the ghostly smell of decay and desire, I run across Cashore's first floor. I find myself at the same exit that earlier today took me and Arthur down to the beach. Or was it yesterday? In my head, the timeline is all jumbled. Maybe I have always lived in this house? Maybe I never left.

I must get out.

I wrap my hand around the strikingly cold handle and turn.

The Fourth Sign.

The reflection of the otherworld trapped in the shallow rock pools, forever cold in the shadow of Cashore. Is that where I'm being lured? But even as I make the connection, I don't stop, don't slow down—I can't.

Mindful of the slippery ground, I step out into the night illuminated brightly by the full moon, the biggest one I've ever seen.

I let the door slam behind me, even though I know all too well that if Vermillion is set on chasing me, no door will stop her.

The rocky steps that lead down into the fog-veiled dark beckon me.

Even from up here, I can already sense the wrongness of the shallow tide pools.

I don't know what the Path will ask of me in return for my next Sign, but I know I can't turn back now. Being on the Path is a covenant. I won't break mine.

I zip up my jacket, hold my breath, and take my first step down.

PART THREE

The Dance

Twenty-Seven

The nauseating smell that chased me out of Cashore eases the moment I commence my descent.

The night air is crisp, but I can barely feel it, let alone enjoy it. I'm sweating through my clothes, my body temperature soaring.

Maybe I have a fever, and this is a fever dream. Because otherwise why would I be going down the steps, alone, at night? Why would I be going toward the smell of the tidal pools, and not running from it?

As a kid, these pools used to draw me in, but I also found them unsettling, eerie. The other day when I went out with Arthur for our revelatory picnic by the sea, I deliberately ignored the existence of the pools darkening the far end of the beach. Now, I'm going there. On purpose.

This is not a dream. Not a hallucination. The elements leave an imprint too vivid on my skin. The moon shines so brightly I can see just enough ahead to choose my steps carefully. The wind batters my face, pushing my hair back. My heart beats uncalmly inside my chest. I'm decidedly awake. I wish I wasn't.

I turn my attention to measuring my steps, keeping my balance. These rock-cut stairs are eternally wet from the fog and sea drizzle. The clusters of alyssums that frame the path stretch across the stone, intent on tripping me. Their whiteness merges with the fog that clings to my legs.

It's easy to pretend that I'm all alone, the last soul left alive in this world, that everything else has succumbed to darkness. It's only me and the sea, and also this mysterious presence, hungering for attention, forever misunderstood, that soaks all of Cashore, down to its cliffside foundations.

I'm twelve again, going down these steps. I have a limp, my injured ankle taking time to heal. It's late in the afternoon, the setting sun's golden glow turning tarnished pink, then dark red, promising a cold night and even colder morning. Layla made me carry a lit lantern; rustic and heavy, it hurts my strained fingers, but I'm not going to let it go. I can't. Filming my descent to the pools, my sister is a silent presence, just off the rocky path in the thickening dark. I hear her as she balances precariously on the flatter sections of the cliffside, her feet slipping dangerously against the dewy shrubbery.

It's shocking how much of these memories I suppressed. Being here is like an extreme version of immersion therapy, and it's working a little bit too well.

I no longer hear my sister's presence next to me. She's gone, vanished into the night. The lantern's weight in my hand is replaced by something soft, slippery, and very, very cold.

A hand, fingers wrapped around mine.

I try speaking, but my mouth is sealed shut.

I try turning my head also, but my neck is stuck, it won't budge.

My body is shutting down, stripping itself to the most basic functions, and yet I'm still walking. My fear is a living thing. It latched itself to my neck and now it drinks, taking my life force away, locking me into this limited state of existence.

I can only move my eyes, but barely so. Not enough to see what leads me.

My memories are a flood, threatening to drown me.

I wondered then, as I do now, whether it was Layla's hand locked in mine or someone—something—else's. Deep down I knew then it wasn't my sister's hand I held.

But now . . . I'm alone. My hands gather into fists so tight my arm muscles ache. No phantom hand holding is going to happen out here tonight.

Fog thickens around my ankles.

I blink and suddenly I'm at the bottom of the stairs, with no memory of how I've gotten here.

I'm shaking. Hot and cold. Burning with fever, or perhaps battling hypothermia.

I remind myself of why I'm doing this. To bring Layla back,

to save her from whatever trouble she's gotten herself into.

As I progress toward the beach and the pools, a feeling builds in my chest, an understanding: Layla might be closer than I thought. I can feel it. I can feel *her*. As if she's right there, waiting for me in the dark.

The final step. My feet sink into the sand.

The desolate beach lies in wait. Even the ocean holds its briny breath.

I begin the trek toward the shallow rock pools. Even from where I am I can tell there's something out there, some thing rising from the surface of the water.

I confuse it for a rock formation at first, a human-sized column in the middle of the pools, but with each new step that brings me closer to that cursed place, I see more disturbing details. The ethereal movement of fabric around the shape of this "formation." The telltale features of a human figure. The lanky drop of long, black hair.

I break into a run.

"Layla!" I scream, my voice breaking.

Her head jerks to attention.

I increase my speed, feet sliding across sand.

I'm so close.

But Layla doesn't move. She makes no effort to come to me, though she can definitely see me. I feel the weight of her eyes on me. Why isn't she running?

I halt to a shaky stop by the pools' uneven edge. Black water glitters in the dark. Unidentifiable things, scaly and sleek, move below the surface.

The moon hides behind the clouds, and the effect is instantaneous, like throwing a blanket over a smoldering fire, extinguishing it in one move. The briny, decaying stench hits me almost immediately. How can no one else smell this, this rot multiplied tenfold? And my sister is right there, in the middle of this festering horror.

"Layla?" I shout her name as I pace along the edge of the pools like a trapped animal, a frustrated beast that fears the water.

She meets my eyes—it's her! It's dark out, but I'd recognize her anywhere. She hasn't aged, but there's a change to her, I just don't quite understand it yet. Her features are . . . washed out. Her outline is uneven, losing particles. She's there and not there.

The moon reappears, releasing a tiny burst of light, but it's just enough for me to see something awful. Hands reach up from the water, grasping at Layla's legs.

My sister is trapped.

A pair of monstrous, rotten hands anchor her in place. They're not just keeping her immobile. They're dragging her under.

The pools are not that deep. And yet, defying the natural order of things, my sister descends into the water right where she stands, pulled into an invisible, underwater hole. Layla doesn't move, doesn't even fight it. The unnatural stillness of her body goes against everything I know about her.

My sister would fight with hands and teeth. She wouldn't just give in.

I wade into the pools, holding my breath, breathing through my mouth—the stench is unbearable. But I have to save Layla. I have to try.

I can barely see where I'm going. My knees keep bumping against the sharp edges of underwater boulders, my feet slipping across the slimy floor. I'm going to have bruises tomorrow. If there is a tomorrow.

I'm a few feet away from Layla; water rises up to her chest. But something holds me back. I might as well be miles away. There's no straightforward path to her.

"Fight it! Why aren't you fighting it?" I cry out.

The moon shows itself once more, and there's just enough light for me to see the despair in Layla's haunted eyes. I'm so close to her now. Her mouth is straining to open, to move, to speak. But she's immobilized, corpse hands dragging her down, slowly but steadily, one inch at a time. Is she alive or is she . . . ? I can't bring myself to think it, let alone verbalize it. I can't let myself even entertain the possibility that my sister may not be . . . alive.

When my right knee hits a particularly sharp rock, the impact nearly sends me flying. My hands flail, my balance hard-won.

But I'm nearly there. Just a few more steps and I can end this.

As if sensing my soaring hope, something in the pool drags Layla down faster.

In a burst of bubbles, she disappears underwater.

Only her coiling black hair floats above the surface.

I run to her, not caring what I hit or how much it hurts. I can still make it to her. I know I can.

There's a lighter spot in the water, under the waning moonlight, where my sister's just been, her skin glinting in the dark.

I reach for her, but before my fingers can find purchase, the last of Layla is sucked into the water, leaving me with only a strand of her long black hair.

I stand alone, in the middle of the festering rock pools.

I'm too terrified to move. If I wavered before, I now believe completely, wholly, irrevocably that whatever dark force exists in Cashore is very much real. And it's linked inexplicably to me, to Layla, and to the amateur film we made here five years ago.

This is not a dream.

I'm frozen in my spot, water to my knees. The Fourth Sign is the last thing on my mind. Hot tears slide out of my eyes. I can't control it. I can't control anything. I had a chance to save Layla, and I blew it. Vermillion is playing with me. Maybe I was never meant to get close enough to grab Layla, and all of this is a sick, twisted game. I'm forever at a disadvantage, barely comprehending the rules.

The moon comes out fully from behind the clouds, bathing everything in its cold, reflective light.

I feel it before I see it, the movement in the water, next to my legs. Something is circling me.

This is *exactly* like that scene from Layla's movie—what happens in it after I'm led down here, as someone who was not my sister held my hand.

After that scene, I don't even remember getting back to Cashore. The next thing I knew, after standing ankle-deep in water, was waking up in my bed the next morning.

In the film though, as Layla's camera captured it, I do reckon with the presence that led me down here; I look down, seeking answers in my own reflection.

And now, here I stand again, once more in these shallow pools, five years later. But this time I'm alone. Still, there's only one thing left for me to do.

I look down.

In the moonlight, there's a fuzzy reflection in the water, but I still see myself. My familiar features are framed by dark hair, not quite as long as Layla's, but getting there.

There's a movement behind me, slightly above me.

I freeze, eyes locked on the water. But the reflected version of me no longer looks familiar. My eyes are completely black, lips snarling.

This is the Vermillion from the movie, the image immortalized as Layla's profile pic.

Breaking my reflection into pieces, a dead hand shoots out from the water and grabs my calf, sharp nails digging in.

I scream. I writhe. I contort myself, anything to shake off this horror that's like a ring of spiked steel around my flesh.

Another arm emerges from the shallow depths of the pool. It reaches for my other leg. It seeks purchase, wrapping fingers around my ankle underwater.

Oh god, oh god, oh god, oh god.

The hands, unnaturally strong, drag me down, and the mulchy floor underneath my tennis shoes gives, sucking me in.

I'm burning, but the pools don't seem to cool me down; instead they're like hot oil, consuming me alive.

I scream at the top of my lungs, but there's no one to hear me.

Twenty-Eight

I sink into the mulchy seabed of the rock pools.

I'm headed where my sister went.

My mouth is numb, trapping the scream within.

I keep fighting against the pull. But no matter what I do, I sink lower, deeper, faster.

It is not death I fear but what's leading up to it, the act of dying.

A part of me, the part that's tired and desperate, kind of wishes I could just black out. Cut to black. If my life has become so thoroughly intertwined with Layla's movie, why can't I benefit from certain bits being edited out? After all, at the end of *Vermillion*, the camera switches to first-person perspective, then blurs to black to indicate my eyes closing. When the camera resumes its external perspective, it floats above me. A split-second before the credits roll, my eyes fly open.

Some fans say that in that heartbeat of a moment, my eyes grow all-black, ink spreading from the irises to blot out the white space. I wonder what my sister meant by that ending. I wish I'd asked her when I had the chance.

But right now, this isn't a movie. I must experience all of it in full.

A violent jerk from below sucks me into the sand down to my chest.

I know the water is cold, it should be, but I barely feel it. I'm only partially present in my body. I exert all that's left of my strength to rotate my body, wrapping an arm around the nearest half-sunk boulder. If I can just hold on, maybe I can stay above the water. Maybe. But this force that challenges me for domination is not of this world; it plays by its own rules.

A pair of hands, fingers like a vise, squeeze my ankles and yank powerfully from below. I can't hold on anymore.

I let go, and sea water rushes in, filling my mouth and nose.

Twenty-Nine

Pressure crushes my chest. I struggle to breathe. Something soft but unyielding parts my lips. Air. I'm filled with air. My senses return. I breathe. I breathe.

I cough, sputtering water. My throat aches, like the inside is sandpaper. Everything's raw.

Arthur's silhouette is sharp against the rising sun; there's a dark aura around him, clinging to his shoulders with shadow fingers. I struggle to clear my vision, and the shadows disappear. Arthur's curling hair frames his face. Moving of their own accord, my lips stretch into a half smile. Strange images rush in—they're shaped like memories, but dreamlike. Images of things I know didn't happen, things I don't remember.

"Sophia—"

Arthur's been saying something. The sound comes from far, far away, distorted almost beyond recognition.

I blink and try sitting up. Arthur's hands fall away from my aching chest. I twist my head, up and down and side to side, until gravity clears up the blockage from my ears.

"Sophia!"

I hear again, but my relief is short-lived. Arthur's voice is . . . shaken, broken, terrified. "You, you were gone—I thought you were gone," he stutters. There's a deep frown between his eyebrows.

He twists his neck, looking somewhere behind my shoulder and up. And I know what's there—Cashore. I watch Arthur as he watches the house on the cliff, trying to read what's going through his head.

"What are you . . . doing here?" I ask. My voice comes out gasping from my aching throat.

"What am I doing here?? What are *you* doing here?" he demands. He sits on the sand by my side, the ocean reverberating behind him. The sun is nearly up. My clothes are wet. My clothes are . . .

"The hell am I wearing?" My mind comes awake. But there are gaps. The agonizing pain that came with swallowing a lungful of sea water returns. My throat aches. But I'm alive. On the beach, a solid distance away from the rock pools. And it's morning. Arthur is here. What's happened?

I take a deep, rattling breath.

My late night visit to the decaying pools wasn't a dream.

I know what happened there. The Fourth Sign. My sister, her desperate eyes locked on mine, as she was being pulled under . . .

I didn't imagine that.

And yet. Why can't I remember what came after I was yanked underwater?

Shock. I must've fought my way out of that mess, crawled out of the water, then collapsed from exhaustion. Either that, or Arthur pulled me out. I've fainted once, from low blood sugar, so I'm not a stranger to real-life blackouts. But deep down, I know what happened to me last night is not the same thing. Having no memory of escaping drowning is different from hypoglycemia-induced fainting.

And then there's also the matter of my clothes. I remember wearing jeans, a jacket . . . but from what I now see of myself, I'm clad in an old fashioned sleeping gown, white and . . . see-through. A furious blush spreads through me. I shiver. The morning is cold, unforgiving against my damp clothes.

"I saw you on the beach," Arthur says as he wiggles out of his jacket and places it over my shoulders. "I saw you, and then I blinked, and you were gone!"

"You saw me vanish?" I ask in a small voice. "Into the rock pools?"

But it doesn't make sense. How could he see me when it was so dark?

"No. In the water. Right there." He half-turns and points at the ocean, at a random spot where the waves foam at the crest. "Were you . . . sleepwalking or something?" He doesn't sound convinced at all, and I agree. I've never sleepwalked in my life. "You know, Serge won't be happy you went swimming in one of his prized period gowns. He claims this belonged to Adrianna Kashoroff herself."

I can tell he's as rattled as I am. Rattled and scared.

He offers me a hand, helping me up on my shaky feet. I clutch his fingers. His warmth grounds me.

"You need to see a doctor. I'll call for Dr. Patel when we get back to the house."

"I'm fine," I say, holding back a cough. A dull pain aches in my rib cage, but I don't think anything is broken.

It's not physical trauma that concerns me now, and I doubt Dr. Patel can help with my memory gaps. What I need is to get back online, to see what others on the Path have dealt with when receiving their Fourth Sign . . . I don't dwell too much on what I *do* remember, but the images come back to haunt me, circling my mind like vultures looking for a feed. The Reflection. My own reflection in the pool, where my face had transformed into Vermillion's signature snarling visage. What matters is that I have my Fourth Sign—another memory recovered from five years ago—and the rest is of lesser consequence, but of course I know it's not true. My version of the Path is trying to tell me something, whether I like the message or not. Is it telling me that to find Layla, I have to find Vermillion first?

I have no shoes on. My toes curl against the cold sand as Arthur and I begin our trek back to Cashore. The sea breeze bites my face; the wet gown clings to my legs in the most inappropriate places. I'm naked underneath. But thanks to Arthur's jacket, I'm mostly covered.

"You gave me CPR?" I ask as we reach the stairs.

"Yeah," he says. "Not how I imagined our second kiss would go, but . . . sorry, that was totally not the right thing to say."

I stumble, and Arthur's hand flies out to keep me upright. His fingers burn hot against my cold skin. I stop and face him. "*Second* kiss?"

He looks straight into my eyes, preventing my gaze from traveling down to his mouth. The word *kiss* rolls through my mind, finding no corresponding memories. I've definitely *thought* of kissing him, imagined doing so, but surely, I'd remember actually going through with it.

His stare turns funny, then concerned. "What's the last thing you remember?" he asks, that deep frown from earlier returning to claim its spot between his eyebrows.

"Talking with you in my room, and then . . . I was researching the *Book of Ka'schor*," I say. "It gets fuzzy after that."

I push away the burning need to bare my soul to him, to confess what happened at the rock pools. Old suspicion returns. I want to trust Arthur, but can I really? His father is up to no good,

but Arthur hasn't done anything to make me doubt his inten-
tions, and yet . . .

He pales half a degree, something I didn't think was possible.
The smell of the rock pools from last night returns. Can Arthur
smell it on me?

"What—what is it?" I beg him to say it, but I don't really
want him to. I must know but I don't want to know; I'm terrified
to know.

"Sophia, that was two days ago," he says.

Thirty

Two days.

I've lost two days of my life.

That was the cost of my Fourth Sign. Of being allowed a glimpse of Layla.

I waver unsteadily on my feet, Arthur's supporting hands on my frame. As they meet mine, his eyes pierce me with concern. But there's something else, a deeper emotion haunting his face.

"It's the Fourth Sign, isn't it?" he whispers, the words barely audible against the breeze that's picked up since we left the beach.

My hair is a wild halo around my head. I'm balancing on a step, still closer to the beach than Cashore. I want to tell Arthur the truth, to confess how freaking terrified I am, how violated I feel after losing two days of my life to an unexplained blackout, but I remember the price Arthur paid when he broke the rules of the Path. He *lost* a Sign and was pushed back by this unseen-but-felt force seeking to control our lives. I don't want the same thing to happen to me. But I don't want my absence from my own life to be worth nothing in the end.

I give Arthur a long look, hoping it packs meaning. I gather my thoughts. Wishing the wind disguises the quiver in my voice, I ask, "What have I been doing these past two days?"

"You were . . . acting normal? Why? I mean, you were like your regular self, except . . ." He trails off, looking away from me and focusing on the patch of alyssums-strewn grass to the right of the stairs.

"Except what?" My voice is dead, an echo of a life.

"Well, you were . . ." He begins again, finding my eyes and braving a deeper look. "You were more direct, I guess. You've made friends with people. Like, you helped Serge restore an old ballet costume that my dad wants to use in the filming. Somehow you convinced Miriam to give you some camera work lessons, and she's usually so precious with her time. And you, well, you kissed me."

Slowly, I watch his hand go to his lips. A subconscious gesture, as if my kiss has imprinted itself upon his mouth, as if Arthur can still physically trace its presence. His body language is tense, but wistful too. I take it this kiss he claims I've given him wasn't an unpleasant experience. There's a painful twist in my chest, a freezing cold hand wrapping itself around my heart, determined to squeeze it till I'm dead. It's jealousy. I'm still capable of recognizing that, even if I also recognize it's not exactly ratio-nal to feel this way . . . about myself.

"Sounds like I was busy," I mumble.

We start walking again, but I barely feel the cold anymore, though the stones are rough on my bare feet. Sun bathes the stairs with gentle light. My gown is nearly dry, but I keep Arthur's jacket tightly wrapped around my shoulders. The leather's subtle scent clouds my mind.

"Anything else we did? Besides the kiss," I ask, focusing on the terrain.

"No," Arthur says. I feel him looking at me but pointedly ignore him. "Are you going to tell anyone about this?" he asks. "I mean about what happened, that you can't remember the past two days? You really need to see a doctor . . ."

"I won't jeopardize my progress on the Path," I say. "If anyone finds out about my . . . memory trouble, it might end things for me. It'll affect filming." I add the last bit because it's a pragmatic thing to say, but deep down I don't care one bit about the filming. What concerns me is that I'll lose my access to the house. My only chance to find my sister. "I mean, would *you* do it? Would you share something like this with a doctor, knowing it might risk your progress?" I give him a long, sideways glance.

"No," he says. "I would not."

When we reach the top of the stairs, the sun turns blinding. Cut sharply against the light, Cashore is painted vividly alive, a beast poised in wait. There's a new feel to the house too, like it can breathe a little bit more fully now.

I suspect it's not the building but me who is changed. A dark premonition that's been making home inside my chest grows. It expands, threatening to take over whatever space is left under my skin, and I'm being pushed out and away. I'm approaching the end, but when I do reach the end of the Path, will I still be the same, or irrevocably changed?

I hope to avoid the others in the house, but it must be some cruel version of Murphy's Law that sends multiple Cashore inhabitants into my path. Raina gives me a wide smile as she passes by, her eyes clouding with confusion when she takes a closer look at my odd attire. Serge pops his head out of his wardrobe enclosure to tell me my outfit for today is nearly ready. I'm lucky he doesn't seem to notice what I'm wearing. Even Miriam gives me a wink, her eyes unconcealed by her signature aviators.

I plaster on a vague smile, but by the time I get to my room it's already slipping. I'm not okay, and I don't have any energy to pretend otherwise.

The door to my bedroom opens with a familiar creak. When I was a child, this door meant nightmares and fright. Now, I'm relieved to see it. I need the much-needed solitude the room offers.

"Do you . . . need anything?" Arthur asks when I step into

the familiar space of the bedroom. "I don't think you should be alone right now."

"I *need* to be alone right now," I tell him. His eyes briefly land on my mouth, but his energy is confused. It's ironic that, in my book, nothing has really happened between us, but our relationship can already be classified as "complicated." What a way to start. "I'll be okay," I add softly, but I don't sound convincing even to my own ears.

He gives me a sad look. "Dad wants to film the masquerade scene tonight. But it's okay if you're not feeling up to it. I can tell him you need a night off."

I know it shouldn't, but the news of this impending filming catches me off guard. And it's the masquerade scene, no less. It's one of the last scenes in Layla's film, which makes me wonder how we got here so fast. What scenes have we been filming over the past two days while I was absent? I'll have to interrogate Arthur later; for now, I need to regroup, assess damage, understand what the hell has really happened to me.

"I should be okay by then. I hope. I just need a nap," I say, though napping is the last thing on my mind.

It's only when I close the door behind me and hear Arthur's uncertain retreating steps that I realize I'm still wearing his jacket. But I don't rush to return it. I'm grateful for the unexpected sense of safety it provides, so I wrap it tighter around my frame and inhale the lingering scent. An unexpected shiver traces through my body. Seeking warmth inside the jacket's pockets, I stumble upon a firm piece of paper.

My hand returns with its find. A photograph.

My breath catches.

It's the same photo I briefly saw appear online on the CrimsonDreadNet website. The one that places me next to Layla days before her disappearance. I'd begun to wonder if I'd imagined that, if I dreamed it up. In the typical CrimsonDreadNet fashion, the photo disappeared so quickly, and I had no memory of being there with my sister on the day. Just like how now I have no memory of the past two days. Crap.

I shake off the jacket, throwing it next to the photo on the floor at my feet. I'm shivering with rage; this betrayal tastes bitter. And just when I was starting to warm up to Arthur, thinking about letting him in closer, deeper into my world.

I crouch on the floor, my feet in a painful curl, and glare at the image of my sister and me. It taunts me.

Controlling my urge to whimper in defeat, I study the picture, focusing on the surrounding crowd. Their faces, features, expressions. I expect to see Erasmus, his beard a dead giveaway, but if he is there, he's wisely hidden behind the first few rows of my sister's stalkers.

Why would Arthur have this photo? How did he get it? Was he there that day too, in the park, tracking Layla with a camera? To what end?

I slump on the floor, my hands on my face, fingers pressing into my lids. Maybe if I keep my eyes closed long enough, the imprint of this photo on my vision will evaporate?

I'm such a fool, letting myself think Arthur is not like other V-heads, while he's been playing me, pretending to be all sweet and caring, while plotting behind my back, tricking me, tormenting me by posting photos on the website he knows I frequent.

What if I was all wrong about Erasmus being behind Layla's disappearance and it was his son instead?

I feel watched. My head jerks up, I meet the nearest camera's steady gaze. I escape the surveillance by running into the bathroom, where I shed the rest of my clothes, tearing the white sleeping gown off my body. I don't care if the fragile fabric gets damaged.

I turn on the shower and step into the punishing hot stream, closing my eyes tight. I burn inside but am ice-cold on the outside. I rub the soap bar over my skin too roughly, but I need to feel it, this visceral belonging inside my own self. This is my body. *Mine.* I let out a sound, a wild, animalistic growl that vanishes into the stream.

When I step out of the shower and dry off, I cringe at the coarse feel of the towel against my legs. I perch on the slippery, cold edge of the tub and take a closer look. There are near identical ugly bracelets of small purple dots circling my ankles. Each individual bruise is half moon shaped, just like the old, scarred flesh around my wrist. Just like the recent cuts to my wrist, the ones on my legs appear a day or two old, still sensitive but not inflamed. The longer I stare at them, the more I feel out of place. I'm scared, scared for real. The only place where these bruises could've come from is the rock pools. Dead hands dragging me down. Vermillion.

It was real. It was real. It was real.

And if *that* was real, then so was the glimpse of my sister before she'd vanished beneath the rippling surface.

I saw my sister in the water. Was she alive or dead?

Layla came to Cashore—of her own will or not—but what if she's never left? And where does Arthur fit in with all this?

I'm moving toward the end of the Path, but the ground is sinking beneath my feet. I feel farther away from my goal than ever before. I haven't seriously thought about it until now, the personal cost of completing the Path. As I study the purpling bruises on my legs, I ask myself once again if the price is too steep to pay.

Thirty-One

I force clothes over my damp skin. The jeans resist, but I persevere. I refuse to risk being naked again. I get into bed, my hair dripping wet and my hands shaking. My phone is on the nightstand, charging. Did I have it with me when I went down to the rock pools two days ago? Was it in my pocket when I went under? Well, here it is now, miraculously undamaged.

As I type my passcode, I half expect it to have been changed. Maybe the stranger who's been living inside my skin for two days wanted another way to push me out of my own life. But the code works, and my phone unlocks. As I check my messages, I find nothing of note. Maybe nothing really did happen while I was out of it. Well, my kissing Arthur is not *nothing*, but . . .

A vague sense of déjà vu draws me toward the camera app on my phone. With a finger hovering over it, I wonder why the act feels fresh, like something I've done recently, though I don't remember filming anything or taking pictures after I came to Cashore House. There was a time in my life when I was obsessively into video journaling. A psychologist might have recommended it at some stage, positioning it as a sense-making mechanism, another way to ground myself in the present, to affirm my reality. At the time, I chose not to see the obvious irony in seeking the reaffirmation of my reality by capturing it on video. And for a while, it worked. Seeing myself recorded, describing my day and whatnot, imbued me with a sense of calm. But then I gradually lost interest in the act, and much of my old discomfort returned. What if a recording caught something else, a presence behind me? What if my eyes glinted black? They're not exactly rational thoughts, but once the idea was planted, I was done with video journaling for good.

So, when I give in to the impulse and open the camera app, it takes me by complete surprise to see the latest recording's unfamiliar thumbnail. A cold feeling of dread, of terrible premonition, awakens in my chest.

I stare at it, the image of my face captured in the thumbnail.

When I open the recordings library, there are three new videos. Recordings I have no memory of making.

I dread pressing play. But I must. I have no choice, really.

Video Recording, Timestamped Two Days Ago, 7:13 A.M.

It starts with a close-up of my face in profile, then the camera moves quickly in a blur until it assumes a stable vantage point overlooking the spacious room which appears to be a ballet studio, complete with mirrors and a barre. The effect of mirrors reflecting mirrors creates an endless corridor, with me in its center.

I wear casual attire, black tights and a large, loose tee tied to one side. My hair is up in a messy bun, and on my feet, there are ballet shoes. I stare at the mirror for an eerily long moment, then move, my eyes meeting the camera. I say, "Let's see if I still remember how to do this."

I stand *en pointe*, then lower myself into first position. I repeat the move, up and down, up and down, the muscles of my legs flexing against the tights. Without a warning, I bend in a semicircle, twisting at the waist, arms flying in a well-practiced move. I unfold, and then I dance.

My moves are precise, slowing down at times and reduced to the smallest components, as if I want to make sure I'm getting it right, the sequence, the angles, all of it. A couple of tentative practice jumps morph into impressive leaps, carrying me almost too high. This must be a trick of the camera, an illusion of flight. I am recreating the Dance of the Unquiet Spirits, moving swiftly across the space I recognize as Adrianna Kashoroff's ballet studio at Cashore House, vanishing from view, then reappearing, vanishing again, until I come to face the mirror once more. Hands on my waist, I lower my head as if in a prayer.

I raise my head, meeting my reflection's eyes, and smile.

End of recording.

VIDEO RECORDING, TIMESTAMPED ONE DAY AGO, 8:27 A.M.

The studio again, but this time I am not alone. Arthur is also here. While my camera's rolling from its vantage point, Arthur films me on his own phone as I move across the studio in a familiar series of complicated steps. While slowly rotating in my spot, I say something (the sound is muffled) and Arthur laughs, his eyes not leaving me. Freezing halfway through a rotation, I come down roughly on my left leg. Arthur winces.

"Are you okay?" he asks.

"I'm more than okay," I reply.

I walk up to Arthur. He lowers his phone and looks at me. I place my hands on his shoulders and tip my head up slightly. Standing on tiptoe, I bridge the distance and bring my mouth to his.

End of recording.

VIDEO RECORDING, TIMESTAMPED TWO HOURS AGO

I am alone in my bedroom, staring into the camera.

"I don't know if you'll ever get to see this," I say. "And it's not that important whether you do or not. It's only a matter of time, and your time is almost up. I don't mean it in a sinister way; it's just how things are. I don't want to be like this anymore. I didn't ask for it. I've lost too much, lost everything. And now I'll take . . ." There's a pause where I look away, focusing on a spot beyond the phone. A scuffling noise. Off camera, someone lets out a hoarse moan, cries out. The camera shakes, the view partially blocked by fingers, as if someone's wrestling for control. I let go of the phone and it falls flat, recording the room at a crooked angle. The corner with the blind spot formed between the wardrobe and the wall is in partial view.

Layla's face appears over the camera, her eyes wild and red-rimmed.

"You have to fight it. She can't win," Layla cries out, and then she's dragged backward by an unseen force into the tight space, into the blind spot. There's a sound of nails scratching against the wall. And then my face claims the screen again. There's something wrong with my eyes. My lips move but the sound that comes out is mismatched. And yet, the words are clearly heard. "You are mine."

End of recording.

I sit on my bed, still, unblinking. My eyes starting to water. I want to press play again on the last video, though the action goes against my every impulse of self-preservation. I want to throw the phone away and never look at it again. I thought seeing myself, this stranger wearing my skin, kissing Arthur, was painful, but that was before I saw my sister being dragged into the corner.

If before this moment I still doubted whether what I saw in the pools was real, here is actual proof. Something to take to the police, to my parents.

Layla was in this room. Two hours ago.

But can I really trust my memory? Can I trust my own eyes?

With shaking fingers, I hit the play triangle but the recording refuses to start. A bad feeling forms in my chest. I press play again and again. I leave the app and navigate to my phone's video folder, but it doesn't seem to have the file either. When I go back to the video queue, the last recording is gone. *No, no, no, no, no!*

What is going on, am I dreaming? Can technology be possessed, haunted, manipulated by a ghostly hand? What is this, a nightmare? I go through my phone again and again, but the video is gone. Disappeared without a trace. Like Layla.

I leave the bed and trace my sister's path through the room. I stand there by the wall, facing the narrow passage. It's shadowy and dusty, but very much empty. There's nothing in here, nothing to suggest a struggle took place here just hours ago.

That is, until I take a closer look at the wall.

Four distinctive, rugged lines mar the wallpaper, stretching deep into the blind spot. I trace the lines with my fingers, the wall as cold as ice to my touch. When I exhale, my breath is clouding white before me.

"Layla?" I say into the narrow space.

No response. But . . . there's a weak draft coming from the corner, which makes no sense. Yet, it should be clear by now that Cashore has rules of its own. It waits. I wait. I know deep down in my heart that this tiny corridor, tight enough to barely accommodate me, is important somehow. It beckons but also repels me.

I don't give myself an opportunity to think too much about it as I wedge myself between the wall and the wardrobe. Before, when I crammed myself into this tight space to use my phone away from the cameras, I didn't go far, and I faced the room the entire time.

This time, I turn my head toward the far wall as I exhale, trying to make myself more compact. Holding my panicked breaths in, trying to ignore the unyielding pressure on my chest, I stretch my right hand, expecting it to go through the wall when I near the end of this passage but . . . my fingers meet solid barrier. I lose control and suck a deep breath in, my chest expanding into the wardrobe. I'm stuck! Pressure steals my breath.

"Layla . . ." I call to my sister in a low, hoarse voice as my fingers rap against the back wall, imitating the beating of the heart that serves as Vermillion's soundtrack in a few parts of the movie. I listen. I repeat the simple rhythm.

Something raps back.

I whimper, repeating my sister's name, as I squeeze a little bit closer to the back wall. My body aches and my chest complains, unable to fully expand, but all I want is to contort myself and place my ear to the wall. Because I think I can hear something. *Her.* A distant voice whispering. It whispers my name.

But even when I come close enough to the back wall to hit it with my fist, it doesn't change reality. Unless my sister is a ghost who can go through bricks and mortar, there's no way to break through to the other side. I suspect even if I took an ax to the wall right now, it'd simply take me to the next room, not to where my sister is stuck. And yet I feel her call to me . . . or maybe not . . . not just yet.

I need the rest of my Signs first, so I can be admitted to the next level of this game.

And if Erasmus wants to film the masquerade scene tonight, so be it. I'll be ready.

Arthur's jacket is where I've left it, on the floor. Since everything that has to do with Layla disappears the moment I come back for another look, I expect the photo I've found in the jacket's pocket to vanish, turn to ash or smoke upon touch. But it's still there. A reminder of Arthur's secrets. A proof of his betrayal.

The video of me kissing him is like a smack in the face, sobering me up. I want to destroy the photo, to crumple it in my fist, but I resist the temptation. I hide the photo in my luggage among a few random things I haven't bothered unpacking. And that's when I find my ballet shoes, the pair I brought with me for a reason I couldn't understand at the time. The shoes are no longer brand-new, clearly this pair has been worn, even bled in. As I hold the shoes in my hands, I can't shake the image of *her*, my talented doppelgänger wearing my body like a costume, twirling with unnatural grace and lightness and ease.

Even with the video gone from my phone, I'll never forget her eyes, dark with meaning, when she looked at the camera and said, "You are mine."

Thirty-Two

"So, how did she do it? All those people were added in post-production? CGI, right?" The question comes from Raina as she follows me to wardrobe, keeping up with my brisk pace. My outfit for tonight's filming awaits. According to Raina, it's "authentic" and true to "Layla's vision." The idea equally triggers my curiosity and terrifies me. So many people claim to understand my sister's creative vision, the moving force behind her art, but Layla herself rarely talked about it. The movie *is* her vision, and she refused to interpret it for the press and the fans.

"I—I'm not sure." I look away so that Raina can't read anything revelatory from my poorly guarded expression. "It's one of those scenes I barely remember. I must've been half asleep or . . . sleepwalking."

The scene in question is the infamous ghostly masquerade, or the Midnight Reverie, as the fans call it. Like most *Vermillion* scenes, it was filmed at night, and I was there—those are the only things I'm sure of. The rest of it? I remember the empty, cavernous space of Cashore's lobby that maybe wasn't empty at all. I remember swirling and dancing like I was caught in a hurricane, my limbs moving of their own accord. And I remember whispers, glimpses, and a presence . . . a terrible, cold presence that dogged my every step, every move, every breath.

But when fans watch the movie, what they see is a crowded masquerade extravaganza—I'm at the center of it all, surrounded by semitranslucent revelers in period gowns and lush masks sprouting swan feathers.

Fans and video experts wonder: Was it another video spliced with the footage of me, a little visual Frankenstein's monster my sister concocted in post-production, or was it real ghost photography? Layla never came clean. Having now seen the blood-chilling footage captured on my phone while I was checked out for two days, I believe the latter. Layla's camera captured what was really going on around me, while I thought—or pretended—I was dancing alone.

"I personally believe in the crowdsourcing theory." Raina seems genuinely excited.

I wish I shared her enthusiasm. I recall how on day one of filming she was terrified of saying the V-word. I assumed she was a V-head or at least someone favoring the supernatural explanation behind *Vermillion*. But if she really thinks my sister, a teen at the time, hired a bunch of random people to recreate one of the Baron's and Adrianna's infamous parties while our parents slept in their bedroom upstairs, then maybe I've pegged Raina all wrong.

I don't respond. As she catches on to my dark demeanor, her excitement fades. If Arthur's to be believed, Raina and I became friends during my two-day blackout. I wonder what we bonded over. I may never know.

The Fifth Sign is all that matters now. Amid my abrupt return to the land of the living from the haunted tidal pools, I didn't have a chance to consult CrimsonDreadNet on what to expect next. I suspect the Fifth Sign is coming, but I'm not sure whether I want it or not. I'm so close to the conclusion, I can feel it. The darkness at the end of the Path grows solid, becomes tangible in my grasp. But there's a cost. Vermillion gave me a preview of that cost at the pools—my time, my body. Will I be able to complete the Path without losing myself to it completely? I'll deal with this when the moment comes. Assuming I'll have retained enough autonomy to decide, with hopes that Vermillion hasn't consumed me whole.

From my memories of five years ago, Vermillion wasn't always set on harming or scaring me. Most of the time she just . . . watched. But during the Midnight Reverie she became . . . more. Wanted more. Showed herself more. Like she suddenly grew impatient.

In my jumbled recollection, the night of the Reverie begins with Layla waking me up. Actually, now that I think about it, I'm not sure it was Layla's hand that reached for me and pulled the blanket off my still form. The digital clock by my bed appeared stuck on thirteen past midnight. "It's time," a voice said close to my ear. Same voice as *Vermillion*'s voice-over.

Eyes half closed, I walked downstairs and into the reception hall, the stretch of it empty but not desolate, dramatically lit by moonlight filtered through the mullioned windows. One step and I was bathed in silver light, and in another step, submerged in darkness.

At first, I remember there being no sound but my own shallow breathing. Layla added a mismatched electronic beat later, mixed with the unsettling noises of rustling clothes and pattering feet sliding against the parquetry. As I study this space now, the reception being readied for this scene's reenactment, long-ago memories return, sweeping me up anew.

A pressure of a cold hand against my back. Bony fingers splayed, she pushes me into the center of the room. Panic flowers in my chest, but I dance, I dance because I must. I feel her presence, but I don't see her—she's behind me, by my side, holding my hand as she swirls me around in an off-beat waltz. Where is Layla? Does she film this? Snowflake-like particles of dust float in the air. And through this wall of deathly shimmer, I begin seeing them, revelers showing themselves in electrified glimpses and shocked moments of there-not-there. Some are fully formed, I can barely see through them, others are suggestions of a presence—look at that pair of ghostly hands curled over the back of an ancient stuffed chair—disembodied hands, impatient fingers tap-tap-tapping against the upholstery. I know they must belong to someone, to something.

As their pressing presence can be ignored no more, I begin seeing details and fragments I'd rather not see. The revelers are wearing disguises, prosthetics, fake hair—creepy things from the Baron's Preparation Room that twist faces beyond recognition. I glimpse the fluff of swan feathers, black and white, sticking out here and there—a fan, a collar decoration, a mask. But what really sends my knees shaking and my blood pumping adrenaline is that what I can see of faces through the gaps in makeup and masks is... dead, carious. Rotten, skeletal. Milky eyes. Empty sockets. Sunken cheeks. I might be the only living thing in this party of the dead.

I scream. I try to run. But just like in a particularly unruly, scary dream, my legs don't obey, and my voice grows weak, reduced to barely a whisper. I freeze. The Baron and Adrianna's undead guests swirl and dance around the room, a demonic merry-go-round wound by a relentless, wicked hand. The circle tightens around me, shrinking smaller and smaller until they entrap me with their funeral gowns, drown me in their rot. Once more, I try screaming, the intent of it forms at the top of my lungs, but no sound issues from my useless throat. I am no longer able to tell what is a memory from five years ago and what is the version of that night I've seen on the screen, Layla's masterpiece. It doesn't matter *anymore—I'm lost in the moment. I'm lost. About to be consumed, torn to pieces by the ravenous dead.*

A red-clad arm reaches for me from between the gyrating bodies.

Vermillion pulls me out of the shrinking circle of revelers and deposits me on the stairwell. Safe, for now.

Did she save me out of the goodness of her heart? Or did she have her own reasons?

And now I'm back at it, ready to reenact this scene of the movie, ready to join the dance of the dead once again.

The outfit awaiting me tonight is a balloon-sleeved, shimmering white gown that falls past my ankles to the floor, swallowing me whole. The fabric smells of mothballs and itches against my skin. I catch Erasmus looking at me, but when I nod in acknowledgment, he doesn't move. I grow cold under his gaze until I realize the director isn't really looking at me but rather through me, focusing on the wall behind me. When I move, the spell Erasmus is under breaks, and he jolts to attention. He avoids my gaze, so I take this opportunity to keep an eye on him, half expecting him to produce a weathered, old book and start reciting demonic incantations. But all he does is talk to Ivor, both men gesticulating as they point out angles of the room. Arthur is a no-show, which disappoints me more than I care to admit.

I expect my hair to be styled to match the gown's old-fashioned extravagance but apparently my lanky, flat do is perfectly enough for tonight, or so Raina says.

When I don the gown and study my reflection in the mirror, I can sort of see what Erasmus and Serge and Raina have in mind for the look: I'm a party crasher, a pretender, a living girl wearing an undead disguise, playing dress-up. It's as if I've stumbled upon this outfit in the Baron's Preparation Room, but it is my hair, still flat from sleep, which gives me away.

I wonder how the Fifth Sign is aligned with this scene, and what I'm supposed to learn from it. Based on V-heads' interpretation of the Midnight Reverie, by this point in the movie, it is no longer certain whether I am alive or dead.

Was I indeed a living impostor crashing the Midnight Reverie, or did I deserve my own place among the ghosts?

I fear I'm about to find out.

Night invades Cashore's every nook and cranny.

Erasmus is elusive, and it's now been hours since I've last seen Arthur. I suspect both are avoiding me. Can Arthur sense my simmering fury at finding the incriminating photo in his jacket's pocket? Can Erasmus feel the bitter aftertaste of my suspicions about him?

I can't speak for his father, but perhaps it's Arthur's self-preservation instinct that's keeping him away. The non-memory of kissing him returns at the most inopportune moment, right as I'm instructed to start coming down the stairs into the lobby. It's been such a long time since I've kissed anyone. Having the memory of kissing Arthur wiped from my mind feels like a personal slight. My mind is all confused.

I need to focus. I need to focus.

I think of my sister, of the horrible sound of nails scratching against the wall as she was dragged to hell.

The lobby below me is smothered in darkness, but I can hear people there. Just a few more steps. But before I can clear the stairwell's final twist and see what awaits me, what's left of the light behind me goes out with a clap. I'm left with just the outlines of the house, revealed in the weak glow of moonlight. My heart beats hard, but the sensation is lost to growing noise coming from downstairs.

I take my final steps and . . . enter the truest reenactment of Layla's movie to date.

The scene unfolding makes me dizzy, my perception split into then and now. It's like my own memories of this scene, ghosts absent at first and then appearing as sinister suggestions, become intertwined with Layla's footage.

Erasmus went all out with extras. A throng of white-clad dancers are trapped in constant movement. At a gliding first look, their motions appear human, becoming more and more odd the longer I stare. Their faces are hidden behind grotesque, off-putting masks—plague doctors, human-animal hybrids, unspeakable monsters—but it's their exposed arms and hands that are truly terrifying. Their skin, what I can see of it, gives off a decaying feel, and the air smells the part.

The hope of receiving my Fifth Sign keeps my feet moving, bringing me closer to this Ball of the Dead. It is somewhere here, in the depths of this crowd that I know I can find my prize, my answer.

In my mind, I conjure my sister's face, the way she appeared to me in that disappearing video on my phone. Real or not real, her red-rimmed eyes plead with me. *You have to fight it. She can't win.* I keep Layla's words close to my heart as I enter the moving crowd.

They don't talk, and there's no music, but their feet must sense a rhythm that unites them. I fall into step with them, swirling and moving as part of the bigger whole.

Someone wedges a mask into my hand. When I study the offering in the weak beam of moonlight, I realize the mask is the face of Vermillion, captured in one of her scariest moments in the movie. Lips curling over teeth, eyes black.

I press the mask against my face, and someone's featherlight hands tie the silk straps in the back of my head. When I turn to see my timely helper, the crowd must've reabsorbed them, because there's no one right behind me. The mask's insides smell faintly of glue and dust, and it helps ground me in reality, reminding me that this is a movie. Serge likely crafted the mask. Still, there are moments during the reverie reenactment when I feel as if my bare feet levitate from the ground, as if I shed my corporeality with each second that I twirl among the dead. But still, I dance.

The crowd shifts around me, forming a narrow corridor of bodies, leaving me face to face with a man who wears the mask of a red demon. He's the only one here not wearing white. An old-fashioned black tuxedo clings to his tall frame. There's not much for me to do but move toward him. I take his proffered hand. The moment our fingers lock, he leads me to the center of the room. His hands trap me in a chaste embrace, fingers gentle around my waist. He brings me close, our chests touching.

"Arthur?" I ask, a tragic whisper in the night, when his scent, attractive and very much alive, draws me in. Temporarily, I forget my anger at his betrayal, cherishing the gentle, considerate boy I've befriended. Perhaps for a moment I can simply enjoy this dance, this closeness, before reality rushes in.

He chuckles, twisting his head sideways, so that I only get a glimpse of his mouth, pale teeth a tad too sharp. "Not quite. Try again, Sophia-the-Wise," he says, but the voice is not Arthur's at all, it doesn't even come from his mouth but rather from all around me, from *inside* me.

I try breaking free of him, but his hands, no longer soft, hold me firm in their steely embrace.

Non-Arthur leads me into a dizzying turn, rotating me away from him in a rapid spiral. And even before I return to face him, I know something's wrong. His hand in mine is no longer human, no longer alive. And it's no hand at all—I'm holding on to a swath of dirty red fabric, still attached to the bigger whole.

When I spiral back, I come face to face with Vermillion.

She is transformed, unmasked.

This time, I know it's not Francesca in makeup. No, this creature is real—as real as any ghost can be. Perhaps there's a parallel universe somewhere out there where I'm simply an actor being filmed surrounded by a bunch of dancing extras. But not here; in this world, in this reality, my lot is to face the real ghost. To dance with her.

My ghoulish dance partner smiles as she leads me away from the crowd, up the stairs, down the corridors, left turn, right turn, backtrack, the house fast-forwarding around me, my rapid breathing deafening, my feet barely touching the floor.

When we spill out onto the patio, the ground quakes beneath me.

"Why are you doing this?" I cry, trying to break Vermillion's hold on me. But her skeletal fingers trapping mine are not giving in. "Where is my sister?"

She tries to open her mouth, strain showing in the ridges that run through her skin, where muscle gives way to decay. Her mouth is hardened by death, rotten lips sewn together in silence.

"With. Me."

That's all but it's enough. The sound out of Vermillion's mouth is a bone-stripping wind that lives in the tunnel between worlds.

"What do you mean?" I cry out, my mind frantic.

The entity meets my eyes and holds my gaze, while I grow cold. Standing next to her is like opening the door into the arctic desolation; there's beauty there but also death. She says nothing, all silent eloquence only the dead have mastered.

I imagine I can hear Vermillion's voice inside my head, like it's been there all along: *What makes you think she wants to leave?*

I don't believe it! I can't. I can't. I can't. I know Layla is resisting Vermillion—I've seen the evidence of it, in my sister's eyes, in her attempts to contact me. Even if at some stage, for whatever desperate reason, Layla wanted to join Vermillion, I know deep in my heart she's since changed her mind. She wants to live.

In my interaction with this spirit, I haven't noticed how close to the edge of the patio we've moved in our unnerving dance. There's a fence around the perimeter, but it wouldn't take much to overcome it and . . . the rock pools await. Only this time I don't think I'll get to return to the land of the living.

I want to scream for help, for Erasmus, for Arthur, for Miriam—someone is filming this, they must be!

Or is this a Sign, the Path beckoning me on? What happens to all those who realize their Path is leading them toward their end, their undoing, their death? Do they try to stop it, to slow it down—but is it like trying to slow down a runaway locomotive?

I pull at Vermillion's hand, her fingers wrapped around mine. I jerk back with all the force I can muster. But it's like my hand is trapped inside a vise, the metal jaws unyielding.

"Let me go! I don't belong here! I don't belong with you!" I attempt a scream, but the result is an angry hiss.

The ghoul holding on to me is silent, yet her lips move against the strain. Without sound, she communicates: *You are mine.*

She pulls at my hand, hers imbued with unreal, unhuman strength. With growing horror, I watch her as she steps off the patio, walking right through the fence and falling backward over the edge, into the rising mist, dragging me with her.

I scream and cry and hiss in protest, but my hand is locked in hers, and she pulls me with her, down, down, down. My thighs meet the barrier of the fence, but my reprieve is short-lived as I proceed to tumble over it, driven down by the momentum of my sinister dance partner.

Wind slams against my face, pushing my hair back.

There's that moment early on in the fall, before I see the ground approach, when I think I'm actually flying, but that moment doesn't last. The ending comes. It always does.

Thirty-Three

I remember reading somewhere that dreams in which you are falling indicate the dreamer's inner turmoil, unresolved anxieties, and slipping control. No shit. I'm anxious about everything, and I control nothing. All I want is to wake up, my sister to be there when I do, and my family to move on from its self-imposed slumber. I want my life to be my own, for it not to rotate around Layla. For once, I want to be selfish, unhaunted. I want the ghosts, real and imaginary, to leave me alone.

One might propose that my fall from the patio would be most logically concluded with me waking up. I'd come awake in my bed, awash with stress, but also relief.

That's not what happens.

I do reach the bottom, the inevitable conclusion of my fall.

I break the water of the damn rock pools, but instead of bone-pulverizing pain and a merciful blackout, I feel the shock of cold water. Brine rushes into my mouth.

These pools are deceptively deep, bottomless even. I wonder what'll happen if I swim down instead of up. Will I resurface in another reality that mimics my own, but with things shifted around in just the right way to seem familiar at first but irrevocably alien upon a closer look? Where do those who complete the Path end up?

My lungs are threatening to burst, and I don't want any treacherous, salty water inside me. I reorient myself, fighting against the entrapment of my ball gown, seeking the light. Because you always swim toward the light.

I remember reading somewhere that sound carries differently underwater; it vibrates through skin and bones rather than ear canals. So, with my skin and what's underneath it, I hear Vermillion's voice ringing clear and insistent while I fight for my freedom and breath.

You. Are. Mine.

Not today.

Thrashing, I break the surface.

My ears are blocked, my eyes stinging. But I remember everything. The dancing, the falling, the almost drowning.

As my vision clears and my senses rush back, I draw a bizarre conclusion: I'm sloshing inside a slippery bathtub, indoors. It is true what they say, you can drown in the shallowest of waters. I sit up, expel the water from my lungs in inelegant heaves.

The flickering light overhead stabilizes. The walls are closing in.

The tub. It's the one from the bathroom Layla and I used to share five years ago. The clawfoot monster.

I grip the tub's slippery sides, my knuckles a shock of white. I hold on like my life depends on it. Like at any moment, I'll get sucked right back in, into that parallel reality where I'm drowning in the rock pools.

I breathe greedily in gulps. I'm still wearing the balloon-sleeved ball gown Serge had bestowed on me before the last filming session. Soaked beyond recognition, it expands. In a bout of blinding fright I contort, hands reaching around my back, tearing at the zipper until it gives. When the fabric slides down my shoulders, I climb out of it, like it's a discarded chrysalis.

Towel wrapped around my shoulders, water dripping down my hair, I leave the bathroom, already shivering. Did I lose time again? How much?

Before something important slips away from my memory, I limp to the bed. I riffle through the unmade blankets and sheets till I grab my phone. I train the camera at my face, cringing at my unraveled look. I hit record.

Video Recording

My face claims the camera. Without much inflection, I speak. "V said I would soon remember and that I'll understand. She said

I belong with her, to her. And that Layla is with her right now. Likely imprisoned. Kept against her will? She must be. I don't believe Layla wouldn't want to be free, that she'd choose to be with ghosts. But I don't understand . . . was this my Fifth Sign? It had to be. But is Layla dead or alive? Some state in-between? And what about me?"

If this recording is real, so am I. If it stays in my phone's library after I hit stop, it means the girl who made it is real.

After watching the recording, I set the phone aside. I take in my surroundings, focusing on things I've barely noticed before. The lamp. The bedside table. My unzipped luggage sitting on a chair. If this was a dream, a nightmare, would these objects seem as real as they appear to me now?

Aside from the one I've just made, there are no new recordings in my phone's video library, and the lack fills me with hope. Perhaps this time I haven't lost any days in payment for my latest Sign. But if not time, what did Vermillion take from me in this instance? Did I dream it all—the masquerade, Vermillion disguised as Arthur, the blood-chilling fall from the patio? A memory comes, saltwater rushing into my mouth. The state of my roughened tongue tells me that was no dream.

How do the dead communicate with the living? They can't

send us letters or just tell us things. We don't speak the same language. Meanings become twisted in translation, as they leak from one plane of existence to the next.

Vermillion appeared to understand me, but she struggled to speak, only managed a handful of words. Perhaps she can't communicate when she's among the living. Perhaps to speak with her I need to meet her on her own ground. The thought fills me with dread that settles like lead in my stomach.

I lie down and study the ceiling. Turning to my side, I notice a small, neat stack of pages on the nightstand. Were they there earlier when I looked around the room?

The pages appear to be torn from a book. The script is a mix of the Cyrillic alphabet and English—or Latin, I guess. My fingers stiff, I sift through the pages, coming across the photograph from Arthur's jacket mixed in among them. Didn't I leave that in my luggage? I set it aside, my hands cold with premonition. The pages have notes penciled in the margins, in Layla's unmistakable hand:

She can't remember. She wants to forget. Died tragically, young. Brought back but it backfired. Trapped. Craves a body. Can she be reasoned with?

My skin ripples; this feeling is terrible, of the gloomiest kind. Is someone out there really walking over your future gravesite when you shiver? Before I gather my panicking thoughts into a semblance of an order, there's a knock on my door, Arthur's voice calling my name.

I stuff the pages and the photograph into the nightstand drawer. The irony of the act is not lost on me. I keep hiding things and someone—or something—keeps unearthing my secrets and putting them on display.

"Just a sec!" I rush to put on whatever clothes I can find: a sexy, black sweater with shoulder cut-outs I was saving for later, a pair of washed girlfriend jeans ripped at the knees. My hair is still damp, but there's no time to dry it, so I just run my fingers through it, hoping for a tousled beach look.

I open the door, my silly heart fluttering at the sight of Arthur.

"Come with me?" he asks instead of hello. He looks like he hasn't slept in . . . a while. Perhaps he's even been awake the entire time we've been at Cashore. *@SleeplessReveler* indeed.

"Come with you where?" I don't move from my spot, keeping the door barely open enough to stick my nose out. Seeing Arthur, getting close to him will cloud my judgment, and I don't need that complication on top of everything else.

"For a drive. Out of this house. Somewhere where no one and nothing can overhear us."

The way he says *nothing* triggers a deep-seated fear in me. Vermillion is real, even if it feels impossible. I don't know if there are other ghosts out there, but I know there's at least one ghost that exists, and she haunts this house.

I study Arthur, taking him in, a brief but intense moment. It is almost a conscious effort on my part to maintain the required level of hostility against him when he's right here, so close I could reach out and touch him, and do more than touch.

"Where have you been?" I ask. "It feels like I haven't seen you ... in forever." I watch him. His face doesn't do anything suspect, but looks are deceptive. Charm can be weaponized.

"We *really* need to get out of here," he says, ignoring my question. "This might be our last chance to ... talk. Dad wants to film the Unquiet Spirits sequence tomorrow morning."

"Unquiet Spirits?" I snort. The very idea of me attempting to reenact the incredible physical achievement of my younger years, before my damaged ankle put an end to my ballet aspirations, is ludicrous. "I haven't put on ballet shoes in years. Erasmus can't expect me to ... nobody wants to see *that*, believe me."

"But I've seen you dance," Arthur says, appearing genuinely confused at my indignation. "Recently, I mean. In Adrianna's studio. You're incredible ... you're in great shape. I mean, for ballet. And in general." His face turns redder by the end of the sentence.

I wish I could erase the fact that I did find that damn photograph in his jacket. But I can't.

"That dance in the studio, it wasn't me, and you know it," I say, my voice dry and biting.

Arthur pales. I have to confront him about the photo. Now. Before another blackout. Before he tries to kiss me again.

I leave him hanging while I step back to extract the damning photo from the nightstand drawer. Returning to the door, I kind of hope Arthur has left, so I don't have to do this. But he's still there, looking as confused as when I left him.

I bring the photo into his line of vision, angling it away from the corridor cameras. "I know it was you who posted this on CrimsonDreadNet. What game are you playing? Are you and your dad doing this together?"

He looks startled, like I've slapped him, as he zeros in on the photo in my unsteady grip. When he reaches for the photo, I pull back my hand.

"Where did you get that?" Arthur sounds fascinated. Not the reaction I was going for. Why doesn't he appear guilty, or even mildly anxious about being caught? "This is . . . incredible," he says, eyes glued to the photo. "You're not in the original shot, right? If this one's a fake, it's a damn good one. But who'd make it and why?"

"*Why?* I was hoping you'd tell me." I barely have half a mind to keep my voice down to a murmur and my face away from the cameras. I won't put it past Erasmus to try and read my lips. "And drop the act, please. I found it in *your* jacket pocket."

"My jacket?" he asks. The whiplash from his innocent-sounding question freezes the blood in my veins.

"Seriously?" I retreat into the room, stuffing the photo into my jeans pocket.

Like we're tethered by an invisible thread, Arthur follows me inside, his eyes never once leaving me as I search for the damn jacket. I know it's in here somewhere! I just don't see it. Growing frustrated and feeling a bit like the tormented protagonist of a psychological thriller who knows what she saw was real, but struggles to make herself heard, believed.

I upend my luggage and nearly rip out all the hangers from the wardrobe.

The jacket isn't here.

I face Arthur. He's looking at me in that concerned way of his that makes me want to scream.

"Did you take it?" I ask. "You took it while I was filming."

"I really don't know what you're talking about. Why is this jacket so important?"

"You were wearing it when you found me on the beach and gave me CPR." I don't sound that certain anymore. The visceral memory of awakening to Arthur's hands on my chest, to his lips leaving my mouth makes it my turn to blush, even if being revived like that is a far thing from a romantic encounter. "You let me borrow it after."

"Oh." He's relieved, like he'd solved a puzzle. I glare at him, packing all my frustration into the act.

"That wasn't my jacket!" he says. "I grabbed it from wardrobe."

I can't help my glare softening. Damn it. The way he said "wardrobe," I doubt he means the closet in his room.

"If the jacket's not yours, then whose is it? Serge's?" A new wave of suspicion leaves me with chilled skin and an elevated heartbeat. There must be more to the hyper-focused costume director than meets the eye. All my prior interactions with Serge turn into a confused film reel in my head. We've barely talked, but all our conversations were strictly professional, related to Erasmus's film. Unless something else had occurred while I was lost to the blackout?

"Sophia," Arthur says, calm nearly gone from his voice. He's grown as agitated as I feel, his hands a nervous jumble. He doesn't seem to know what to do with his fingers. "That jacket is not Serge's. It belongs to the set. Anyone in the house could've borrowed it."

Thirty-Four

There's noise in my head.

I'm falling off that cliff again, breaking the rock pools' surface like a stone, and going under, to a place that offers no returns, no second chances.

It's this house. The Path. The Signs. The ghost. My sister.

Somewhere inside Cashore's walls, the red demon sleeps.

My relief is palpable. Arthur is not some mastermind. He's just as mixed up in all of this as would be expected of someone whose father's making a movie about *Vermillion*, and who is obsessed with my sister and the occult. My need to believe Arthur's innocence is visceral; it fills me with both adrenaline and hope.

"You're right," I say. "We really need to get out of here. I can't think properly in this house."

I take Arthur's hand, a gesture of trust, and lead him out and away from my room, not caring what Erasmus's cameras—

and whoever else is watching—make of it.

On our way out of the house, we pass a small group of crew members who move furniture, piece by piece, back into the lobby. I don't recognize anyone, but the looks they give us are odd, even pitying. Maybe I'm projecting my own uncertainties and fears onto others.

I look away, desperate to get outside to where sunshine creates a world of its own, free of ghosts and lost memories.

A scared, anxious part of me wonders whether Cashore will let us go.

When we reach the front door and I turn the creaky swan-shaped handle without resistance, I brace for the pushback, for an unknown force to trip me over and drag me back inside by my ankles, but when I step over the threshold, nothing slows me down or holds me back.

The sun is blinding and alive. It seems to follow me, sliding into my eyes no matter where I look or twist my head. Sunglasses would be nice, but the only pair I've brought here with me lies forgotten at the bottom of my bag.

After being trapped in a cave for months, surviving on water and algae, people return photosensitive. But I've only been inside a day. Two? I'm pleasantly warm and disoriented by the light. A rush of gratitude shivers through me when Arthur's hand finds mine. He directs me toward the compact silver Honda parked next to the production van. In the bright light of day, the van that brought me to Livadia a small eternity ago is too real.

"Your car?" I ask when Arthur lets go of my hand to search his pockets for the keys. The broad expanse of his shoulders draws and holds my attention. He's wearing a black polo shirt and jeans. Bathed in sunlight, for a moment I can pretend like we're just going out for a drive, maybe even a date. We have just the right kind of tension between us, the good kind. I know I'm not the only one who feels it. Whenever I'm near him, I'm physically aware of him, affected by his gravity.

"A rental," he says, opening the passenger door for me.

I climb in. The seatbelt's pressure applied to my chest is painfully familiar and yet strange, like I'm a spirit only recently made flesh, still perceiving visceral sensations from a faraway place beyond life.

Arthur gets in next to me and wastes no time getting the car started. As we drive away from Cashore, I feel my persistent connection to the building. Not a tangible restraint designed to keep me in place, but a ball of black yarn unspooling as the car speeds away. No matter how far I go or where, I'll always be linked to this place.

We don't talk at first. I watch Arthur indirectly, via sideways glances. He's a careful driver. As he takes us down the mountain, diligently slowing down before each turn, his eyes never leave the road. Earnest and open. Which makes it even more difficult to imagine him as a scheming liar.

"Where are we going?" I ask after he clears the last of the dangerous turns and we pass by a security point his father set up for the duration of the filming.

"There's a café in town. It should be deserted at this hour. I don't want anyone overhearing us talking about the Path. And I wouldn't put it past Dad to bug the car."

"I thought we weren't supposed to talk about the Path," I say as I mull over the possibility of Erasmus going as far as to install surveillance cameras or mics in rented cars on the off chance I might slip up and say something revelatory.

"That was before you started losing days and memories. This is not normal; I mean not even by the Path's standards. I've been reading up on the CrimsonDreadNet and no one's ever mentioned blackouts. They do talk a lot about 'a price to pay' though, but I haven't seen anyone specify what it actually cost them to get their Signs."

Aside from urban legends, there's suspiciously little known about those who have completed the Path. What happens to them? Where do they end up, especially if their Path experience goes sour? I've always assumed there was an unspoken conspiracy to keep the details about the Path secret. But what if there's so little information because so few people who complete the Path live to tell the tale? Was the price they had to pay to receive their final Signs too high?

None of that explains my blackouts. Maybe those are unique to me because my Path experience is so irrevocably linked to Cashore itself. After all, I was there as the material that informs the lore of the Path was being created.

"What do you think is going on?" I ask, sounding more scared and fragile than I care to admit.

Arthur doesn't respond for a long moment. The sun starts bothering me, so I lower the car visor. As we follow the road along the coast, Livadia flickers by in the window. Bathed in golden afternoon light, the town looks normal. Idyllic, summery. A little seaside paradise. An invisible demarcation line is drawn between Livadia and the brooding house on the cliff. By an unspoken agreement, the town's residents do not venture anywhere near Cashore, not even to the pristine beach nearby. There's no cult around my sister and her macabre film here, no museums dedicated to her art, no festivals devoted to *Vermillion*. The house is a shadow cast upon this Californian heaven, and the brighter the sun gets, the darker the shadow grows.

"I don't know what's going on," Arthur says. "But it does feel like we're about to cross over some kind of event horizon."

The point of no return.

I'm surprised to hear this fatalism come from Arthur. My own twisted tangle with Vermillion and the Path is deeply personal, but what is Arthur's stake here? For all I know, despite how earnest and cute he is, he's just another fan, a V-head moving along the Path because that's what V-heads do. They obsess. This brings me back to the question of his goal for the end of the Path. When I open my mouth to ask, he's parking the car next to an adorable beach café. Its walls are painted dreamily blue, adorned with surf boards and seagulls hovering over white-cresting waves.

We leave the car and make our way to the order window. Minutes later, we carry iced coffees to one of the outside tables, overlooking the gorgeous surf. Arthur was right earlier: This place is nearly deserted. Aside from an ice cream–devouring family of five at a far table, it's just us.

"Do you feel it?" Arthur asks, lowering his mouth to capture the cup's straw. "How different it feels to be out here, far from the house?"

I know exactly what he means. Even the air out here feels more real. The suffocating pressure I wasn't quite aware I was carrying inside Cashore is lifted off my shoulders.

"Do you think the house has something to do with it?" I ask. "Never mind, a rhetorical question." I sip my coffee, the freeze shocking my brain into extra-sharp clarity.

Arthur nods, giving his coffee cup an almost thoughtful look. "I've pretty much stopped sleeping. But I'd rather hallucinate than have nightmares. Yes, I know exactly how it sounds. But I've been seeing my mom. At least, I think it's her. I hope."

"Your mom?" I ask, gently, carefully. "You never talk about her." I remember reading in a rare online interview with Erasmus Sawyer that he's a widower. Until now, I didn't connect that to Arthur. I saw Erasmus's loss as separate from the mysterious boy before me now.

Arthur appears fragile, less certain, as if leaving Cashore has stripped away his corporeality. I wonder how I look to him in the sobering light of day.

"You've been seeing her in the house?" I ask gently.

"My mom is . . . you might know this, she passed away. A few years ago." He looks at the ocean, deep in thought. I wait. I don't rush him to speak. I want him to be certain he wants to share this with me.

I'm grateful when he does.

"She's the reason I'm on the Path. But . . . I'm not even sure anymore, not sure if I should keep going. Maybe I should stop if I can. I think maybe she wants me to stop."

She's the reason I'm on the Path.

I zero in on his words. Quiet but certain, they roar in my head like thunder. Arthur and I, we're alike more than I thought. Both of us are seeking closure, and for both of us the Path is personal. This revelation spreads its intoxicating energy through my body. I feel this pull toward Arthur; it's stronger than gravity.

"You don't have to tell me if you don't want to."

I reach for his hand across the table. The gesture, its boldness, surprises me, but I don't retreat. I cover Arthur's hand with mine, my fingers sensitive against the warmth of his skin. When he looks at me, his eyes are lit up, but some cautiousness remains. He moves his hand away and my heart falls, but then he shifts his fingers so that they wrap around mine. My heart flips in my chest.

"Your mom's passing. What happened?" I know so little about Arthur's family. Erasmus's online profiles focus on his career, his art. It's like the man doesn't exist outside of his work. Perhaps that's how he prefers it.

"It was a heart attack. Just over two years ago. I didn't know it at the time but . . . she died *while* on the Path," Arthur says. "I learned that by accident. She kept a journal, and I found it before my father made it disappear. I knew then that I had to find out what happened to Mom. A friend helped me hack into the coroner's report—there was nothing suspicious about her passing, but . . . she had no heart condition, no history of that. In her journal, she wrote about watching *V* with my dad for the first time, and then she started getting these recurring dreams in which Layla would talk to her from the dark, inviting her to come look for her, that kind of stuff, very creepy. It was like your sister was haunting my mom.

"I don't know whether Mom ever posted on CrimsonDread-Net, or how far down the Path she progressed, but I think in the end she was frightened to death by the experience. She didn't choose to walk the Path, she wasn't a V-head, though she was married to one—whatever you want to call my dad. And after she passed, whenever I manage to sleep, I dream of her, like she's trying to communicate with me.

"Maybe it's my mind attempting to explain her death. I mean, I know there's a pretty good chance it was just that, a heart attack, a random, horrible thing that happened, but the night I got my first Sign, my Invitation, I could swear Mom was there too, in the room with me, trying to tell me something. I knew then I had to walk the Path too. I hope that in the end I get to see Mom again."

Despite the sun's generosity, I'm cold. *Vermillion*, it seems, is a family business. It doesn't just affect one person; it affects everyone and everything linked to it.

I flinch when Arthur speaks again. "When Dad reached out to you and you agreed to be in this movie, it was like a bulb lit up in my head. I was just starting on the Path, and it was my chance to get serious about it. I mean, I'd get to be on the Path *and* have access to the very building where V was filmed—how much more serious could one get? And then I met you and it finally felt like everything was falling into place. But now I'm beginning to wonder . . ."

"Whether the price is too high to pay?" I say. His doubts are my doubts, his fears my fears. I understand what he's going through. "I didn't believe in ghosts before I came here," I say.

He gives my hand a gentle squeeze that sends excited shivers through me. I have to keep it together, no matter how inviting his touch feels. "But now I *know* that V is real. I mean, she must be. I've been experiencing things I can't explain. Forgetting things. Like she's been feeding off me, taking me apart, little by little. And then she got greedy, and I lost two days. It's dangerous. We don't know what we're dealing with. But then if V is real, then maybe she really knows things, like what happened to your mom, and where the hell my sister is." *If my sister is still alive.*

Our hands linked, we sit in silence. My impromptu confession reverberates inside of me like the howling of a hurricane. A hurricane that's far from over.

"I believe you when you say you don't know anything about this photo of me and Layla," I say. "But someone wanted me to see it. Likely, the same someone who left torn pages from the *Book of Ka'schor* in my room. What if those are the same pages, in translation, that you found among your dad's notes?"

Arthur's eyes focus on me anew, but he stays quiet.

I regret leaving Cashore in a hurry, not taking the pages with me. But I remember the words penciled in the margins.

"Don't ask me for proof, but I know those pages came from Layla's copy of the *Book of Ka'schor.* She left notes in the margins, she wrote something like *she wants to forget* and that *she died young.* And there was something else . . ." I strain to visualize the writing. "Arthur, my sister wrote that V *needs a body.*

Do you think that's it? The reason I've been losing time and memories? Is V . . . possessing me?"

My question sits unanswered, a little black hole, festering between us.

"How far along on the Path are you?" Arthur asks.

"Waiting on my Sixth Sign."

"Me too. And despite what I've been saying earlier, I'm not giving up. I need to face V if I'm ever going to know the truth about my mom."

"You're not worried that V will punish you again, for sharing this with me?"

"If she does, I'll just keep on coming," he says, voice like steel. I know he means it.

"I'm not turning back either," I say. *I wonder if I even have that choice anymore.*

We both cast our eyes over the ocean, some unspoken pact between us. The waves, single-minded and relentless, soothe my heartache.

Arthur lets go of my hand. But instead of walking to the car he rounds the table, coming over to my side. I stand up and face him. He's not a stranger anymore. He understands me, my struggle and my isolation, in a way nobody else possibly can. We're linked now and will stay linked no matter what we do. No matter where we end up. And, I realize, there's something comforting in knowing that.

"You really don't remember kissing me?" he asks, brow furrowed in earnest.

I shake my head slowly. "I've seen the recording of it though." I frown and then blush at the uncomfortable memory my mind still tries to make sense of.

Arthur looks startled at my words. "I-I forgot about that. It must've been such an odd thing for you to watch."

I don't respond. There's a part of me that wants to apply some mental version of bleach to cleanse my mind of ever seeing that video, but . . . "Well, I suppose it was the next best thing to actually being there." I try for a joke, but it just sounds sad.

"Let's fix that?" Arthur says. "God, that was corny." He laughs as he leans into my space, just a little bit. The pull of his gravity is strong. I want to let it take me.

"What is it exactly you're proposing?" I ask, taken aback by how confident I sound, how flirtatious. "Are you saying that despite all this, the haunted house, the ghost, the likely possession, you actually want to kiss me, again?"

"That is exactly what I'm saying."

We both move at once, covering the remaining distance between us, but stop before our lips meet. His warm breath is featherlight on my skin. I'm shivering on the inside, the outside of me covered in goosebumps. Never before have I been this shaken by the moment that precedes the kiss. The moment before everything changes. Arthur reaches for me first. He gently kisses my upper lip, then the lower one, tugging at it in a light tease. And then our lips meet, hungrily and his hands are around my waist, pulling me in. I knew I wanted to kiss him, but it shocks me to my very core how right this feels, how visceral my need is to hold on to him and not let go. The rest of the world retreats, the ocean holds its breath, as our kiss grows deeper, hungrier, more ferocious. For a moment, it's only me and Arthur. The rest can wait.

When we finally come up for air, we don't immediately move away. His hands are still on my waist, fingers splayed over my back; mine are tangled in his hair, tracing the contours of his neck.

"No matter what happens in that house," he says, huskily, eyes not leaving mine. "No matter how this ends, we're going to go on a real date. Okay? I mean . . . if that's okay with you?"

"It's okay with me," I say.

Thirty-Five

We joke about running away, leaving Livadia and not coming back. But we both know we can't just sever the dark thread that connects us to Cashore. And I doubt Vermillion will let us, not without a fight.

So instead, we strategize. Our plan is to stick together, so that when Vermillion finally appears at the end of our joined Paths, we'll be ready. This kind of thing, as far as we know, has never been done before. At least, CrimsonDreadNet is silent on that account. There may be a reason for that. But our determination is strong, a powerful thing born out of shared nightmares and sadness. And when we face the red ghost herself, we'll be able to hold on to one another, to feed each other strength.

But first we need the Sixth Sign. And as per CrimsonDreadNet's next clue, it is linked to the most haunting—and *haunted*—scene in my sister's movie: The Dance of the Unquiet Spirits.

The very same scene Erasmus wants me to reenact next.

There was the fall through the rotten rafters, the injury to my ankle. But there was something else too, something I never thought about. Not until now.

My crooked ankle wasn't the only tangible thing left with me after the fall. The circle of half-moon scars around my wrist was the first thing I noticed after regaining consciousness. Then the throbbing of my ankle kicked in. I had no memory of getting those scars, but I'm certain now it had to be from an encounter with Vermillion herself. Did she try holding on to me, digging her nails into my skin, as my sister brought me back?

Whenever I think of the spirit that dwells within Cashore's walls, my fingers compulsively run over those strange scars, both a reminder of what happened and a harbinger of things to come.

Back at Cashore, Erasmus is the first to greet us. "I didn't know you were going out," he says to Arthur once we're through the door.

"We're not your prisoners, Dad." Arthur sounds friendly, but I can tell he's holding back from being rude.

"That you're not," Erasmus booms. He seems taller and somehow more imposing, even though he's nearly the same height and build as his son. "But you do work for me. And you need to tell me when you're borrowing the car."

"I left a note." Arthur shrugs.

Erasmus turns to me then, producing an unexpected smile. "I have a surprise for you, my star. Will you please come with me to wardrobe?"

Erasmus appears genuinely excited, but my heart is heavy. Maybe it's Erasmus's mention of wardrobe, which brings the incriminating jacket to my mind. For all I know, Erasmus was the one to wear the jacket before Arthur grabbed it on his way out. I feel one step closer to a black hole, Arthur's event horizon.

The damning image of Erasmus blending in with the crowd of V-heads outside of Cashore comes back to rattle me now. As I'm trying to decide whether to confront Erasmus now and potentially endanger the filming and my progression on the Path, the director turns his gaze on his son.

"Arty, why don't you go help Ivor? A couple of the cameras in the studio stopped working overnight. I bet he can use your help."

"Yes, sir!" Arthur offers his father a mock salute. Before he leaves, he gives me a disdainful look, whispering, "Later."

Following Erasmus to wardrobe, I only partially register his excited monologue, something about how pleased he is with all the incredible footage he's been getting for his film. At least someone's happy, things seemingly going his way. I wonder what that feels like, to be in control.

An idea comes as sudden as a dizzy spell, and I want to shout at myself for not trying this before.

"I've been meaning to ask," I start to say. "Can I see the footage from the Midnight Reverie?"

My innocent request sends a dark wave over Erasmus's otherwise benevolent face. I catch the exact moment his eyes turn to steel.

"I never show my work in progress to anyone," he says, words like a knife that cuts with resolute determination.

"No exceptions? Not even for your star talent?" I ask, sweetly. "I'd love some notes before my final performance. I want the last reenactment to be so magical it manifests something real."

He gives me a sidelong glance, his expression difficult to read. If Erasmus heard the accusation in my awkward wording, he doesn't show it. Our brief moment of reprieve as we were filming minor scenes and atmospheric sequences feels long behind us. "Sophia, I don't think it's a good idea for you to see any of the footage of yourself right now. It might affect your focus," he says. "As for notes, just keep doing what you're doing, because it's working."

And that's that.

We're at wardrobe, where Serge greets us with his usual time-is-money smile.

I look around, trying to see this space with new eyes. There's that bit of red I spotted on my first day of filming, the ancient gown that turned out to be Francesca's costume. Where the hell is Francesca? I've had no encounters with her outside of her role, something I suspect is Erasmus's doing.

Then I see the rack of attire assigned to me. The white funeral number I wore for the Baron's Preparation Room scene, the weird flapper look for the balcony encounter with Vermillion. They feel like portals into another dimension. Reality and fantasy entwine in my mind.

It's a jolt when, while waiting for Serge to deliver Erasmus's "surprise," I catch a glimpse of Francesca. She walks by, and seeing her like that, not in makeup, not trying to scare me, is odd. When our eyes meet, she gives me a wave but doesn't stop or slow down. I have this urge to go after her, to follow her, but Erasmus is saying something to me then, and though I don't focus on the words, I know from the silence that follows he's waiting for my reply.

When my attention is back on Erasmus, Serge has joined us. I see a swath of glittering red in his hands.

It's a dress. Or, more correctly, a stage costume.

Before tutus became a thing, ballerinas of the olden days wore delicate, fancy outfits resembling evening dresses. My eyes catch on the intricate beading covering the front of the dress, faceted gems mixed with crystalline sequins in feather-like patterns. Actually, those are not feathers, but rather flames of fire that run across the entire bodice, merging with a gauzy, ethereal skirt. The pattern looks hauntingly familiar, but before I can vocalize where I know it from, Erasmus speaks. His words are giddy; he sounds like a kid in a candy shop, which is out of character for him.

"It's her outfit, from *The Crimson Queen*. Serge managed to get it on loan from the Californian Museum of the History of Ballet!"

I meet eyes with Serge, and he beams at me. I sense no hidden agenda, no ill intent from him, and yet the costume I'm supposed to wear today sends a deep shiver down my back.

I step closer and watch the shimmery fabric in Serge's hands change shape and color in the light. Like liquid fire. Up close, the outfit is not all red. There are thin traces of black velvet shot with golden thread throughout. The effect is like a fireproof salamander from a fairy tale.

The Crimson Queen.

The experimental ballet from the early twentieth century that made Adrianna Kashoroff a star. I remember seeing incomplete recordings of *The Crimson Queen* back when Layla was researching Cashore's complex history for her movie. Cameras were still a novelty back when the ballet was first staged, so there is no complete record of it. What we have instead are edited sequences put together into a bigger whole, showing red-clad Adrianna on stage, leaping, jumping, swirling like a furious wraith set on fire.

The ballet was composed by Russian émigré musician Leon Stanitsky upon a commission by the American ballettmeister Anthony Blakely. Both Stanitsky and Blakely, longtime lovers married in a theosophical ceremony, appear to have vanished from public record after the ballet came into existence. The complete story of *The Crimson Queen* seems to have been lost for good. No matter how much Layla looked, she couldn't find the definitive script for the ballet. But the gist of it, what she could find, appeared to have echoed Adrianna's own tragic fate. The eponymous Crimson Queen is the restless spirit of a woman who dies young and who, in death, transforms into a god of sorts, a Hades that dwells in her subterranean kingdom and rules over the dead. There's a hint of Baba Yaga mythology there too—she is the guardian of the gate, the ruler of souls. But in *The Crimson Queen*, Hades is also Persephone, one and the same, showing her innocent, kinder side in between bouts of wild dancing, symbolic of her fury and rage in the face of her untimely death.

"You want me to wear it tomorrow?" I say as I study the red dress in Serge's proud hands.

"Yes," Erasmus replies. Something odd and unsettling glints in his eyes. "I thought that would be the best way to conclude my film, don't you agree?"

Thirty-Six

Night comes and I cannot sleep.

Cashore is too quiet, and I'm too spooked to lie still.

Tomorrow will come, whether I want it to or not.

But I don't have to be alone right now.

Blanket wrapped around my shoulders like a cape, I leave the freezer of my room and walk the familiar stretch of corridor to where I know Arthur's keeping vigil.

But I lose my brave momentum when facing his door. The light inside doesn't appear to be on. Perhaps Arthur's asleep for a change. I'm listening for any signs of him, when the door slowly slides open.

I swallow back a scream, but it's Arthur's face peeking at me through the crack. "I was really hoping it was you . . ." he says.

I chuckle but I know I sound miserable, uncertain, desperate. "I can't sleep," I say.

"Welcome to the club. I have cookies." He opens the door so I can enter.

I don't know what I expect to happen between us, if anything. I just seek companionship. Far away from my friends, hiding from my parents, cut off from my sister, I don't want to be alone tonight. I find Arthur's eyes in the dark and say, "I'm really scared about tomorrow."

There are so many things he could say in response, but he simply reaches for me and pulls me into a soft, warm hug. I melt into him.

"Do you want to stay here, with me?" he whispers into my hair.

I nod, exhaling my tension into the soft skin of his neck.

I must've dozed off because the dawn's light wakes me from strange dreams of swimming in dark, murky waters. It takes me a few breaths to orient myself. Past experiences make me fear that I've imagined everything, but my current state suggests otherwise. I'm in Arthur's bed, and I can feel the reassuring weight of his arm around me. I freeze up as the events of last night come back to me in full. We hugged. I kissed him. He kissed me back. But then he brought those lips to my ears and whispered, "You need to sleep, Sophia." And as if his words had some magical power of compulsion over me, I fell asleep.

The sound of Arthur's measured breathing surrounds me, and I feel terrible when I wake him up in my attempt to slither out from under his hold. I sense the moment he wakes up.

"Do you want me to bring you breakfast in bed?" he asks, voice still husky from sleep. My stomach growls, which makes Arthur chuckle.

"I should probably go shower first," I say, even if the idea of delaying the start of the day and remaining in his bed for as long as I can is very tempting. "Meet you in the kitchen in half an hour?"

He grunts in agreement and nuzzles my neck, sending me giggling my way out of bed. This feels so painfully normal— whatever that word is supposed to mean—that for a moment I wonder if I woke up in some alternate reality. But no, we're still in Cashore.

"You slept," I say.

"My first proper sleep in a while," he admits.

"I'm glad," I say.

"You're my sleeping charm," he says, smiling. "I should stick close to you from now on."

"Sounds like a plan." I give him a nervous smile. "Thank you for . . . everything."

"Uh-oh." He sits up in bed. "Breaking up with me already?"

I laugh. "Just being polite. I really am grateful. But maybe you should wait until the end of filming before you decide if you really want to go on that date with me."

"Ready?" Erasmus asks.

No, I want to reply, but instead I nod.

Miriam is in the corner to my right, in the only spot of Adrianna's studio that serves as a partial blind spot, safe from multiplication by the mirrors. This place is like the Baron's Preparation Room, Cashore's second psychomanteum. But right now, the only ghost multiplied by the mirrors is me.

I try not to study my reflected self for too long. But from what I see, I look so much like her. Adrianna Kashoroff. Her costume from *The Crimson Queen* combined with Raina's skillful makeup has transformed me into Adrianna's near-perfect lookalike. The dress required minimal alterations, as if it was designed for my body, and the replica of Adrianna's fiery red pointe shoes fit me perfectly too.

If only I could do these clothes justice. The moment I start dancing, the illusion will shatter. But I have to try and do my best in the hope it'll be enough to reveal my Sixth Sign.

The cameras start rolling.

The Dance of the Unquiet Spirits in *Vermillion* begins right here, in this very spot where I stand now.

I close my eyes.

The muscles of my legs tighten in anticipation. My body craves this. I haven't felt this want for ages. Carefully, I assume a shaky en pointe position, stabilizing quickly, finding my balance with each new breath. I wait for the pain, for my injured ankle to complain, but it's strangely quiet, giving me courage to do more, to test my limits. The music starts.

I take my first step, then another, alternating between brief sequences en pointe and then surer, faster moves as I slide across the studio floor. Even five years later, it turns out I still remember this dance sequence. The familiar fire I used to thrive on as a twelve-year-old returns, igniting all of me. I let this memory fill me. As I move, the steps come to me. Everything else retreats, and it's just me and the dance.

Incomplete sequences of Adrianna Kashoroff's surreal dance from *The Crimson Queen* overlay with my own memories of performing this variation. My entire body is lost to the process, my hands moving with unfamiliar grace, morphing into swan wings that entice and cajole and enchant. From the soles of my feet to the top of my head, I'm electrified. Gravity shifts around me.

Where are the cameras? Where are the people?

I don't know, but does it truly matter right now? I'm a whirling dervish trapped in a never-ending rotation, eager to see the face of the dead god that's haunted me for five long years.

The room changes around me as I turn and turn and turn.

The mirrors are gone, covered in black silk, as if in preparation for a séance. I'm the spirit to be summoned and I'm the summoner, the possessor and the possessed, I am the haunted and I am the ghost. A haunted girl inside a haunted house. I dance like I'm going to die tomorrow, like if I stop the world will end.

I remember. Words spoken in Erasmus's deep voice, a warning preceding this filming session. He said something about staying away from the attic. It's dangerous. They don't want a repeat of the old accident.

While my brain acknowledges the danger, my body doesn't care. My lips stretch into a strange grin.

There is a spirit that hovers above me, always near me—I can feel her cold breath on my skin. She's been with me for five years. But now she's closer than ever. Is she what Layla begged me to give back when she appeared in my invitation to the Path, something that isn't mine, that doesn't belong to me?

I expect to leave my body, to surrender my flesh to Vermillion, like I did when I danced this sequence for the first time, my sister filming it from the shadows. But I remain in my body, in part, with Vermillion directing my movements without completely overtaking me. This sharing doesn't come easy. There's an instinctual resistance. I push and I fight, but it's like hitting a thick rubber wall—it yields just enough to give me hope but it never goes away, not fully.

Together, we dance. Vermillion's icy breath never leaves the back of my neck, her fingers dig into my shoulders.

I'm trapped, living out this experience both as a wispy, stick-legged twelve-year-old and as my current self, while another presence looks out from behind my eyes.

When did I leave the studio?

I'm climbing the stairs. Each step, each leap is artistic, strange. I feel the sleek wood of the railing under my fingers, the firmness of marble under my feet. And though the lobby behind me is empty, it is also filled with people, the guests of the Baron and Adrianna. I hear their murmuring voices, their shuffling feet as they dance, and see their faces hidden behind macabre masks. The Midnight Reverie is in progress, Cashore is alive once more. But it is not my fate to join them, not today. I have a path of my own to travel, and it takes me up, up, up. The stairs, the corridor, then up again. Fast-forward, my mind grasping at the straws, in and out of consciousness.

I'm in the attic.

Trapped in an unnaturally lengthy pirouette that doesn't seem to be slowing down, I notice white smoke rising from the spot where my weight-bearing right foot meets the floor. Just like five years ago. Only this time, the idea of this smoke being a special effect is preposterous. There's nowhere here to hide dry ice. The smoke is coming from me, from below my feet. I'm the otherworldly source of this fog. Did Layla know this then? Something tells she did. My sister kept me in the dark. I hope it was to protect me. I have to believe it. I must.

I no longer feel the floor beneath my feet.

Still rotating, my body levitates. I'm only a few inches off the ground but the shift in gravity rolls over me like a fever. My back craves to bend back, to give in to this ungodly force, to surrender, but there's still some fight left in me. I resist until I regain some feeling, first in my hands, then my legs.

My possessor drops me like I'm a fiery ember. I don't expect it, so when my feet meet the floor, I stagger. A sharp pain shoots through my long-ago injured ankle, and I whimper.

But I don't stop dancing, my body already back to its demonic momentum, picking up where it left off.

I swirl across the attic, ignoring the unsteady feel of the wooden planks against my feet. Gaps between the planks are large enough to fit a finger through.

White smoke claims my vision.

I prepare for the next arabesque. And after that comes the unfortunate sissonne. The one that hurt me, that changed me.

"Please, don't!" I cry out, but I don't know if I'm pleading with myself or with the spirit trapped within me. Both are deaf to my plea.

I jump.

I land on a rotten plank. It disintegrates under me.

I fall.

PART FOUR

The Bargain

Thirty-Seven

I remember falling, but everything—the memory and the now—happens simultaneously. When you die, the meaning of time is lost. Time is an ocean washing over me.

Five years ago, my fall happened so fast. It was furious. Tremendously painful. When I came to, unable to tell how much time had passed or whether I was alive or dead, I saw Layla's face first, leaning over me in the dark, relief carved into her features. Yet my sister also looked like a desperate denizen of the underworld. Everything smelled of blood and dust and chalk, and behind Layla I spied weird symbols drawn on the wall in red and white. The air felt electric, charged by energy that didn't belong in this world.

"It's over," I remember Layla saying. "You're safe now."

At the time, I thought she was referring to the ordeal, my fall through the rafters. Because it was indeed over, I was safe, somewhat unharmed, my injured ankle notwithstanding.

But as I'm falling now, I remember more: what came before I saw Layla's face in the dark.

Like five years ago, it's beginning to feel as if I've been falling forever. And as I fall, Cashore turns itself inside out, morphing into a vortex, hungry, oh so hungry.

When I reach the basement, my feet don't touch the floor but rather hover above it, light as a feather. In the uneven thrall of darkness, the house is transformed. Stripped of color, rendered anew in black and white.

I'm not alone.

Like when I was twelve, having fallen to this place, as my eyes adjust to the dark, shapes moving around me. They whisper. The Baron's guests from the Midnight Reverie—still in their costumes and masks—glide around me, *through* me. Are they ghosts? Some sort of remnants of the living? The soul of Cashore personified, multiplied?

Another memory comes. Or is it reality? Can present already be a memory? Depends on one's point of view.

I float above the floor, the revelers moving around me in an eerily synchronized dance. I'm not in Cashore anymore, and if I'm a ghost, I'm a ghost unlike all the others.

I want to laugh in relief and weep in pity for myself when I see her.

She approaches, like a haunting melody, one chord at a time.

A woman in fiery red, she's the only drop of color in this otherwise colorless room.

She comes—*floats*—toward me across the basement floor, through a corridor formed by the revelers' ghostly bodies. Her attire is a copy of mine; we are one and the same. But no matter how long I look at her, her face remains blurred. The only thing I can tell with certainty is that her eyes are closed tight but her mouth is moving. She says, no longer struggling to speak because this is her kingdom:

"Welcome to Shadow House, Sophia. You are mine."

Once the words are spoken, an unstoppable force actualized as a pair of hands emerges from the floor. Fingers wrap around my ankles and pull. It's the tidal pools all over again. The hands bring me down to the ground, but they don't stop there. The floor becomes textured, sand-like; it feeds on me like a hungry mouth, pulling me inside it one inch at a time.

My last thought is . . .

The Sixth Sign has arrived.

Thirty-Eight

Babies don't remember their own birth, or the time that precedes it; they float in amniotic fluid, in relative calm and quiet. My current state is like that, stuck in the in-between, weightless, and stripped of all physicality. Until I feel this terrible pain in my chest, like my heart is about to explode from pressure. My heartbeat shakes my entire body, speeding up.

Thoughts, strange memories pour into my head. There's too much, their mass threatening to push my own thoughts out.

My mind is still my own. I'm still Sophia Galich, nearly eighteen years of age, most recently of Bakersfield, California. I came to Cashore House of my own volition. I believe my sister is alive, and that a being known as Vermillion has her trapped in this house.

I also know, and this is new, recovered knowledge, that my fall through the rafters five years ago was more than an unlucky accident. It was a trick. A trap. Vermillion's way to claim me as hers.

And she did, for a time. It was in death that I was able to enter the chiaroscuro world of Shadow House, a realm of the dead ruled by Vermillion herself.

I hover over my broken body, watching with cold detachment as Layla cries over me, as she begs the darkness for another chance, for a life. In her moment of despair, my sister doesn't care who listens, who answers her prayer. She spills her blood and makes a pact, seals it with an incantation from the Book of Ka'schor *that she finds in the house.*

When I return, made whole again, all but my injured ankle and a bracelet of half-moon scars around my wrist, my rebirth comes with strings attached.

Vermillion is a part of me. But she wants more—all of me. She wants to live again, to feel again. To leave this house that became her prison.

This new knowledge is poured into me against my will, as some unnatural force squeezes my heart in its unyielding grip. All I can think about is my sister, how after my fall she eventually continued filming, how she obsessively stitched the movie together. Did the red spirit compel her to go on or was she too far gone in her obsession to stop? I will ask her when I find her. If I find her.

I try moving a limb, a finger, anything, to blink, to speak. The fluid matter around me comes to life, threatening suffocation. I force my eyes open, fighting the urge to lower my lids again. I'm suspended in darkness, but there's light too, far away, ahead of me.

When I regain sensation in my right hand, I want to scream in triumph. I wriggle my fingers and stretch my hands sideways, testing the limits of my prison. I meet weak resistance, like pressing against a thin sheet of cellophane stretched tight. I use my nails to claw at it, to tear it to miserable shreds.

I writhe and I growl like a beast, fighting for life. My life. Wild creatures, foxes and wolves, chew off their own limbs when trapped in a steel-jawed foothold. I'm prepared to do the same.

The trap gives. I slide out of my embryonic cocoon and land on my ass, twisting my long-ago injured ankle underneath me. I cry out in pain. *If it hurts, it means I'm alive . . . right?*

It's dark, and the air and everything else here feels different. Dust floats in the air, the objects around me come in muted colors, edges blurred. The monstrous shapes of covered furniture.

"Hello?" I ask weakly as I stand up, keeping the weight off my injured leg.

It's dead quiet. Whenever it's like this, empty and desolate, I suspect that's when the two worlds, that of the dead and that of the living, coexist in the nexus of this house, transitioning from one state to the other and back.

The ankle aside, my entire body hurts. *But I'm alive*, I repeat. *I'm here. And I remember everything.*

Why did Vermillion let me go?

Your Path is not complete, a voice says.

I've always known this, even if took me long to admit: The

Path is Vermillion's way of drawing people to her, to hook them in, fuel their obsession, and then pull them into her lair. A fine sheen of cold sweat coats my skin. It may not be my time yet, but there's a curled unease inside my chest, like a tight spring ready to go off. I've used the Path to get close to my sister, but I've also let Vermillion sink her claws into me, deeper and deeper with each Sign, with each turn of the Path.

But I have my Sixth Sign now. The renewed memory of my fall . . . I ended up in Shadow House then. Which means I've . . . died and returned.

And now there's one Sign left. And then Vermillion will appear before me in earnest. We'll meet properly at last.

The last Sign is known by many names. The Appearance. The Oath. The Deal. The Bargain. How do I know this? Did I have a moment to check CrimsonDreadNet before filming the dance sequence? I can't remember. It doesn't matter anymore.

This might be my only chance to ask Vermillion for something. But what am I prepared to give to the red ghoul in return? Is my life even truly my own to give?

For now, I breathe. I breathe and wait.

My vision adjusts. I'm in Cashore's basement, exactly where Layla once found me five years ago after my original fall. But this time I'm alone, no one is leaning over me, no one is checking my pulse. Aside from the creaking and whispering of an old house, I can't hear a soul.

Stepping lightly, I find the stairs. I climb. I turn the basement's handle expecting resistance, but it gives.

There's no handbook to walking Vermillion's Path. Every single experience is deeply personal, grounded in specific memories, doubts, and fears. I have always feared the rock pools beneath Cashore, have always thought that drowning was the worst death, fearing the moment when my lungs would give out, taking in water. So that's what Vermillion made me experience within the course of my Path. She also took two days of my life and stole my first kiss with Arthur, but who am I to keep score? When I'm possessed, in dark unity with this spirit, I know her restlessness and her anger as if those are my own. I know her thoughts as I know my own, her aches, her wants. I sense she's tired and furious. She wants out. I know this because her thoughts leak into mine, just like mine leak into hers. Whatever she really is now, she used to be alive once. She wants to be alive again. To taste that sweetness of life so many take for granted. Can I really blame her for latching on to me, for tricking my sister into linking our lives forever? A part of me understands Vermillion. Another part is furious with her. When I come close to giving in to the latter, I fear exploding from within. This is the part that fuels me now, pushing me forward.

I return to the real Cashore, at least I think it's real. Here's the lobby, bathed in a late afternoon glow. Somewhere not far from me, a phone rings.

My phone. A tune from the *Vermillion* soundtrack, the disturbing melody I assigned to my sister.

My blood chills but hope soars. I break into a shuffling run, ignoring the people popping up in the periphery—Miriam with her camera, Ivor behind her, others. Even Francesca. There's concern on their faces, but I don't care, I don't stop. For them it's just a movie.

For me it's everything.

My phone keeps ringing.

I must pick up, must answer Layla's call before it's too late. Before my sister slips out of my grasp once more, perhaps for good.

It's time for me to bargain with the dead.

Thirty-Nine

"Sophia! Wait!" Arthur's voice is a disembodied cry somewhere behind me. But I can't let anything hold me back now, not when I'm so close. I increase my speed, crying out softly whenever I put weight on my right ankle.

I don't stop until I reach my bedroom. I scramble for the handle. The phone stops ringing the moment I'm in the room.

"No-o-o-o!" The sound that rips out of me is only part human. The door slams behind me, I dive for my phone, but I'm too late.

I stare at the screen, at the missed call notification from Layla's number.

I wait for the notification to vanish, like everything else does that has anything to do with my sister. But a moment passes and it's still there, as real as the pulsing pain in my leg.

I screenshot the notification. And then there's more. Layla is typing a message, three dots moving in a ripple. I blink and wonder if it's my vision that ripples, but no, the dots are real.

Find me in the dark.

I stare at the words until my eyes water.

Arthur is outside my door, saying my name, but I barely hear him.

Find me in the dark? Really, Layla? That's what you're choosing to tell me when I'm so close to finding you? How about something real, something useful, a hint, a clue?

There's a movement in my periphery. I grow ice-cold, scared to take my eyes away from the phone's screen. But when I do dare look up, there's a shadow stretching from that narrow space between the wardrobe and the wall.

I can barely feel the weight of the phone in my cold hand.

"Do you want me to go there? Into that corner?" I whisper, looking between my phone and the dark space that beckons.

Just as I'm about to move, those little dots begin to move again.

Oh hell no. Not another cryptic message. Enough.

I press to dial Layla's number. Dead or alive, she better pick up.

I hear the ringing; it's coming from somewhere . . . inside the house.

My sister is here. She's always been here.

Phone in hand, I rush outside and slam into Arthur.

"Sophia? What's happening?" He falls in step with me. I don't stop, too scared to lose my trail, worried that the phone will stop ringing. "You blinked out from the cameras," Arthur says. But

I'm only partially comprehending what he is saying to me.

"You hear it too, right?" I ask him, without slowing my pace.

The ringing, it's definitely coming from one of the other rooms up here, on the second floor. I expect to discover its source somewhere in the forbidden west wing, but no.

I come to a stop before a door identical to all the rest. Which member of Erasmus's crew is staying here?

I finally look at Arthur then, for the first time noticing how spooked and pale he looks.

"Whose room is this?" I ask.

He just looks at me, and a strange silence mounts and grows between us until it's too big; too powerful to contain. "Whoever it is has Layla's phone," I say. My heart beats so loud inside my chest that it's a miracle Arthur can even hear my words.

The ringing cuts off suddenly. Someone inside the room mutters something that sounds like relief. A man's voice. Low, but still booming.

Erasmus.

I pound at the door and scream a stream of accusations. Arthur takes a step back, doesn't try to stop me or talk to me. I'm grateful for that.

The door opens a cautious crack revealing Erasmus's freaked-out expression. There must be something terrifying in my face because he flinches.

"How did you get it? Who did you bribe?" I glare at the director, packing all the menace I'm capable of into my voice.

"It's . . . I can explain! This . . ." He chokes on his words.

I smell it, his fear at being caught, this charade ending.

I look away in disgust, turning to Arthur. "Please tell me you didn't know."

He takes too long to reply. Or maybe it's just the world is speeding up around me, and Cashore is expanding into a universe of its own, a bloated star ready to implode. I don't wait for Arthur. I'm too fragile right now to risk hearing him lie.

"I found it in this house!" Erasmus launches into an explanation. "I saw your sister that night and I went after her, but she was already gone. She left her phone behind . . ."

Find me in the dark, my ass.

If Erasmus authored this latest message, does this mean the first one I received, the one that pushed me to walk the Path, was also a fake?

What is even real?

"And you just kept it to yourself?" I shout, wincing at my feral growl. "Used it to get me going? To trick me?"

"I'm not a monster," the director pleads. "I'm doing this to save her. She died on the Path, and I know she's stuck. I must free her."

Arthur winces at his father's words. Erasmus is talking about his wife, Arthur's mother.

"I'm sorry about your wife," I say. "But what does any of this have to do with me?"

"I tried walking the Path, but . . ." Erasmus launches into it before I finish talking. "But then the time came for me to pay the price—getting you into this house was the cost of my progress." He looks away, waiting for the words to sink in.

The shock wave hits me, and I'm instantly filled with rage. Luring me into Cashore was the cost of his Fourth Sign then. I knew that the Path demanded a payment—and that the experience of receiving the Signs was deeply personal—but losing two days to a blackout of possession somehow feels like a different kind of stakes compared to manipulating a teen into reenacting the scariest episodes from her childhood on camera.

"Is this even a real movie?" I hear myself asking. Like Vermillion that I danced with during Midnight Reverie, my mouth becomes stuck; it's an effort to move my lips.

Erasmus's hands fly up in a placating gesture, but I'm done here. He may have progressed on to his next Sign, but I'm still walking my Path. Layla is still lost.

I'm nearly back to my bedroom before I realize I'm moving, leaving Arthur and his lying, manipulating father behind.

I squeeze my head with my hands. I want to scream, but all I manage is a whimper.

"Layla!" I croak. "Layla, if you can hear me. If there's a way to help you, please. Give. Me. A Sign."

In my corroded vision, the room turns red. The walls slant, bending out of shape. This is Escher's reality, with twisting floors and stairwells leading nowhere. Cashore is alive, but it is not life as we know it. It is the life of a building burdened with secrets of both the living and the dead. The building, where all the Paths truly end.

The floor bends into a crooked wave underneath my feet, sending me down on my knees.

"Layla, are you there?" I crawl toward the darkness stretching from the space between the wardrobe and the wall. A faraway echo responds, from a basement, or a crypt.

When I peer into the narrow space, the end of it is so black, smothered in shadows, I can't see where it goes or how far. Maybe it stretches into eternity.

Could this be it, the coming of my final Sign?

Time for me to go deep and claim my dark prize. To meet my elusive possessor and demand my sister back.

I turn sideways and plaster my back against the wall. Facing the side of the wardrobe, I squeeze my way in.

Just like before, it's a tight fit. And when I say *tight*, I mean it; the wardrobe's ungiving wooden surface presses roughly into my chest. With the hard, cold wall behind me, I can only take small, unsatisfying breaths.

It's okay. Calm yourself. Calm.

I move into the dark in tiny, sideways steps. The side of me that faces the echoey darkness feels the gasp of freezing wind.

I have this urge to go back, to extract myself from this tomb-like place before it's too late and I'm sucked in completely. I'm still wearing the *Crimson Queen* outfit. But I can't stop now. I can't risk this passage disappearing.

I take another step. The cold air blowing from the dark brings with it memories. Of Layla and me before we came to Cashore, back when we were just two sisters, fighting and making up, but always caring for one another, no matter what. I don't believe for a second that Layla meant for bad things to happen to me in this house, ever. I know deep down that she vanished because she was trying to fix things. I know it because I know my sister. Cerebral, broody, and surly, but full of love for me. If I'm delusional, I'd rather die like this, believing in the best of Layla, rather than learning something terrible and disappointing about her in the very end.

I'm way farther into the tight, dark corridor than I should be able to go. When I flatten my hands against the wardrobe before me, instead of warm wood, they meet wet stone. It is no longer possible to turn and see the room. I can still sense its light, though it's fading the deeper I go.

I hear something. I tense, clenching my teeth. Am I not alone in here, in this place between darkness and light? There's nothing I can do to protect myself, nothing.

But this presence I'm hearing is not emerging from the dark ahead. It's following me.

"Sophia? Where are you? I can't see . . . Please let me . . ." Arthur's voice, coming from my room. Can he see this corridor, or is its existence for me and me alone?

I'm torn. I remember our pact, the decision to walk the rest of the Path together, but the discovery of Erasmus's betrayal hit me hard. Is Arthur here to steal my final Sign from me? Or is he here to help me? To save me?

I don't need saving.

Though I wouldn't mind some company.

I pull air into my lungs.

"I'm here!" I manage a weak shout in the dark.

But it's enough.

He's closer now. A spark of another life burning bright in the cold depths of this lonely corridor.

"I'm coming!" he shouts back.

I can't see him, but I know he's following in my footsteps.

I continue my progress, with Arthur on my heels, until the tight space starts expanding again, and I can take a proper breath. The familiar scent of the west wing hits me, bringing with it restlessness and anticipation.

Forty

I emerge from the corridor, this secret passage, and . . . reenter my bedroom at Cashore. It's not the same as I left it.

There's a stillness to the space that makes me think of a tomb sealed deep underground, its air carrying the scent of life from a millennium ago.

This smell, the west wing smell, used to frighten me. It's a smell from the past, but also . . . a smell from the grave, from the great beyond, the unknown. I wonder what breathing this air will do to my lungs. Will it change me?

Welcome back to Shadow House.

I've been here before, and more than once, most recently today when I fell through the rafters for the second time in five years. And now I've returned, of my own free will.

I look around.

There are no clothes stretched across the backs of chairs, the bed is made, the coverlet is not one I recognize. Heavy and regal-looking, its fabric shot through with golden thread. But there's one familiar thing: the portrait of Adrianna Kashoroff. It's on the wall, overlooking the bed, just like it was when I returned to Cashore and was shown to my childhood bedroom. Adrianna's eyes follow me. And she's not alone. Next to her is the portrait of the Baron. Has the Baron always been here, right next to his doomed lover? If not together in life, then united in death, in the Shadow House?

I look away from the portraits, my unease growing. This is their place, and I'm sticking out like a drop of blood marring the snow.

The door that connects my bedroom to Layla's is open wide, but there are no signs of any presence other than my own. I keep expecting someone to enter the room, a Shadow House resident. Who are they? What do they want?

I flinch in fright when I hear scuttling behind me, a movement displacing the dead air of the room.

"What is this place?" Arthur's voice enters Shadow House first, followed by the boy himself. Wild-eyed, he looks around. "How did we get here?" When his eyes meet mine, he says, "I swear to you I didn't know he was doing that, that he even had her phone. Please believe me. He's suspicious and doesn't trust anyone, and he's gotten worse. He hasn't been the same since Mom died. His grief has twisted him."

Shadow House absorbs Arthur's words, distorting them into a strange echo.

"I trust you," I say. "But we have other things to worry about." I indicate the room in a broad gesture and watch his face pale as this place sinks in. There's nothing terribly wrong about the things in this room, they are mundane, regular objects, but there's an emptiness here, a hunger. Something watches us. Silky wallpaper ripples, sending an army of black floaters across my vision. Before I blink the confusion away, it's as if the walls have myriad eyes, black dots, unblinking.

"We need to find her. Face her." Arthur sounds way more balanced than I feel. "We need our final Sign. The Confrontation."

The Bargain.

I nod in agreement and offer him a hand, which he takes. I give his cold fingers a reassuring squeeze. I think this time I'm the one grounding him.

He's never been here, in this twisted version of Cashore, never come so close to the world of the dead. But I have, and I escaped it once, though not without giving away a piece of myself as my toll, my payment of coin to Charon. Shadow House has marked me as one of its own. I dig deep, excavating my lost memories of this place.

A scream shudders the hollow silence. Distant, it comes at us from far, far away, but I know it's somewhere in the house.

"That's my sister," I say, filled with this knowledge, its certainty.

I must run to her, leave this room's shaky sanctuary, and give it all I've got. I must run the labyrinth of Shadow House until I find Layla. But Arthur holds me back. He approaches the door with caution, and because our hands are joined, I follow.

There's shuffling noise, a suggestion of movement, and it's coming from right outside the door. This must be the reason for Arthur's sudden tension. He plasters himself against the door and listens. Indeed, there's something out there. Unbreathing but real, as real as things here can get. Some more shuffling. Like someone light and ethereal is passing by or pacing outside.

"Maybe it's Layla," I whisper. In response, Arthur's fingers loosen.

He looks at me. "We should've had this conversation before we came to this place," he says. "But I guess better late than never. How much do you actually know about the people who lived here?"

I rewind my mental tape. "You mean, the new owner of the house? Whoever hired my parents five years ago?"

"No, I mean *before*. Like, the original tenants. The ones who built this place."

I feel a thin drip of cold sweat, one tiny line, tracing a path down my back. Behind me, Adrianna's and the Baron's eyes zero in on me, their attention settling on my shoulders, pressing down.

"Just what's in the public record," I say. "And on Crimson-DreadNet."

He nods, a gesture of encouragement. What is this, a lesson?

"Just come out and say it." I do my best not to snap at him.

"Well, the main hypothesis as to V's creation is that the Baron *dabbled*, right?" he says, unperturbed. I nod, practically sick with impatience. Every V-head out there worth their salt knows this: The Baron von Hahn loved all things occult. *The Book of Ka'schor.* The mirror room. Legend has it, every single one of the Baron's infamous soirees concluded with the summoning circle, guests later reporting speaking in voices and losing chunks of time, their memories . . . And of course, there are stories of the one demon the Baron allegedly managed to summon.

The demon who refused to go back.

"V is the demon, that's what you're saying? But . . ." I don't get to finish the thought because there's a double knock on the door. From the outside.

Someone's out there in the corridor, waiting.

Arthur and I exchange a wild look. For a moment that stretches and stretches, I can't hear anything but the beat of my own heart.

Like moving in water, I step past Arthur to get to the door. His hand captures my shoulder, in warning or encouragement, I can't tell.

The door handle is colder than ice. Fog clouds my vision, but it might be my own breath in this cold, cold space.

I open the door and find Adrianna Kashoroff.

Forty-One

I t's as if she came straight out of the painting over the bed.

Her raven-black hair is parted in the middle and sleeked into a high chignon. Her eyes are blue, glacial. Her lips are unmoving, yet impatient somehow. But instead of some spectacular stage attire one might expect from Adrianna, she is wearing an elegant black dress with gauzy form-fitting sleeves. Her only decoration is a silver brooch in the shape of a swan pinned to her dress's Peter Pan collar.

I suspect it's only for a fraction of a second that she and I stand like this, staring, but it feels longer, as long as a life. I brace for something, a supernatural assault, some scary transformation to mar Adrianna's features. She died young after all, and tragically. They never found her body. What really happened to her?

I suspect she can read my mind. She raises her left arm, the movement as ethereal as a slow-motion unfurling of a wing, and places it on my right shoulder. Somewhere behind me, Arthur protests, but I'm already being whisked away from here, into another time, another life.

Adrianna may be a silent ghost, but she definitely has a lot to say.

Her light touch sends a stream of images into my head. Her life unfolds before my eyes, as if I'm the one living it, inhabiting the world in her skin.

Here is Adrianna, young and talented, falling in love with the dashing, enigmatic Baron. She: an artist. He: powerful and compelling.

There's a wedding, a glittering affair. After their honeymoon tour in Europe, Adrianna tells him she wants to keep dancing, but her new husband wants her all to himself, in this house he built for her, named after her. In his bed, at his parties. She misses ballet but she loves him too. She chooses him, but it costs her. A part of her withers away.

Deprived of a stage, she dances in the house. In the studio the Baron built for her, in the corridors, out on the patio that hangs precariously over a cliff. Adrianna dances like she is possessed— repeating over and over the main sequences from her beloved ballet, *The Crimson Queen*. She remembers the steps with her eyes closed. Sometimes she wears the red dress.

But the Baron wants more, he wants other things, all of it, all of her. And he fears things too. Losing Adrianna. Losing his wealth and power. Dying.

He seeks to overcome his fear of mortality with his occult sessions. Séances, invocations, esoteric prayers, the Baron uses all of it as he reaches out to the other world for answers. For *the Cure*, he calls it, as if aging is a disease.

He invites the best mediums and psychics of the time to Cashore, beseeching them to bring forth an entity that can give him what he wants. He doesn't stop until one of them does. When, draped in black and smelling of dried roses, Lady Beverly Parschalli arrives to Cashore, she brings with her a well-read copy of the *Book of Ka'schor*. The name of the book intrigues the Baron—it echoes his wife's family name, and perhaps it's fate.

"We'll bring forth Ka'schor himself, the god, the demon, the granter of wishes," Lady Parschalli promises.

The Baron cuts her a generous check.

The olden ways of his ancestors appeal to the Baron. After all, he claims to be a relation of Madame Blavatsky herself, tracing his lineage to Wolgadeutsche nobility. Magic is his birthright, he truly believes it.

But when the medium summons the being, it is something beyond human understanding.

This, this *thing*, makes many promises as it settles into Cashore, feeding on its warmth and its liveliness, merging with shadows and tainting its windows. This being, whatever it really is, is pure rot, decay. But to the Baron, it promises life eternal.

The time comes to settle the bill. The creature that calls itself

Ka'schor refuses to leave. It cries and roars and shakes the earth on which the house stands. Adrianna fights it, but it drags her to the patio, and then . . .

The earthquake. The patio's collapse. Adrianna's fall.

The stream of images in my head ceases, leaving me bereft, out of balance.

As I return to my own body, into my own head, I find Arthur facing me, holding me by the shoulders and saying my name. When I blink, his relief is palpable.

"I'm sorry . . ." I say to Adrianna's ghost, my voice weak, uncertain.

Still, her story feels incomplete; there are gaps in her memory too, or there are things she holds back. As for the things she did show me—I believe those were true. There was really a demon, an entity that held Cashore in its grip. Shadow House was its domain, or perhaps the consequence of the entity's existence. "I'm sorry," I repeat, finding my voice.

I force myself to stare directly into Adrianna's eyes, a big no-no according to *Vermillion*'s mythology. "What happened to you was awful. But I need to find my sister, Layla. Do you know where she is?"

When I think she isn't going to answer me at all, Adrianna moves from her spot and retreats from the door. In her true undead ballerina fashion, she doesn't walk but floats above the floor, the back of her dress trailing behind her like black fog.

"I think we should follow," I say to Arthur. He nods, though there's a hint of hesitation in his movement.

We leave the room and follow the ghost.

I hope she's leading me to my sister, and not to my death.

With Adrianna in the lead, Arthur and I traverse the length of the corridor and proceed to the west wing. I keep my eyes in front of me, too unsettled to study my surroundings. But even without looking I know Shadow House only appears empty. Its darker corners are alive, like black-and-white static squirming inside a TV screen, like octopus tentacles writhing in the dark. The walls' eyes, unblinking, follow our progress.

There are people here too. Not fully fleshed out, they are like sketches, or long-ago actors partially erased from deteriorating video tapes. Some wear masks and odd, unsettling makeup that surely came from the Baron's Preparation Room. Others are dressed like stage characters, possibly from *The Crimson Queen.*

And then there's a third kind of Shadow House denizen: people without stage makeup, many of them young, in modern clothes. Most would pass for a regular person I'd see on the street. Whenever my eyes wander, and I make a mistake of looking at them too closely, it is these regular people who appear the most desperate. They are also the most fleshed out, not as erased as those from a century ago.

What really happens to people who complete the Path and get to face Vermillion in the end? They have a chance to make a bargain, that much I know, but what if they fail? What if Vermillion wins and they end up under her control, in this place, Shadow House?

One of them, a young woman, in skinny jeans and a pink hoodie, reaches for me, her wispy fingers curling around my wrist, leaving no imprint. When I make a mistake of looking at her, I nearly drown in her haunted eyes. Her mouth shapes into a silent shape: HELP.

"I can't!" I shout, moving away. What *can* I do? How can I save them all?

Turning to Arthur, I find him studying the faces of these beings, desperate determination on his face. Sadness too. He looks so sad that it affects me as well. I don't need to ask him what he's thinking, who he's hoping to find in this crowd of ghosts. He's looking for his mother.

We've been walking for hours, or at least it feels that way. Is Adrianna taking us in circles?

"I need to find Layla. Please take me to her!" I plead with our silent guide, and my voice is like thunder in this muted place.

Ahead of us Adrianna flinches, some powerful emotion ripping through her. The reality glitches and fast-forwards, expelling us outside, to the patio.

Catching my breath, I blink in disbelief.

The patio is the last tangible piece of Shadow House that I can see and feel. Beyond it: nothing. Just a wall of black, like that of the inkiest night. No matter how long I stare into this darkness, waiting for my eyes to adjust, there are no shapes, nothing there to discern. Being this close to emptiness shakes me to my core. If I'm to survive this experience, if I'm to return to the light, I know I'll never stop dreaming of this darkness, not until my time comes to face it again. For good.

I look for Arthur.

I've let go of his hand. I panic when I don't see him near me at first but . . . there he is. At the far corner of the patio, to my left.

He's not alone.

Arthur is talking, all in hushed tones, with one of those partially-erased beings. I watch as this being, a woman in her mid-forties perhaps, stretches a see through hand to touch Arthur's face. Can he feel it? He must, because the contact transforms his expression, bringing out one of those genuine smiles that warms up the place. The moment I make the connection, I see the resemblance between them. Their features, a mouth that wants to grin, clever eyes. Arthur's mom, she's been stuck here. But is Shadow House a trap or a final destination?

A weak voice, barely a whisper, says my name. The sound comes from behind me, but only a few seconds ago, there was nothing there, only inky darkness. I turn around slowly, just as my name is spoken again. I know that voice.

I see her then. My sister.

She's sitting on the cement floor, just a few feet away, her head hanging low. Black hair. Jeans torn at the knees. Green and black lumberjack shirt. Feet, bare. Layla's casual at-home style. Was this what she was wearing the day she left her dorm room, got into her car, and drove all the way here?

I say her name. Call her. And my voice is like the water of life; it revives her. Layla.

She lifts her head, blows her hair away from her face. Her eyes are on me, disbelieving. Instead of relief at seeing her, finding her at last, my insides fill with dread.

"Sophia, is that you?" My sister's voice. "No, no, no, it's not real, not real . . ."

I run to her, she's so close, but the patio expands underneath me, my feet sink into cement. What is this nightmare? And why can't I just get to Layla?

Finally, I get close, as if by sheer force of will.

I kneel by her side. Go in for a hug.

It hurts me worse than any ghost can when she pushes me away. "You shouldn't have come."

She cries.

Forty-Two

"I made a deal, I made a deal," my sister moans, repeats, her voice recognizable one moment, then distorted by static the next. Tears run down her cheeks.

I reach for her, desperate for proof of her solidity. When my fingers take hold of her, tears burn my eyes from the inside. Warmth seeps through Layla's clothes. Alive! She's alive! And though all the old anger and frustration uncoil within me, all I want, more than anything, is to hug her.

But first I need to get her out of this place before it devours us both. If Layla's been here for the past two years, it's a miracle she's not like those half-shadows, wandering these halls unaware.

"Can you walk? Can you stand up?" The words come in a rush. "We have to get out before the door closes."

I have no idea where I'm getting this from, perhaps it's leftover from the trove of information Adrianna Kashoroff transmitted into my head with a touch. Shadow House is unstable, it plays by its own rules, it changes things. This, I know.

I attempt to pull her up, but she's like a marionette without strings. Limp and loose, I can't carry her, and Arthur is no help. I see him in the periphery, his hands joined with those of his mother. Can he feel her touch? I hope he can, and I hope the contact gives them both closure.

But now I have my own closure to worry about.

"Layla, you have to try," I beg.

She nods; she understands.

When I manage to get her semi-vertical, she freezes in my grasp. With her head resting on my shoulder, she has a direct view of whatever is going on behind my back. I freeze with Layla. We're out of time.

I feel someone, *something*, approach. I know it's not Arthur.

It's like I'm standing with my back to an open freezer.

Here's that displacement of air again, a barely-there sensation of a being that doesn't need to breathe but manages to exist nonetheless.

With Layla clinging to me, I'm too chicken to face whatever it is head-on. My body wants to give up, even with Layla in my grasp, as if I've been running on fumes up until this point.

"*No, no, no, no, no,*" Layla whispers obsessively into my hair. "Leave her out of this. We had a deal. We had a deal. We. Had. A. Deal."

I reclaim some control over my body. I force myself to turn, and then I see.

I see her feet first.

How odd that a terrifying spirit that haunts this house and my life has such human-looking feet. Thin ankles. Crooked toes. Discolored nails. A dancer's feet.

As I look up, the rest of her comes into focus.

On the surface, she's still Adrianna Kashoroff. Elegant, clad in shimmering black, alert. Human. But she's trapped inside a flaming cage; violent red flames surround her in a deadly embrace. She tips her head back and burns, the transformation lifting her off the ground. Change vibrates through her.

When her feet touch the floor again, Adrianna is gone. What's left is only darkness. A thing of evil looking out into the world.

Vermillion is here, just as I remember her from Layla's movie.

The Baron's demon: the one who was summoned, refused to go back, and who is now stuck in between.

And now this entity, desperate for another chance, another body to take over after its botched possession of Adrianna, is here again.

"Adrianna!" I cry out, still nurturing the hope of bringing back the ballerina. "You have to fight this. Please, please fight this."

Next to me, Layla grows silent. But her fingers dig painfully into my wrist. The same one Vermillion scarred five years ago when the demonic spirit grabbed me and wouldn't let go. Until my sister made her. That I'm sure of. Because that's why Layla's here. As some punishment she bargained to save me from this ghoul. Did she come back to Cashore that fateful night because her payment was due? Was she out of ways to avoid the fate that was dogging her after she brought me back from the dead?

The time for pleas is over.

Vermillion, fully formed, rushes at me, hands outstretched. She hits me square in the chest, sharp fingers digging in.

And it hurts, it burns.

Our connection is pure pain and hellish fire, and I get the rest of Adrianna's story through this torment. The missing pieces she couldn't share.

She was the collateral damage, the bargain made and lost to the Baron's desire for immortal life. The demon the Baron summoned tricked him, but Adrianna paid the price. As the patio cracked underneath her feet, sending her to her death, the Baron was left alone. Suddenly, without his beloved, he was begging the entity to bring his lover back instead of wanting to live forever. The demon obliged. But when Adrianna returned, she was only half alive. The demon possessed her in payment. So, Vermillion was born, an entity stripped of memories and identity. A thing that didn't remember itself and only knew hunger and rage.

Kids don't usually fare that well in horror movies. They're always first to experience the terror that lurks in the dark, but nobody believes them. And then it's too late, because it's the parents who are succumbing to the terrible evil that dwells in the basement, or the attic, or the walls. Mom is possessed! Dad's out to get you with an axe! And I don't even want to think of those poor house pets, the fate that awaits them.

But when the terror is over, or when the viewer thinks it is, we almost never get a glimpse of what those traumatized kids have in store for them. Years of therapy, nightmares, and suppressed memories popping up in the most inopportune moments. What of the actors who played them?

Whenever I think back to my experiences filming *Vermillion* with my sister, it is Layla's explanations that I remember the most. *It's not real*, she'd say whenever my eyes filled with tears. *It's a special effect.*

That noise did not come from the dark corner behind the wardrobe.

It was a nightmare, Sophia, you dreamed it.

Even now, I cling to those words. But I also know that my sister lied to me. To protect me. Maybe I'm a fool, but I believe it, one hundred percent. Otherwise, what was Layla doing in this house the night she went missing if not trying to set things right, to bargain with the demon who was going to claim my life but who claimed hers instead?

As Vermillion, the entity who became the unwitting antagonist of Layla's movie, has her ice-cold hands deep inside my chest, my recovered memories from five years ago rattle through my mind.

Everything that happened in Cashore House five years ago was real.

The haunting was real.

My terror and my nightmarish encounters, real.

Whether my family's arrival and subsequent restoration work reawakened the slumbering demon or not, Layla happened to be there, ready, her little camera rolling. And I happened to be there too, my unguarded reactions there for the taking. But remembering the terror on my sister's face, the evidence of fear as she hid in the corner with her camera, tells me she lied to protect me from the truth. She said she set it all up, that she controlled everything, and that I was safe. But then the unthinkable happened.

When I fell through the rotted rafters, I didn't just hurt myself. I died.

Was that Vermillion's doing or just an unfortunate accident? I'm still not sure.

With Vermillion's cold, cold hands moving things inside my chest now, contaminating my bloodstream, some things are made suddenly clear, and some less so.

Possession spreads through me like wildfire. It burns, it cauterizes life.

A different kind of movie is playing out in my head as Vermillion-the-demon takes hold, a new sequence of recovered memories. Things that took place immediately after my fatal fall five years ago. Before today, what I remember was a brief flash of pain, then a fade to black. But where I really went for a time was Shadow House. The limbo, the in-between, a place no longer here but not yet there.

Through our painful connection, I get a glimpse of Vermillion's frustration from that day. She nearly had me. I was lost, but my sister wouldn't allow it. After finding my body, she invoked the entity of the house, and just like it did in response to the Baron's summoning more than a century ago, it came to Layla.

Drenched in red. The demon, the being, the *thing*.

And just like with the Baron, the entity tricked my sister.

It brought me back, but it slapped Layla with a bill she couldn't afford to pay.

I was to become Vermillion's vessel.

But real possessions take time.

For years, I was oblivious. But now as I think back, in retrospect, I've always known. I could feel it, this piece of Vermillion dwelling inside of me, her anchor. The piece that is now strong enough to take hold of me and hold on forever, for as long as I breathe.

With Vermillion's hands deep in my chest, I begin losing myself to another blackout, one from which I may not return.

I hear Arthur's voice—what is he saying? It's like he's behind a rippling cascade of water or separated from me by glass.

I hear music, the familiar notes of a famous *pas seul* from *The Crimson Queen*. When the music starts, Vermillion's claws inside me loosen, just a bit. The horrific stream of demonic consciousness ceases in my head.

This music is the beginning of the Dance of the Unquiet Spirits, slow and cautious at first, before soaring into the wild bacchanal of movement, turning frantic in the end. This music has always triggered something in me, made me uneasy on the most primal level of being. But now, the complex melody is all that keeps me grounded within my own body. It's coming from Arthur, or rather from his phone, which he's raised to the entity's eye level. How is Arthur's phone even working here?

I dare to seek out the spirit's gaze. For a flickering moment, Adrianna appears. Her eyes come alive, an ember of her soul refusing to die, bringing life to this washed-out corpse before me. Adrianna's eyes follow the movement on the screen of Arthur's phone where the assembled footage of the ballet that made Adrianna a star is playing out to the haunting score.

"Remember yourself," I let out, struggling to speak, our connection muddling my thoughts. The entity's face is unreadable, but there are red tears making wet paths across its cheeks. Adrianna.

Abruptly, the entity's hands retreat fully, letting me go, and leaving me fighting for balance.

Layla catches me before I fall.

"What do you think you're doing?" she asks, voice flat.

"Saving you!" *Isn't it obvious?*

"But who's going to save you this time?" Her words are a pained murmur.

"I didn't think of that," I whisper back.

I'm too afraid to move, to break Vermillion's fragile trance.

"When I tried to save you, this is where it got me," Layla says. "I bet you don't even remember when she took hold of me that night and made me come all the way here from the dorms."

My insides turn cold. Layla is talking about the night she vanished.

That photo of us, in the park. The photo I don't remember being taken. In it, Layla held the *Book of Ka'schor*. Later, when the police described the scene of my sister's disappearance, they said her dorm room was filled with occult implements.

Layla was trying to summon the entity of Cashore, her last attempt to save me before the possession could fully take hold. Was I there with her when she attempted the summoning? Regardless, whatever Layla tried to do backfired in a major way. Vermillion took control of *her*, made her come here, enter the house, and be devoured.

"We have a lot to talk about once we get out of here," I whisper to my sister.

If we get out.

The music stops.

I look from my sister to Vermillion just in time to see the demon return. Its eyes are back on me, its tears dried. It snarls, giving me a terrible view of its rotting teeth. But Adrianna fights it, her face flickering back and forth, features trying to settle, to take control. My only hope is that she will prevail.

If not, we're all screwed.

I can only imagine the headlines when this news breaks: *Sophia Galich Disappears from Cashore House While Filming a Tribute to Her Vanished Sister.*

I can't do this to our parents. And I won't have Arthur's death on my hands.

I have to help Adrianna, fight the demon she has become. I have to do something.

"Play it again!" I shout to Arthur. Shadow House tries swallowing the sound, but Arthur must understand my intent.

The video starts again, that familiar music, tentative in the beginning.

"Vermillion, let's make a deal," I say.

The thing snarls at me, its hands reach for me again. It wants to restore our unnatural connection, to regain its control over me. My sore chest throbs in anticipation.

"Don't you want to be free of these chains, of this trap?" I ask.

A violent gasp of wind slams at me. Shadow House is shivering, shaken down to the core. Like a terrible special effect, the reality wavers around me, a gauzy curtain moving in the wind.

It seems I've got Vermillion's attention. It waits, dirty fingers lingering, not burying themselves into my chest. Not yet.

"What if you could leave here for good?" My words rush out; I'm afraid that if I stop speaking, the demon will change its mind. "Isn't it clear by now that you can never fully possess anyone? Bodies are imperfect, they fight, they suffer, the merging can never be complete. What if I can help Adrianna remember herself? That way you'll be able to untether yourself from her?"

I'm partially bluffing here—I don't know if this plan will work. My plea is part desperation, part instinct. Am I getting through to Vermillion? Is freedom what it wants, or have I grossly miscalculated the intent of its demonic desires? Those who tried to make deals with Cashore's demon have failed before me, the Baron first, then my sister. And every single faded soul here, trapped in Shadow House. But what do I have to lose if I don't try? Only myself.

I wait for a perfect moment in the flow of music from *The Crimson Queen* to stand en pointe. As a child, I dreamed of being a ballerina; this might be my last chance to dance.

Sore tendons stretching, my ankle hurts like never before. My neck creaks when I move it. My hands are not fully my own.

But I'm at the end of the Path, and I've made my wish. Now the only thing left to do is dance.

So that's what I do.

Forty-Three

Even when we begin to forget, we remember.

I remember the dance, the all-consuming trance of it. The falling in sync with Adrianna and the entity that latched on to her more than a century ago. The three of us know the steps, *The Crimson Queen* being the only thing that united us, aside from our desire to be free.

Before I can completely lose myself to the dance, I have half a mind to scream at my sister and Arthur to get out, to leave Shadow House and not look back. I don't know if they listened. I hope they did, because I can't stop now, my feet carrying me back into the house, to the place where it all began.

Landscape changes around me, losing shape. Shadow House convulses, its walls crumbling, starting to collapse on themselves, white dust raining down from the ceiling, blinding me. Could this impending collapse be the sign that the deal with Vermillion is working in my favor? Because Shadow House, the stronghold of the Baron's demon that exists in the reflection of Cashore, is coming apart.

Everything hurts, but I keep going. I must.

I blink and I'm up in the attic, with no recollection of how I got here. Am I in the movie, or is this real? Is Miriam filming this? Is Layla? Does it matter?

Will I fall through the rotten rafters for the third and final time, to my doom, or will I wake up, before it's too late?

My mind is not entirely my own. I proceed deeper into the attic, unsteady planks creaking underneath me. There's no more music, only my terrified breathing.

"Sophia! Come back!"

I know that voice.

A warm hand lands on my wrist like a brand of fiery iron. A touch shouldn't hurt this much. A scream erupts from within me and wakes me up.

I'm on the precipice. About to twist and leap and land on that fateful piece of rotten wood again.

Arthur stops me, he pulls me back.

"I think it worked," he says. "What you did worked! But we have to run. Now."

"Where is my sister?" I whisper.

"I'm right here," Layla says from behind Arthur. Her impatient eyes burn, and their fire exorcises the rest of my trance.

"Your mom?" I ask Arthur, but he's shaking his head.

"We've said our goodbyes," he says. "At least, I have that."

Arthur leads me out of the attic. Wooden planks break and collapse behind us.

Chased by dark silhouettes, we run. As Shadow House dies, the inhabitants of this place are fleeing their trap. I hope Adrianna is among them. I hope I've liberated her too.

We make it back to the tight corridor in my bedroom and squeeze inside it, one by one.

The way out of here is longer than the way in. The tunnel has shrunk. It wants to keep us, but our collective will is stronger.

I'm the last to leave the corridor and emerge on the other side. When I find my breath again, and my eyes adjust to the weak late afternoon light, I see that we're not alone. Erasmus is here. His bewildered eyes are locked on my sister.

"You're alive," he says. "I saw you enter this house and then you were gone."

Layla stares him down before shifting her attention to the object in his hands. It's a phone. Her phone. The phone used to manipulate me. I don't know what conclusions Layla makes or whether she even knows who Erasmus is, but if her eyes could kill, the director would be bleeding at her feet.

"I'd like my phone back. Now." She reaches for it. Erasmus gives it up without a fight.

My sister is back.

Forty-Four

The moment we emerge from the corridor between the worlds, the dusty portal collapses behind us.

Cashore shakes, dust raining from above, as a solitary crack forms across the ceiling. I can hear them—the trapped souls roaring as they are released. Without the hungry demon to hold them in their prison, they can move on. At least, I hope that's the plan.

I hope Cashore will be given another chance at life. This place has been through so much, it deserves to hear laughter again, to watch its residents sleep peacefully at night.

"An earthquake!" Erasmus shouts against the rattling of walls. But there's nowhere to hide.

The moment the words leave his mouth, the shaking stops. I exchange a glance with Arthur. I bet he's thinking what I'm thinking: that was no earthquake but an aftershock from Shadow House's destruction.

All is quiet now, too quiet.

My sister stares at the unlocked screen of her phone like it contains all the wonders of the universe. She browses her contact list, fingers moving in a sluggish way that suggests they've become unused to the shape of the device.

"Who are you calling?" I ask. I expect Layla to disappear any moment. But she's still here, solid and edgy.

"Mom and Dad."

The words hit me with too much force. I've been masterfully avoiding thinking about our parents, but I knew this moment was coming. Of course, Layla would want to talk to them, to hear their voices. But that also means the end of my charade. I try calculating how much trouble I'm in and conclude that it's a lot.

Layla ignores me, staring hopefully at the dialing phone.

"This is a family-only meeting," Layla drops as an afterthought, barely even sparing a glance in the direction of Erasmus and Arthur.

The director, still appearing shell-shocked, doesn't need to be told twice. He heads for the door and doesn't look back. We'll deal with him later. The police might want to hear about him taking possession of a missing young woman's phone and using it to trick her underage sister. That kind of stuff is a career killer, I bet. Although oddly, I don't even feel that vengeful toward Erasmus. Maybe my ordeal in Shadow House drained me of rage and fear, or maybe there's a part of me that's secretly grateful. Erasmus brought me closer to my sister.

On his way out, Arthur meets my eyes, and we exchange a half smile. His hand brushes against mine. I watch the door close behind him.

Put on speaker, Layla's phone rings loudly, not going into voicemail. I picture our mother, shaking, pale in shock, as she stares at her missing daughter's caller ID.

The phone connects, someone picks up.

"Yes?" Mom's voice packs everything I imagine she's feeling in this moment. Disbelief, rage that someone's playing a cruel joke, wild hope.

"Mom, it's me," Layla says, her voice unstable but unmistakably hers. "I'm back."

A pause stretches. I begin to wonder if Mom's still there. When she begins crying—loud, unrestrained sobs—I sense the power of her relief, the exhilaration of it.

The rest of the conversation is barely coherent. Our father joins in a few seconds later, adding his own subdued cries to the mix. Mom's questions to Layla ring in my ears—*Where have you been? What happened? Can we come and get you now?*—and I brace for my sister's response.

"I-I don't remember anything." Layla's eyes meet mine and don't let go. "I'm in Cashore House, in Livadia. Sophia is with me. She's safe, we both are. She's the one who found me."

As our parents speak at the same time on the other end of the line, Layla holds the phone away and reaches for me. I wrap my hands around her and press my forehead to hers, inhaling a lungful of her scent. Underneath that lingering smell of Shadow House, dust and dried blood, Layla smells the way I remember. Of forest after the rain, of wilderness.

We've never done this before, hug like this. The gesture feels both organic and too intimate. Even in my most private memory of Layla, that moment five years ago after she brought me back to life following my fatal fall through the rafters, I didn't feel this close to her. Now, we're equals, sharing a secret, a bond, a covenant.

"Thank you," Layla says, barely a whisper but in my ears it's as loud as the oceanic roar. "You brought me back to life."

"I guess that makes us even." I say in a lighthearted way, though I feel anything but.

I don't know how long we stand there, in the middle of my old bedroom in a house that used to be haunted, but when we untangle, the silver evening gloom spreads across the sky.

I have found my sister, but the outside world is still the same. Same air, same ocean. The town of Livadia goes on with life, unaware of what went down in the house on the cliff.

Forty-Five

FIVE DAYS LATER

Days that follow blur as we transition back into the world of the living, where time moves like a river and air tastes of sunshine. For me, this is a period of wild emotions. There's deliriously happy relief—my sister is back. I made it happen. I won. But then, an afterthought—is this really it? We're free to go, just like that?

In the hours that it takes our parents to drive to Livadia, two important conversations take place in Cashore House. One involves Layla, Arthur, and me. We agree to keep our time in Shadow House a secret. No one would believe what happened to us anyway—only diehard V-heads. Layla is sticking to her shock and amnesia story. Dr. Patel seems unconcerned after she checks my sister's vitals and has a private chat with her. But I suspect this is only the beginning of Layla's journey as far as doctors and psychologists are concerned. Given her fame, there's also the added complication of whatever stories are going to be told by the media. But we'll worry about that when it happens.

The second conversation involves Erasmus and my sister. As they talk, I'm in the room with them and my role is to make sure Erasmus comes completely clean, that he doesn't keep information from Layla. The director seems genuinely apologetic—he didn't mean to take the phone, etc.—but I don't trust him, and I don't think Layla does either. Erasmus really fancies himself a magician, I think. Someone who wants to know the workings of the world beyond the veil. His persisting grief for his late wife is at odds with this sinister intent and general self-aggrandizing. He has questions for us too, about where we went, what we saw. He doesn't ask about his wife, but I can read the question from the terse silences between his words. Maybe Arthur will share his Shadow House experience with his father. It is not my place to insert myself into this family drama. I have enough of my own.

Our parents arrive at night and insist on checking us into a hotel with them. My parting with Cashore is abrupt, I don't even have enough time to pack up. Mom says we'll come back later for my things, but I know when the time comes, she'll try her hardest to keep me away from that house. My parents have suffered in the two years Layla was missing—I've seen their pain, witnessed their grief—but I can only guess at their experience five years ago when we lived in this house as a family. Do adults see ghosts too? Do those ghosts take the same shapes as perceived by children?

Arthur comes to see me in the hotel the next day. My parents reluctantly let me go with him. Layla wiggles her eyebrows at me and makes a ridiculous kissy face when our mother is not looking. Arthur drives us to that same beachside café, where we shared out first kiss—or second, depending on perspective. We barely talk, just sip iced coffee while staring at the ocean.

Our time spent in Shadow House was mercifully short, but still, we are shaken to the core. It'll take time for us to recover, to regain our vitality. I hope those images of dead spaces, of souls in agony will fade from my mind. I also hope I'll never forget.

Layla is a different story. My sister is . . . not the same. She can't stand the dark, can only sleep with a nightlight. Our roles have reversed, and I'm now the mature, older sibling, looking after her, sitting by her side until she falls into a fitful sleep.

Is there a support group specifically for kids who survive haunted houses?

Later, when I'm alone for the first time in ages, I grab my laptop and navigate to CrimsonDreadNet. The site takes time to load, as if it's debating whether I should be admitted now that I've been to the other side and back. But eventually it lets me in. Nearly all the threads have been updated multiple times since the news of Layla Galich's return rocked the V-head community.

__LookingForLayla has been updated most recently. How can the site already know about my sister's return?

When I click on the thread, the most recent post is a screenshot of some obscure news blog, no URL provided.

Missing Cult Filmmaker Returns?

Fans of Vermillion rejoice as Layla Galich returns after mysteriously vanishing two years ago. What happened and where was she all this time? . . .

More questions and speculations follow. I wouldn't be surprised if the post disappears the moment I look away from the screen. CrimsonDreadNet plays by its own rules. Perhaps Vermillion herself, wherever she is now, is still pulling the digital strings.

I hover over the __OnThePath link next, but something holds me back. Call it self-preservation instinct. Or maybe I've become so oversaturated with everything related to the Path that I can't stomach another bite. By the time I make myself click on the link, the site has logged me out. The site's ghostly authority must know that this particular Path is now completed, even if I never got to write my last post.

As I close my laptop, a feeling of forgetting forms in my chest, a small gap where a memory is supposed to be. As the feeling spreads, I become uneasy. Mom and Dad were swift in getting

Layla and me out of Cashore, so it's probably just me worrying about my things I had to leave behind. Why then do I feel like I've left a hair straightener on—the kind that doesn't know when to turn itself off, the kind that burns the house down?

I've heard somewhere that the best way to recover a lost memory is not to think about it, to forget that I've forgotten. As a distraction, I pick up my phone and scroll through recent messages and videos. The camera folder that used to contain little souvenirs Vermillion left for me, evidence of her taking control of my body, has no footage from my time in the house. The most recent video is something I've filmed weeks before returning to Cashore—an abruptly-ended attempt at a video essay for a college application. Maybe I can pick up where I've left off, finish my application, go to college.

Whatever it is I think I forgot will come back to me, I'm sure. For now, the ghosts in my blood have calmed enough and I can hear myself again. It's a lovely sound.

Epilogue

Localized Earthquake Damages Historical Cashore House

A mysterious 3.7 magnitude earthquake hit the Californian town of Livadia yesterday. Residents reported minor tremors, but there was no serious damage except for the external patio of the historical Cashore House, which developed a crack. Restoration work is scheduled. Baron von Hahn built the allegedly haunted Cashore for his ballerina-wife Adrianna at the turn of the twentieth century. At its height, it attracted many famous artists, writers, and spiritualists, including the famed medium Lady Beverly Parschalli. Most recently, Cashore was made famous as the set for *Vermillion* (dir. Layla Galich). For the past few weeks, Cashore hosted the production of Erasmus Sawyer's new documentary *Vermillion: The Return*. The earthquake did not injure anyone on set.

LAYLA GALICH, CREATIVE FORCE BEHIND CULT SENSATION *VERMILLION,* IS WRITING HER NEXT FILM

Catapulted to fame at seventeen, Layla Galich has recently returned after a mysterious two-year absence. Fan theories abound as to her whereabouts during this time. Our sources confirm that the famed filmmaker is already busy with her next project. It is not yet known whether this new work will be a sequel to Galich's debut horror feature *Vermillion* or whether her younger sister Sophia will resume the role that made *Vermillion* so popular with its dedicated viewers. [Story continues on page 7]

LARA CASHORE, SOLE DESCENDANT OF THE FAMED BALLERINA ADRIANNA KASHOROFF, VISITS THE SET OF *VERMILLION: THE RETURN*

Several photographs leaked yesterday show Lara Cashore, the sole descendant of Russian American prima ballerina Adrianna Kashoroff, on the set of Erasmus Sawyer's new documentary. Sawyer's experimental feature titled *Vermillion: The Return* was filmed in Cashore House (Livadia, California), where more than a century ago, Adrianna died in an earthquake. Cashore was also the set for Layla Galich's cult debut feature *Vermillion*, which drew on the lore surrounding Adrianna and the demonic entity her husband allegedly summoned. New property owner Lara Cashore says she and her wife plan to transform Cashore into a museum dedicated to Adrianna's legacy. Photographed with the director, the crew, and sisters Sophia and Layla Galich, Lara Cashore (in the center) is shown wearing a vintage red dress belonging to Adrianna; the resemblance to her famous ancestor is uncanny.

ERASMUS SAWYER TO SHARE DIRECTOR CREDIT WITH LAYLA GALICH IN *VERMILLION: THE RETURN,* A DOCUMENTARY STARRING GALICH'S SISTER

In a statement posted today on his website, award-winning director Erasmus Sawyer revealed he will share directorial credit for his new documentary with Layla Galich. Sawyer's documentary—which reenacts key scenes of Ms. Galich's debut horror masterpiece *Vermillion*—stars her younger sister Sophia. [Story continues on page 2]

CRIMSONDREADNET@__ONTHEPATH*

Sophia stares directly at the camera. She is outside, her hair moves gently in the wind. A blue patch of the ocean can be seen behind her, a shade lighter than the gunmetal sky. The camera drifts away from Sophia's face, taking in the view and the shift reveals the location as the partially collapsed patio of Cashore House. The railing is gone, the stone floor of the patio tapers straight off into a drop. The camera shakes.

"I win," Sophia says, back in the view. "It's over."

"Hey. I was looking everywhere for you," someone says off camera. "I don't think it's a good idea to be here. The patio is unstable."

"I'm not going too far. Come here," Sophia replies.

There are light steps, followed by another shift in perspective.

The camera is now stabilized, facing Sophia and Arthur. They are standing close, her hands resting on his shoulders. "Thank you . . . I'm—" Sophia starts to say, but the rest of her words and Arthur's reply get lost in the sudden gust of wind. They share a smile.

"Do you hear it?" Sophia asks. Arthur shakes his head. "I swear I can still hear the score of *The Crimson Queen*. It's worse than an earworm. Can a sound haunt you?"

The response is inaudible. Arthur kisses her. Sophia closes her eyes.

Right before the recording ends, both Sophia and Arthur look directly at the camera for a split second. In a certain slant of light, Sophia's eyes appear to go completely black.

End of recording.

This video recording was uploaded on the fan site Crimson-DreadNet, where it remained for less than an hour. The video had no time stamp, and comments have been disabled. The protections placed on the video prevented downloads and screen-capture. Website users who allege they watched the video reported later seeing an apparition of a young woman in a red dress. The woman appeared in distress, silently calling for help. Some V-heads say such a sighting is the first Sign of the new Path that will lead seekers to a world beyond this one, if only they are brave enough.

The End

Acknowledgments

Here am I again, writing acknowledgements for my third book, staring at a blank page in fear of forgetting someone important. So many people have been there for me, and I appreciate every one of you. If I forget to include you here, please forgive me and my overloaded brain.

But firstly: I wrote this book while living on the ancestral lands of the Wurundjeri People of the Kulin Nation, who are the Traditional Owners of what is now known as the City of Yarra. I now live, teach, and write on the lands called Merri-bek, where the Wurundjeri Woi Wurrung people are the Traditional Owners. These lands have never been ceded. This always was, always will be, Aboriginal land.

And now, let's begin! My heartfelt thanks go to Rena Rossner, my brilliant agent and friend. You are a light and a star and a fighter. You never give up. I'm grateful to have you in my corner.

Lauren Knowles, my insightful editor. You are smart, thoughtful and have great taste in books (I mean, of course, you do—you've acquired this one ☺). Working on *Ghosts* with you has been a blast and I can't wait for more.

Everyone at Page Street YA—Rosie G. Stewart, the brilliant designer and art director behind the cover of this book (WOW), Lauren Cepero, Cass Costa, Lizzy Mason, and so many others!

My Pan Macmillan team—thank you so much for your

enthusiasm and all your hard work. I knew I was in excellent hands from day one.

Dolce Paganne, for drawing this book's mind-blowing cover art. I could write a whole essay dedicated to it, analysing its layered meanings, sinister hopefulness and overall perfection, but no words can truly do it justice. I mean. Look. At. It. Thank you, Dolce, you're a genius.

My author friends: Astrid Scholte, Ella Dyson, AJ Vrana, and so many more; and the talented Queens of YA horror I'm also lucky to call friends—Sarah Glenn Marsh, Erin A. Craig, Kelly deVos, and Alison Ames.

Everyone at Deborah Harris Agency, for being so great to your authors.

The foreign rights team, the audio rights team, the film rights team: I know how hard you work and I appreciate it.

Melanie Schubert and Angela Montoya. You are both bright stars and I'm lucky call you my friends!

My friend, Narrelle Harris. You are among the most talented authors I know. Co-editing our anthology with you has been the most rewarding experience. I'm so grateful we got to do it together.

My family: Olga, Vitaly, Angela, Paola, Simi, Clery, Roberto, Miguel, and the little ones: Jaxson and Alexis. Much love to you all.

Those who are not with us anymore: Lydia, Tamara, Viktor, Vladimir, and Augusto. I miss you every day.

And, of course, Jorge, my most favorite human in the whole universe.

About the Author

KATYA DE BECERRA writes atmospheric young adult horror featuring determined characters, complicated families and enigmatic places. Critics called her debut *What the Woods Keep* "a thoughtful and compelling horror fantasy" (*The Bulletin*) and "a narrative that will keep readers enthralled" (*Booklist*), while her second novel *Oasis* earned a starred review from Booklist. Katya regularly publishes short fiction in anthologies and literary magazines. She is also coeditor of the anthology *This Fresh Hell*, which reimagines and subverts horror tropes in new and unexpected ways. As a child, Katya wanted to be an Egyptologist, but instead she earned a PhD in Cultural Anthropology and now works at a university, where she teaches and researches as well as supervises graduate students in Anthropology, Creative Writing, and Education. Katya is a short version of her real name, which is very long and gets mispronounced a lot. *When Ghosts Call Us Home* is her third novel.